book eleven

CARRIER
Nuke Zone

KEITH DOUGLASS

JOVE BOOKS, NEW YORK

CARRIER 11: NUKE ZONE

A Jove Book / published by arrangement with
the author

PRINTING HISTORY
Jove edition / September 1998

The Penguin Putnam Inc. World Wide Web site address is
http://www.penguinputnam.com

ISBN: 0-515-12253-X

A JOVE BOOK®
Jove Books are published by The Berkley Publishing Group,
a member of Penguin Putnam Inc.,
375 Hudson Street, New York, New York 10014.
JOVE and the "J" design
are trademarks belonging to Jove Publications, Inc.

PRINTED IN THE UNITED STATES OF AMERICA

10 9 8 7 6 5 4 3 2 1

After twenty-two years in the Navy, I know this: Teamwork is everything, whether you're working on the flight deck or just writing about it.

Meet the rest of *my* team:

Jake Elwell and George Wieser, the finest agents in the world. John Talbot, the next-finest agent and superb new-writer mentor. Tom Colgan, my editor, who'd make a great fighter pilot. Cyndy Mobley and Ron Morton, technical advisors and war consultants.
Lynette Spratley, who types faster than I can talk and reads my first drafts.
Hewlett-Packard and "E.G." on the technical support line—dynamite printers and excellent support to fix operator error on the eve of a deadline!

And finally: to the men and women who go to sea in the service of our country: BRAVO ZULU.

I like to hear from *Carrier* readers. Drop me an E-mail at KFDouglass@aol.com (the F stands for Francis) or write to me at:

Jove Books
Attention: Tom Colgan
The Berkley Publishing Group
375 Hudson Street
New York, New York 10014

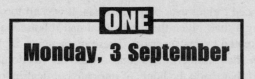

ONE
Monday, 3 September

0400 Local
MiG 42
Five Hundred Feet above the Black Sea

Fog streamed past the single-seat cockpit, cloaking the MiG-31 in a shroud of condensed moisture. Ukrainian Commander Yuri Kursk could barely make out the tendrils streaking past, writhing and weaving themselves together in an unholy white blanket that seemed to suck the warmth out of the cockpit. He shivered, as much from the stark realization that the mission was finally underway as from the chill insinuating itself through layers of flight suit and heavy undercoating to penetrate his bones.

He kept up his scan, glancing continually from the dimly lit green status indicators on the panel in front of him to the fog outside. Had it not been for the reassuring thrum of his two Perm/Soloviev D-30F6 turbofans, he could have believed that he was alone in the air, suspended motionless above the Black Sea.

He goosed the throttle slightly just to feel the change of vibration radiating through the fuselage. It was reassuring, a link with reality, a reminder that he was not some alien creature forever entombed in fog, but a warm-bodied, living human surrounded by the most advanced fighter ever built in Russia. It was all too easy to forget that, given the mechanical and robotic way he was treated by his superiors. These moments in flight— longer than moments this time—were his freedom, the payoff that made the hours of intricate political indoctrination, psychological testing, and continuous intrusive watchfulness of the Ukrainian Psychological Services all worthwhile. They might believe they owned his mind and body on land, but screaming through the darkness, he knew the truth.

The MiG-31 Foxhound was pure freedom in motion, an advanced strategic interceptor that had been intended to take the Soviet Union into the next century as its primary carrier-based aircraft. It stretched seventy-four feet from the tip of its Flashdance phased-array fire-control radar housed in the nose to the tips of its slightly canted vertical stabilizers. With a wingspan of forty-four feet, it possessed a vastly increased range over its predecessor fighter airframes. Carrying external fuel tanks and lightly loaded, it possessed an unrefueled range of almost 1800 nautical miles.

He'd need every inch of that too. While the Foxhound was capable of reaching Mach 2.35, its most economical cruising speed was Mach .85. If he were detected, forced to evade, or even to engage in real combat, his effective range would drop dramatically. As it was, he would be running on fumes by the time he returned to the Crimean Peninsula.

Just like the rest of Ukraine. He snorted, thinking how apt the analogy was, congratulating himself on his own wit. The remnant of the former Soviet Union had been out of fuel for years now, as loath as its current leaders were to admit that. But no amount of political denial could conceal the truth forever, just as his engines couldn't run on wishes and hopes. He shifted slightly in the ejection seat, keeping the blood flowing, settling in for a long flight. No, as fiscally and politically bankrupt as his country might be, it wasn't dead yet. It still could pull some surprises out of its ass from time to time.

Like this one.

The MiG-31 was proof of it. In addition to the advanced power plant, it possessed a host of subtle and deadly avionics carefully crafted by Ukrainian engineers working with pirated U.S. Stealth technology. Every inch of its thin fuselage was wired into the central counter-detections module. It was less a coating for the aircraft than an oddly shaped phased array of electromagnetic detectors and transponders. Capable of intercepting radar signals and generating out-of-phase canceling waves, the MiG-31 had the ability to virtually disappear from the scope of any radar operator within range. Additionally, the integrated suite of sensors and transponders could easily mimic the radar characteristics of a wide range of commercial—and nonthreatening—aircraft.

As it would shortly. The MiG-31 was currently flying in full stealth mode, and Yuri felt confident that none of the radar sites ringing the Black Sea had the slightest inkling that he was transiting through their area at Mach 1. Yuri intended to stay in this mode during his transit across the Black Sea as well as his overflight of Turkey.

After that, as soon as he was over the Aegean Sea, the invisible night marauder would assume the identity of a Turkish commercial air flight departing Istanbul for London. If all went according to plan, the Americans would merely think that their copy of the published Turkish commercial air flight schedule was in error. Yuri knew that that happened often enough for it not to be alarming to either USS *La Salle,* the Sixth Fleet command ship now loitering in the Greek Isles, or her Aegis cruiser escort, USS *Shiloh.*

He could have continued the entire flight in stealth mode, but to do so would defeat the entire purpose of the exercise. It was not only necessary that the United States be reminded who owned this portion of the world's oceans, but that they also be convinced that the cause of their sudden disgrace was Turkey. By simulating the appropriate size, altitude, and IFF codes of a Turkish aircraft, Yuri would catch them completely off guard.

Yuri eased the throttle back down to the economical Mach .85, then fished around in the upper-leg flight-suit pocket until his fingers closed around a foil-wrapped chocolate bar. He pulled it out, shucked off the protective covering, and bit greedily into it.

It was one of the true luxuries of being part of this elite strike force, being issued precious Swiss chocolate bars for in-flight meals.

0430 Local
Combat Direction Center (CDC)
USS **La Salle**

One hundred miles off the coast of Greece, USS *La Salle* steamed slowly north. Forty miles ahead, the island of Samothrace was visible only on the SPS-10 radar that echoed its images to the bridge on the SPA-25G repeater. The fog that had plagued her around midnight was slowly dissipating, responding to the gentle easterly wind that had sprung up around 0200. The massive vessel sliced easily through the sea state two swells, throwing off curling bow waves of churning white bubbles and aqua water. Overhead, the first few stars were starting to peek out through the clearing sky.

"How about some coffee, sir?" The operations specialist extended the white disposable cup to the young black lieutenant. "I made it myself."

"What, no latte? I'd expect better on the Sixth Fleet flagship." The lieutenant smiled as his fingers curled around the white stippled surface.

Operations Specialist Third Class Matthew Carey grinned ruefully. "Some espresso would be damned fine about now, wouldn't it? These mid-watches . . ." He shrugged.

Lieutenant (junior grade) Jules "Skeeter" Harmon took a sip from the steaming cup. He grimaced. "Better than most, bearing but a slight resemblance to JP5 this time."

"We aim to please, Lieutenant. The customer's always right, even if he is a TAD nugget hiding out from the carrier."

Skeeter set the cup down on his TAO console with a little more force than necessary. "Damn it, Carey, I'm not hiding out! I told you before—some idiot in D.C. screwed my orders up. I'm supposed to be on *Jefferson*, not *La Salle*. Can I help it if they decided to leave me stashed here while they figure it out? Don't you think I'd rather be on the bird farm than trapped on this gator?" He gestured around the Combat Direction Center, which was only half manned under peacetime steaming conditions. "Do you think any self-respecting aviator would want to be here?"

Carey grinned. "You're here."

"For another two weeks." Skeeter kept one hand curled around the coffee cup just in case the ship lurch unexpectedly, a holdover habit from his midshipman cruise days aboard much smaller ships. "Besides, that gives *Jefferson* time to prepare, seeing as how I'm such a hotshot aviator. You know, hate to embarrass the admiral by showing up before he's ready for me."

Carey stifled a snort. The lieutenant was a good guy, better than most of the black-shoe surface officers that inhabited the amphibious command-and-control ship. You could talk to him, and he didn't get all bent out of shape over the small stuff, like the "shoes" did. That made the mid-watch hours more endurable, a fact for which every member of Watch Section Two aboard the Sixth Fleet flagship was grateful.

Still, there were times when Carey wondered whether the newly minted aviator had any idea of what he was getting into. Sure, he knew Skeeter had been through the training pipeline, and had already completed the required carrier qualifications while assigned to the RAG—the Replacement Air Group—that gave the nuggets their first practical look at the intricacies of landing on board their floating airfields. And from what he'd heard, Lieutenant Harmon was supposed to be one damned fine pilot. Mess-decks intelligence—MDI—had it that he had graduated at the top of his class, both in basic and at the RAG. The enlisted troops liked him, about as much as they were prepared to like any junior officer who hadn't yet proved his worth on a six-month cruise. Sometimes it was better not to get too attached to officers until you knew what they were really made of.

How much of his own growing reputation did the lieutenant himself believe? Carey wondered. All of it? He shook his head, and his congenial expression clouded ver. He hoped not. After two years in the Navy, Petty ﬁcer Carey knew what Lieutenant Harmon had yet to learn—that the sea held surprises of its own for the men and women who sailed on her.

"I expect they'll be glad to get you on board," Carey said finally. "There's bound to be some junior officers who are getting tired of pulling Alert 15 sitting on the flight deck." He glanced slyly at the lieutenant j.g. "You'll be the 'George,' won't you, sir?"

Lieutenant Harmon frowned. "Yeah, and I'm not looking forward to it." Being the most junior officer in a squadron carried with it a host of collateral duties that took away from flying and sleeping time. Movie officer, welfare and recreation officer, and general all-around shitty-little-jobs officer—that was the domain of the George.

"I think they call it an opportunity to excel, an OTE," Carey said, affecting the slight drawl that so many pilots used when airborne. Even aviators born in the northernmost sections of Maine sounded like Chuck Yeager over tactical, and the enlisted technicians who supported them picked up the habit.

Harmon shrugged. "They can load me up with all the collateral duties they want to, but I joined this man's Navy to fly. And once they see me . . ." The aviator let his voice trail off and shot a significant look at the young operations specialist. "You don't believe me, do you?"

"Now, sir, I didn't—" Carey started to protest.

Skeeter cut him off with a lazy wave of his hand. "That's all right. You haven't flown with me. And neither have they." He pointed at the large-screen display that dominated the forward part of the compartment. "VF-95 doesn't know it yet, but I'm about to set a Tomcat record for most consecutive good traps on board. Mosquitoes don't bolter—and neither do I," he said, referring to the maneuver a carrier aircraft executed when it missed catching the wires on the aft of the flight deck.

"I'm sure they—what the hell?" Carey's head snapped forward to stare at the large-screen display. "What's that?"

Skeeter spun around in his swivel chair to face forward, and his fingers reached for the trackball to position his cursor over the new air contact flitting across the upper edge of his screen. His fingers fumbled for the right buttons, and finally the relevant tactical information appeared on the small screen at the side of his desk. He took a deep breath, then let it out slowly. "Damn, Carey—you're gettin' jumpy. Nothing but a commercial air flight."

Carey shook his head, his frown deepening. "They're not scheduled for one, sir. This is dead time—the ninety-minute gap when there's not any civilian flights scheduled." He took a quick look at the status display. "And it's moving too fast."

"Five hundred knots? That's well within speed range of a commercial aircraft," Skeeter countered. "Besides, IFF indicates it's a commercial air flight."

"Like I said, he's not on my schedule. Besides, they're usually at four hundred and fifty knots," Carey said, "not five hundred. Why would he be going fifty knots faster than every other COMMAIR flight that outchops Turkey?"

Skeeter shrugged. "Fast is good."

"It's out of parameters, Lieutenant," Carey said stubbornly. "Recommend we designate it as a contact of interest and ask the cruiser what they think."

"Might as well, seeing as how you've got a bug up your ass about it. Besides, it'll give those shoes something to do besides play video games on that Spy 1 system. I'll designate it as a contact of interest—if I can find the damned—ah, there it is." The display changed the symbology associated with the contact and sent the data out to the other ships over Link 11, the tactical net that allowed the ships in the battle group to share information. "But the cruiser is net control. When she starts howling, you're going to have to talk to them."

"Be glad to. The track supervisor on *Shiloh* is an old shipmate of mine, and he'll be thinking exactly the same thing."

Skeeter glanced up at him. "Bet?"

"You got it, sir. Loser buys an espresso machine for the winner's mess."

Skeeter smacked his lips. "Can't wait."

0440 Local
MiG 42

Yuri extended the retractable infrared pod housed under the cockpit and stared at the display. Useless, as he'd suspected it would be. Still, the admiral had been quite adamant about conducting an IR search before activating his radar. Soviet tactics, Soviet thought processes. He sighed. Until they overcame this institutionalized mandate to control every small tactical detail on a mission, Ukrainian air would continue to be hampered. Especially on missions like this. What was the point of even trying the IR sensor in fog as dense as this? None.

Moreover, the aircraft was already adequately configured to search for the Sixth Fleet flagship without revealing its own identity. The Flashdance radar had been meticulously modified to provide an alternate

operational mode, one that closely simulated the ubiquitous Furuno surface-ship search radar found on most
other world ships. At five hundred feet, he could easily
be mistaken for any one of the thousands of tugs, fishing
boats, or other commercial vessels that plied these
waters. And the contrast between a radar blip emitting
the characteristics of a Turkish commercial air flight and
an electronic signature mimicking a civilian surface craft
would undoubtedly add to the confusion. In theory, the
flagship's electronic-warfare specialists would simply
assume that the target-processing algorithm had inad-
vertently attached the electromagnetic signature to the
wrong blip.

In theory, at least.

And really, all he needed was four minutes. Four
minutes of precious time to close within range of the
amphibious flagship, fire his weapon, and get the hell out
of there.

Yuri felt the adrenaline flooding his system, noticed
the tingling in his fingertips and the light, giddy feeling
of overconfidence it generated. It was an all-too-familiar
sensation, one that he'd learned to ignore in Afghanistan
while flying more primitive Soviet fighters.

He glanced over at the GPS—the Global Positioning
System indicators—and watched the green luminescent
digits slowly click over. Based on the Ukrainians' best
intelligence and the Americans' public announcements of
their own deployment schedules, the flagship should be
located within one hundred miles of a point immediately
in front of him.

One hundred miles. Still a hell of a lot of ocean to
search, and visual and infrared would certainly be useless
today. He reached over and toggled on the radar, flipping
the switch into the commercial-air-simulation position.

Even better than being part of his deception, the radar would actually work in this mode, providing a complete lookdown-shootdown picture of the water below him.

He eased back on the yoke, gaining altitude. Eight thousand feet, he decided. A brief foray up to that altitude to get a good, solid picture of what was around him, then pop back down out of counter-detection range. With any luck at all, it would all be over in ten minutes.

A slight additional whine haunted the airframe as the radar spun up and came on-line. His heads-up display sprang to life with a speckling of green clutter that quickly resolved itself into the fuzzy-edged lozenges indicating radar contact.

There—it had to be *La Salle*. The large one loitered in deep water. A smaller contact, probably *Shiloh,* was positioned twenty miles astern of the massive flagship. Yuri calculated the intercept, then dove back down to the deck for the concealment of sea clutter.

0441 Local
Combat Direction Center
USS La Salle

"Sir! You've gotta listen to me!" Carey's voice was deeper, harder. "There's something going on with this contact I don't like." He pointed to the automated status board.

Skeeter stared at the display and frowned. "The altitude—it's not matching up, is it?"

"No, sir. And look at the EW—the electromagnetic-warfare signal going with it. A Furuno."

"That's not right—not at that altitude. Unless it's a fishing boat with—"

"Sir. With all due respect, you're letting your conclusion drive your analysis." Carey stabbed a finger at the display. "You've got a contact radiating commercial IFF, going too fast, displaying a radar it shouldn't have, and now bouncing back and forth between five hundred feet and eight thousand." Carey's voice took on an urgent note. "Sir, you'd better get the TAO in here. Now."

"What if it's just a commercial flight after all? Or a computer-processing glitch?" Skeeter replied uneasily. As a junior officer stashed on board the flagship, he'd been pressed into duty as the Combat Direction Center TAO only because the ship was in peacetime cruising mode. Nobody was expecting anything to go wrong, not in the familiar confines of the Aegean Sea and just off the coast of a friendly nation. Besides, the admiral's Chief of Staff had expressed full confidence in Skeeter and told him it was an opportunity. "What does the Aegis say?"

A flicker of movement on the large-screen display drew their eyes toward it. The Aegis response was clear—the blip had been redesignated as an unknown, potentially hostile contact.

"I know Lieutenant Commander Boney," Carey said. "If you call him and wake him up for no reason, he's not going to be pissed. He expects it—hell, if he'd known you'd hesitate to do it, he wouldn't have left you here alone on watch, sir!"

Skeeter reached for the telephone and punched in the four-digit code that would ring the TAO's stateroom. He stared at Carey as the phone rang twice, then quickly briefed the Tactical Action Officer on the scenario. Color drained from his face as he listened to the response. He slammed the receiver down and turned to Carey. "You and your counterpart on the cruiser better be right.

Lieutenant Commander Boney's on his way down here, and he told me to ring the captain."

Carey nodded, immensely relieved. "Better safe than sorry, sir. Always."

0442 Local
Tactical Flag Command Center (TFCC)
USS **Jefferson** *(CVN-74)*

TFCC was one of the smallest compartments on board the supercarrier, but it was the fusion center for every sensor on every platform assigned to Carrier Battle Group 14. Radar, electromagnetic, and a variety of other sophisticated detection and countermeasures systems fed their electronic data into the processing center. Tiny waverings in the electromagnetic spectrum, fuzzy contacts that might have been sea clutter or actual contacts, were correlated with national sensor data from satellites and other top-secret assets to produce a chillingly accurate bird's-eye view of the airspace and sea for five hundred miles around the carrier. A satellite data link with the Sixth Fleet flagship extended her range to well within the Aegean Sea.

The compartment was dimly lit, red lights glowing softly from the overhead while a giant blue large-screen display covered the far end. Two tactical consoles were positioned in front of the screen, each with its own automated status board, keyboard, trackball, and associated communications circuitry. The Flag Tactical Operations Officer occupied the right-hand one, while his assistant sat in the left. Both wore headsets linking them to the command circuit, and a dial-up switch in front of them allowed them to change to other circuits as necessary.

At the moment, both were studying the large-screen display. Just seconds before, the "unknown, possibly hostile" designation had flashed before them as the Aegis cruiser had revised her opinion on the identity of the air contact. Lieutenant Commander "Gator" Cummings, an F-14 Radar Intercept Officer, or RIO, slued his cursor over to capture the offending blip. His status display indicated the contact had been designated a COI (contact of interest) by *La Salle,* now loitering two hundred miles to the northeast.

"Raw video," he muttered. "That's what I'd rather see than this. If I could see just exactly what the radar is painting, I'd know—"

"Just what you know now," his assistant finished tartly. "Gator, you RIOs always believe you've got the only calibrated set of eyeballs in this Navy. Don't you figure those operations specialists on the cruiser know their jobs?"

"Sure they do, but I know mine even better."

"Well. What do you want to do about it?"

Gator stared at the symbology on the tactical screen. It was tracking southwest, headed directly toward the Sixth Fleet flagship. Behind it, a shadow trace indicated its previous path. From its track history, it appeared to have left Ankara and been detected as it went feet-wet off the coast. "Could be a commercial air—time's wrong, but it might be a charter flight." He changed his mind as soon as he said the words. "Or something else."

The other officer, an E2C Hawkeye pilot, nodded. "I don't like this."

"Anything from Intel?" Gator asked.

"Let's find out." The pilot picked up the telephone and

punched the numbers. He spoke a few short sentences in the receiver, then hung up. "Commander Busby's on his way down right now. He sounded worried."

"My sentiments exactly." Gator picked up the Bat-phone located to his right. "Get the Alert 30 Tomcats rolling. I'll brief the admiral."

0444 Local
MiG 42

One hundred miles. It's time. Still, he hesitated.

Why? Was it the enormity of the act he was about to commit? Or simply lingering doubts about the viability of the entire operation? He shook his head, pushing the questions that had plagued him for the last five months away. There was more to this plan, more than he'd ever been told or would ever know. It was the old Soviet way—that he know only the small portion that was required for the successful execution of his mission, not the broader strategic implications. He took a deep breath, focused on the radar screen, and toggled the weapons-select switch on his stick. Not that it made much difference—he carried only one missile, and an odd variant at that.

He punched the button on top of the stick, releasing the weapon from its hard-point station on his right wing. The MiG heeled, suddenly unbalanced by the loss of six hundred pounds of—of what? As he broke off from the approach and heeled back in a tight turn toward Turkey, he felt the question grow more insistent in his mind. What had he just fired? And why?

0445 Local
Flight Deck
USS Jefferson

Minutes after the TAO's wake-up call, the flight deck was teeming with a rainbow of jerseys. Two decks down, the Alert 30 Tomcat crews waiting in their Ready Room were slipping into their ejection harnesses, double-checking kneeboard data, and trying to figure out why the hell they were scrambling.

The yellow-shirted flight-deck control personnel swarmed over the Alert 30 Tomcats, conducting final preflight checks and readying the aircraft for their crews.

Inside the carrier, the duty tower crew stampeded up eight decks to Pri-Fly, the glassed-in control tower on the inboard side of the island. CAG, although his presence was technically not required in the tower, rousted himself out of his rack and hastily tossed on his yellow jersey over his khaki pants.

In TFCC, an atmosphere of controlled chaos was developing. Admiral Edward Everett "Batman" Wayne, commander of Carrier Battle Group 14, strode into TFCC. The admiral's cabin was located on the same deck, just thirty feet away.

"Good morning, Admiral," Gator said crisply. He followed his greeting with a concise summary of the contact's track history. "I'm having them spin up the Alert 30 aircraft—just to be on the safe side. If it *is* trouble, though, we're going to be too late to do any good."

Admiral Wayne nodded. "Good thinking. Better safe

than sorry. We're too near our old hot zones to take anything for granted at this point." Batman stifled a yawn as he slipped into his elevated brown command chair. "What does Sixth Fleet think it is?"

"They're not talking yet, Admiral," Gator answered. "Based on the traffic and Link data, they're treating this as a threat."

Batman shook his head. "They've got the Aegis with them. An aggressive little bastard, from the looks of his contact designations. I like that in a cruiser. If this contact makes trouble, the Aegis ought to be able to deal with it."

"*Shiloh* has a sharp crew," Gator agreed. "I suppose I could have let them handle it alone, but— "

Batman waved off his suggestion. "Always better to have more firepower than not enough. It's probably just a civilian aircraft off track with a misassociation of the electromagnetic signal. Still, you did the right thing."

Gator nodded, slightly relieved in spite of himself to find out that the admiral agreed.

Batman turned to the Intelligence Officer lurking in one corner of TFCC. "Anything to add?"

"No, sir." Commander "Lab Rat" Busby looked slightly chagrined. "Nothing. But the absence of data doesn't mean there's nothing to worry about—just that we don't know about it if there is."

Batman studied Busby for a moment. A strong officer, a superb intelligence specialist. But if ever an officer had an appropriate call sign, it was Commander Busby. Large blue eyes behind steel-rimmed frames, close-clipped blond hair so light as to be invisible, pink complexion— whoever had hung that name on him in his first assignment had nailed him cold appearance-wise. But the aggressive, scalpel-sharp mind housed beneath his un-prepossessing exterior belied the meek nickname.

"Better safe than sorry," Batman said. He turned back to Gator. "Tell the Air Boss to get those Tomcats up *now*."

0447 Local
MiG 42

The fog enveloped him again, closing around the canopy like a welcoming blanket. Stealth technology might hide him from radars, but the enveloping low clouds made him *feel* safe, as well as preventing visual contact.

As soon as he'd started executing his hard turn toward Turkey, Yuri had slammed the throttles full forward on the Foxhound, kicking the light aircraft up to Mach 2.3. They'd factored it in, this mad dash for home, during the initial mission calculations. He should have enough fuel—just barely.

Thirty miles behind him, the missile he'd just launched was still heading for the *La Salle*. He watched the digital time counter on his console, counting down until deto-nation. His mission planner had been specific about run time and distance at launch. Moreover, he'd harped incessantly on the necessity for executing as much of the mission as possible at a bare five hundred feet above the hungry sea below him. Yuri had wondered about it at the time, wondered even more now, but was not about to disobey his orders.

One more hour and he'd be back over the Crimean Peninsula, having made a circuitous route again over Turkey cloaked in his stealth technology. One hour, if nothing went wrong.

0448 Local
Combat Direction Center
USS Shiloh

"Oh, Jesus, we've got separation. *Missile separation.*"
The operations specialist's voice went high and wavering, then dropped immediately back down into a more
controlled register. "TAO, incoming Vampire."

The young lieutenant on watch felt the blood draining
out of his face. How had the situation gone to shit so
quickly? Sure, he'd designated the contact unknown
and possibly hostile, but that was standard target-
identification protocol. You don't know what it is,
something looks odd about it, you call it a possible
hostile. It was the Aegis way. The captain had sounded
drowsily satisfied when he'd reported it to him, evidently
rousing from a sound sleep.

What in the hell—? The symbology for target-fire-
control designation popped into being on his screen, and
he slued his chair around to stare at the weapons
technician manning the fire-control console. It was
happening fast, too fast. There wasn't time to—

"Sir, sir! Request weapons-free authorization." The
voice of the chief manning the weapons fire-control
console was firm. "Lieutenant, I need permission now to
make certain we have enough range to catch it."

A cold calm settled over the young lieutenant. This
was it, the moment he'd trained for, the moment they'd
memorized and anticipated and dreaded in equal proportions. This was why he was the Tactical Action Officer—
the captain trusted his judgment enough to give him

complete control of the awesome weapons inventory that his ship carried. If he froze now, it would be more than a black mark on his fitness report. "Weapons free." One small part of his mind was pleased to note that his voice sounded steady and professional.

Seconds later, the cruiser shuddered as an SM-2 surface-to-air missile exploded out of the vertical-launch-system tube and arced away from the cruiser. The noise was overwhelming, almost drowning out the insistent bonging of the General Quarters alarm. The TAO could hear people moving around CDC, the General Quarters crew pounding down the passageways and into the compartment located on the third deck of the ship, taking in the tactical situation at a glance and starting turnover with their on-watch counterparts.

He heard the cacophony, but it didn't register. His eyes, his mind, his entire being was fixed on the blue symbol arcing away from his ship and toward the incoming missile. "Fire two," he ordered.

0449 Local
TFCC
USS Jefferson

Aside from a few whispered oaths, TFCC was silent. Batman stared at the SM-2 missile symbology with its long blue speed leader pointing out in front of it. The incoming missile carried the same symbol with the same long speed leader, but was colored in red. The tips of the two speed leaders were already intersecting, as though they were some obscene beginning to a game of tic-tac-toe.

"Flight line manned and ready," Gator said quietly. "Estimate five minutes until Tomcat launch."

"Make it three minutes," Batman answered. "I think we're going to need them."

0450 Local
Vampire One
Thirty Miles North of USS La Salle

The Sunburn missile inbound on the USS *La Salle* was a one-of-a-kind variant. Its internal mechanisms and warhead were adapted from a sea-launched version of one of the United States Navy's most dangerous threats—a tactical nuclear warhead. While American technology was more than adequate to supply such a weapon to U.S. forces, American doctrine forbade its use, even though Ukrainian combat doctrine specifically dictated the use of tactical nuclear weapons at the earliest possible point in any decisive battle.

Traveling at just under Mach 3, the missile tracked along a line of bearing dictated by its maneuvering circuits. After one minute of flight, its final-approach radar activated, illuminated the water below it, and spotted its target off on the horizon. It made two minor course corrections at its current altitude before descending to two thousand feet and continuing on its trajectory.

Had Yuri Kursk known what tactics were embedded in the pathways of the warhead's electronic-control mechanism, he would have had even more reason to be concerned about his mission. Not for the strike on the American battle group, but for his own odds of escaping unscathed.

Thirty miles from the USS *La Salle,* the missile detonated. The warhead's explosion punched through the steel alloy casing, the intense heat of the burgeoning nuclear explosion vaporizing the metal into a thin layer of molecules that would ride outward on the fireball's leading wave. The after part of the missile disintegrated microseconds later. There were no intact portions of it to form the deadly shrapnel that accompanies most missile detonations, but it was not necessary. Even thirty miles from the carrier, the missile was close enough to inflict the damage intended.

The EMP—electromagnetic pulse—was far more destructive to the ships in the vicinity than the relatively small blast effect the missile produced. It killed silently, without warning, and its target was not the human beings inhabiting USS *La Salle,* nor the structural elements of the ship, but the delicate electronics housed within.

0450 Local
Starboard Lookout Station
USS **La Salle**

The starboard lookout had just begun his slow, methodical track toward the bow of the ship when the missile exploded. His involuntary reflexes took over—his eyelids slammed shut, and a piercing scream ripped from his throat. He dropped the binoculars from his eyes and plastered his hands over his face. Pain lanced through his eyes and back into his brain, a thin silver needle of agony. He dropped to his knees, not feeling the impact of soft tissue on the hard metal deck.

He could hear the screams of the others on the bridge

faintly, as though coming from a long distance away. But the pain, the all-encompassing pain, ate every shred of reality other than the lancing agony boiling in his brain. He rolled over onto his side and curled up on the bridge wing, still screaming. His eyes were wide open, tears flooding down his face, and completely unseeing. The nuclear flash had blinded him.

0450 Local
Combat Direction Center
USS **La Salle**

"Holy shit, it—what the hell?" Skeeter's question transformed itself into a shout as the screen in front of him lit up with an unholy brilliance. Something on the port side of the compartment snapped out an angry, electrical sound.

Every light in the compartment except for the emergency battle lanterns went dark. Skeeter jumped up, ripped the headset off his ears, and took one step back. There was only one type of missile that would cause that type of damage to a modern battleship without a concussive explosion that would have rocked the deck that was so steady under his feet. Only one.

A tactical nuclear explosion.

The ship was oddly quiet, the all-pervasive electronic hum that normally permeated every compartment silenced permanently. From the corridor outside, he could hear feet pounding down the passageways as sailors raced for their damage-control positions, their General Quarters stations, and the myriad other underway positions that the ship assumed when it was fighting for its life.

In a few minutes, they would all know what Skeeter knew—that USS *La Salle* was no longer a Navy combat vessel but merely a silent, dead hulk.

0450 Local
TFCC
USS Jefferson

"They got it!" Gator crowed. He turned to face the admiral. "Right smack on. That Aegis must have—" He broke the sentence off as he studied the admiral's face.

The admiral had the microphone for the command circuit in his hand and was doggedly, quietly, and desperately calling up *Shiloh* and *La Salle*. Gator stared at the speaker as though trying to make it answer.

The normal background electronic hum was noticeably louder, and spiked with violent electronic peaks. Electrons chittered all over the electromagnetic spectrum, violently roiling in the aftermath of the weapon.

"Admiral?" Gator said finally, a note of uncertainty in his voice. "I thought the Aegis shot it down."

Batman replaced the handset in its metal bracket holder. "I don't think so." A look of deep agony settled on his face. "No, I don't think they got it at all. Every communications circuit we've got is blanked out by full-spectrum electromagnetic distortion. There's only one kind of weapon that does that. And I never thought I'd see it used. It hasn't been—not since Hiroshima."

0600 Local
MiG 42
The Crimean Peninsula

The fog was thicker at the boundary between land and sea, obscuring the Naval Aviation base and the two long runways that ran east to west along the northern portion. Yuri vectored in along the tactical radial, switching to approach-control frequency as he entered controlled airspace. At the same time, he secured the stealth gear. His superiors had decided to continue normal activities on the base, and at this hour of the morning the first routine training flights were already cluttering the approaches.

He heard several startled exclamations over the ground-control frequency as he popped into being on their radarscopes, but there were no suspicious inquiries or demands for explanations. He smiled slightly, imagining the consternation that the Psychological Services officer— the new term for a *zampolit*—would be causing in the control tower.

He requested approach instructions and received priority clearance into base, as he knew he would. Five minutes later, the Foxhound alighted gracefully on the tarmac and rolled smoothly to a stop.

Yuri paused for a moment, his engines still turning, at the far end of the runway. Even on the ground, he still had the sensation of freedom, and these were the last few moments of it before he returned to the control of his superiors.

The mission—he mentally ran through his actions and

decided that the entire evolution had been executed exactly according to instructions. Even if it hadn't been, he would have reported it as such—there would be no excuses, could be none. Finally satisfied with his version of the events, he took one last, long deep breath of the purified and filtered air circulating in the cockpit, tasting the oddly sterile flavor of it. Then, using his nosewheel steering gear, he executed a precision turn toward the flight center and the group of men waiting there.

0800 Local
Flag Briefing Room
USS La Salle

"There was nothing else you could have done, sir," OS3 Carey insisted. "Nothing."

Skeeter stared at the clutter arrayed on the table. The last hour had been an inquisition, a demanding professional look at every second of time from the moment he detected the incoming aircraft to the attack. The admiral's questions had been pointed and direct, the Chief of Staff openly accusatory. Maybe that was not what the admiral had intended, but it certainly sounded like it if you were the individual doing the answering. In the end, the admiral had concluded that his performance at TAO had been inadequate, and had ordered the COS to place a letter of reprimand in his service jacket.

Not good enough. He hadn't made the grade.

Paper charts and tracing paper cluttered the table in front of him, and the entire control of the flag battle group had shifted to ancient methods men had used for centuries to sail these waters. They were moving in closer to the coast of Greece, waiting for instructions on their next port call for repairs. Work crews scampered over the superstructure, trying desperately to resurrect any bit of combat capability left in the shattered gear. Deep in the bowels of the ship, some of the spare electronic components had survived, and the engineering officer and combat-systems officer had said they thought they might be able to jury-rig a rudimentary Furuno radar and one radio circuit in the clear. Secure, encrypted communications were out of the question. The radio components were stored too far above the waterline to have survived.

Shiloh was in better shape. The Aegis cruiser had been specially hardened to withstand EMP, and most of her vital combat circuitry was located well below the waterline. According to the helo that had ferried her XO over ten minutes earlier, she'd have to replace some exterior antennas, but would probably be fully operational within a matter of hours. *Shiloh* would be coordinating the medical evacuation of the flash-blinded lookouts and other casualties, including the bridge watch-standers from both ships, as soon as she could raise *Jefferson* to provide a helo.

"I should have. . . ." Skeeter's voice trailed off, uncertain and wavering. He stared down at the paper, the lines delineating the Aegean Islands and surrounding waters blurring as his eyes drifted out of focus, clouded with tears. "I should have—" he tried again, searching within himself for an adequate definition of how he'd failed the ship.

"You couldn't have." Carey was emphatic. "He stayed outside of our engagement zone, and there was enough ambiguity in the situation that anyone might have made the same decisions. You did your best."

Skeeter finally looked up at him. "It wasn't good enough."

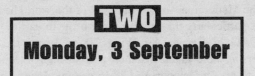

TWO
Monday, 3 September

0400 Local
Washington, D.C.

Even at this early hour, the Beltway was a diamond necklace of headlights. Unmoving headlights. The attack on USS *La Salle* had occurred late evening Washington time, and by 0400 all roads leading into the Pentagon were tied up in what amounted to rush-hour traffic.

Rear Admiral Matthew "Tombstone" Magruder throttled his cherry GTO into neutral and set the parking brake. The traffic ahead of him had not moved in ten minutes, and he was tired of holding the powerful engine in check with the brakes. He'd spent too many hours restoring and maintaining the car over the last twenty years to take for granted the possibility of obtaining spare parts for any component in it.

Hot-and-cold-running admirals—you hear it all the time but you don't believe it until something like this happens. Every flag staff on every deck and ring is busting ass to get in the office and show the Old Man how on top of things they are. Politicians, half of them. Wonder how much time they spend thinking about the men and women out there on the front line.

For Tombstone, the question was more than academic.

The Mediterranean was one part of the world he knew well, particularly this small corner of it. In earlier years, as CAG of Carrier Air Wing 20 on board the USS *Jefferson*, he'd taken his men and women into harm's way to give air support to UN forces involved in a civil war.[1] It had been about this time of year too—no, wait, a little later. October and November, if memory served. The water had taken on an icy sheen as winter approached, a harder, more brilliant shade of blue. The islands themselves were still green, basking in the warm waters that eddied and flowed around them as they had since the days of the Peloponnesian Wars. And the entrance to the Black Sea itself—the narrow funnel of Bosphorus that opened into what the Russians had once considered their own private lake.

Not that Turkey had agreed. He grimaced at the memory. The Battle of Kerch as it was now called had ended with a clear victory for the American battle group and the Marine expeditionary unit that accompanied them.

However, the odds of maintaining a permanent peace among the nations bordering the Black Sea seemed slight. To the north, there was Ukraine. Once a part of the Soviet Union, this newly independent state was suffering the ravages of decades of Communist rule. Its people were an odd mixture of European and Asian cultures. It was also the home of the legendary Cossacks he'd confronted so recently in the Aleutian Islands.[2] In that conflict, he'd found that the legendary savagery of their warriors had not been exaggerated.

---

[1]*Carrier 7: Afterburn*
[2]*Carrier 9: Arctic Fire*

The recent political maneuverings between Ukraine and Russia gave him no reason to feel confident about the Black Sea nation's future. Politically and culturally, the two nations were close. Russia had already provided some evidence of her determination to re-form the former Soviet Union, albeit encompassing a slightly smaller area. Belarus had already been reabsorbed into the Russian hegemony, and Ukraine appeared to be not far behind. Despite Ukraine's protestations of democracy and prayers at the altar of capitalism, the tenets of socialism were too deeply ingrained in its culture for anyone to expect any miracles.

The other nations surrounding the Black Sea were just as worrisome. Turkey held the southern coast of the Black Sea, and for that reason had been for years the recipient of massive American foreign aid. The pundits in Washington called her the gatekeeper to the back door of the Mediterranean, and permanent military missions as well as ongoing technical support were a routine part of the relationships between the two nations.

However, like many nations in the region, Turkey was moving away from the centered, global approach to politics and toward a hard-line fundamentalist Islamic approach. With it came the ever-so-subtle realignment of attitudes. While formal treaties and alliances remained in place, in recent years Turkey had begun to view American support as an unwanted and unwelcome intrusion. Not the money, not the technology—just the influx of Western culture. As a result, Turkey appeared to be moving away from the Western world and reestablishing her ties with Iraq and Iran.

Finally, the west coast of the Black Sea. Bulgaria and Romania shared that coast, and both had substantial ties to Ukraine.

And Greece. The ancient nation, with its smattering of islands and reefs, comprised the western border of the Aegean Sea, the entrance to the Black Sea, while Turkey held the east. Since ancient times, the Aegean Sea had been a naval battleground of renown. Through the Aegean and into the Black Sea via the Bosphorus was a trade route as old as history could record, and it had been the site of the final battles between the Greek and Roman empires.

No, there was no reason to be surprised that trouble was brewing again in this part of the world. History has a memory, and those lessons that nations failed to learn they were doomed to repeat.

The car ahead of him moved forward several feet. Tombstone pulled the gearshift back to Drive and closed the gap between them. Traffic stopped again. He sighed and reset the parking brake. No sense in wasting time. He reached across the well-cared-for vinyl seat and drew a small notebook out of his briefcase.

"At least some skills you learn as an aviator come in useful later," he remarked aloud, more to keep himself company than for any other reason. "Keep up the scan—that's the first rule." He positioned the legal pad on his lap and began making notes, shifting his gaze between the paper and the traffic ahead.

Thirty minutes later, following a check of his ID card by the Marine guard, Tombstone pulled into his designated parking spot near the main entrance to the Pentagon. At the entrance, he went through another ID check line, which included a check of his briefcase. The Marine Corps guard was polite, formal, but doggedly thorough.

When he finally reached his temporary office, it was almost 0500. The rabbit warren of temporary offices and cubicles that comprised the floating working staff of the

Chief of Naval Operations was already lit, with at least half of the spaces occupied.

Tombstone parked his briefcase in the private office he'd been assigned for the duration of his temporary duty, and headed for the Chief of Staff's office. Not surprisingly, the captain was already in.

"Morning, sir," the Chief of Staff said. Tombstone noted he already looked drawn and haggard. How long would it be before *he* looked the same way himself? Not long, he suspected. Along with every other officer assigned to the Pentagon, Tombstone would be living at his desk or in the command center until this crisis was resolved.

And as for Tomboy—her recall to her squadron had come only moments after his own notification of the incident in the Aegean Sea. Her flight back to Pax River would leave at 0700. Any chance they'd had of stealing some time away from their busy careers for each other had vanished as quickly as that unknown contact had blipped onto *La Salle*'s radar.

"Is he in?" Tombstone asked, gesturing toward the Chief of Naval Operations' office after acknowledging the Chief of Staff's greeting.

The Chief of Staff nodded. "He just got back from the JCS briefing. I'll let him know you're here."

Tombstone paused outside the paneled door, wondering how many other nephews in the world had to be announced in to see their favorite uncles. Not many. But then again, not many uncles were Chief of Naval Operations, one of the most powerful positions inside the Pentagon.

The captain replaced the telephone receiver and gestured toward the door. "He's got a few minutes, Admiral." A small frown crossed his face. "I need him back in ten, if that's convenient for you."

"Having trouble keeping him on schedule?" Tombstone asked.

The Chief of Staff shrugged. "Well, he's been better than most, but you know how it is—any problems that reach his desk are tough ones. In the last six months he's been here, he's never had to make one single easy decision. And now . . ."

Tombstone nodded. "And now it just got tougher. I'll do what I can, Captain." Tombstone turned the knob on the heavy door, tapped lightly, and shoved it open. He took one step into the room and waited for his uncle's greeting.

"Stoney," Admiral Thomas Magruder said. "Come on in." He gestured at the piles of ubiquitous red folders already crowding the edge of the credenza. "I was looking for you. Come on, have a seat." He pointed at the leather chair positioned in front of the desk.

"Good morning, sir. What can I do for you?"

The CNO grimaced. "You can tell me why the hell the Turks took a shot at us, for starters. And after that, explain the theory of general relativity, the quantum physics in a black hole, and what the hell it is that women really want from us. Is that enough for starters?"

His uncle's wry, self-deprecating voice coupled with his self-assured gestures touched something ancient in Tombstone. It was a feeling of déjà vu, as though he— Of course. His father. Tombstone's father, like most of the Magruder men, a Navy pilot.

Tombstone stirred uneasily in his chair, uncomfortable with the memories that came flooding back. He'd been young, so young, the last time he'd seen his father. Could he even have comprehended at that age that it would *be* the last time?

Military service was more than a career choice for a Magruder. It was a way of life, the hard lessons and dangers that came with it the backbone of their family traditions. His grandfather had served on Nimitz's staff during World War II. His great-great-grandfather had commanded one of Farragut's monitors at Mobile Bay. His father and the man sitting behind the massive desk had continued the tradition, both attending the Naval Academy. They'd both been fast-tracked—both, at least, until his father had been shot down above the Doumer Bridge in downtown Hanoi in the summer of 1969. Sam Magruder had finally been listed as killed in action, and the family had long since given up hope that he was still alive.

"I'm relieving Sixth Fleet," the CNO said bluntly, interrupting his nephew's reverie. He fixed Tombstone with that somber, unreadable stare that all of the Magruder men possessed. His slate-gray eyes, a shade lighter than Tombstone's, revealed no trace of emotion.

"Loss of confidence?" Tombstone asked, referring to the standard Navy reason for relieving officers of command absent cause for disciplinary action.

"Yes. The early reports indicate he damn near pulled a *Stark*," the senior admiral said.

Stark. One of the most critical failures of naval leadership in the last several decades. Coupled with the USS *Vincennes* shootdown of an Iranian airbus, the two incidents neatly bookended the delicate line a commander was required to walk between caution and recklessness.

In the case of the *Stark*, an Iranian P-3 Charlie in an overflight had approached the vast frigate in a threatening posture. The *Stark*'s TAO had treated it as a routine mission, relying on their past experience with Iranian maritime patrols. The captain, in fact, had been in the head during the actual first attack on *Stark*.

Closing to within tactical range, the Iranian P-3 had fired an antiship missile at the USS *Stark*. With the close-in weapons systems masked by her aspect to the attack, the *Stark* hadn't had a chance. The missile had plowed into the ship's midsection. The resulting explosion had killed a number of men, and the *Stark* herself had managed to stay afloat only through the superb professionalism and damage control of the remainder of her crew.

"How bad is *La Salle*?" Tombstone asked. "The EMP is something we've been worried about for a long time. Were there any personnel casualties?"

The CNO sighed. "It's bad. Real bad, I suspect. Every bit of electronic circuitry on the ship is fried. She's underway—just barely—en route to Gaeta for full damage assessment." He shook his head gravely. "We're looking at a full refit of all combat systems, of every bit of twidget equipment on board *La Salle*. Fortunately, *Shiloh*'s EMP hardening worked like it was supposed to, and *Jefferson* was out of range. We've got fifty-one sailors with either complete or partial loss of vision from the nuke flash. Which brings us to the critical question— why?"

"It makes no sense whatsoever, sir," Tombstone said immediately. "Turkey is an ally—an uneasy one at times, perhaps, especially since the fundamentalist Islamic forces began dominating her politics. They've always been hard to figure out—a primarily Muslim country that elects a female, Tansu Ciller, as Prime Minister. As a practical matter, they're heavily dependent on the foreign aid we provide, both militarily and in the civilian population. Aside from our disagreement with them over the Kurds—and we've been damned weak-spined about that—we tend to see eye to eye on things. It just doesn't make any sense."

The CNO nodded. "The Intelligence wienies agree with you. It makes no sense—yet they've opened a Pandora's box of tactical nuclear weapons as a *first strike*. That seems to indicate that everything we know or think we know about Turkey misses the mark. Quite frankly, my immediate inclination is to order a devastating counterforce strike against them. But that's going to meet with some resistance from both State Department and the president."

Tombstone leaned back in his chair and stared at the world map dominating the wall behind the CNO. The intricate politics, the ebb and flow of loyalties and alliances, all driven by the vast machine of religious fervor in that part of the world—how were a couple of pilots supposed to make sense of it? The State Department sure as hell didn't have the answers.

But there'd been an attack on American forces at sea. Aside from any other political considerations, that matter had to be dealt with. Decisively and immediately. To do less would simply open the floodgates, encourage every tin-pot dictator anywhere in the world to take his best shot at American forces, lulled into security by the United States' failure to retaliate against Turkey. He shook his head. No, that would never do. Many more would make similar attempts in the years to come if America demonstrated any lack of resolve or inability to avenge herself. That must not be allowed to occur.

"Any word from State?" Tombstone asked, knowing he was not going to like the answer.

The CNO sighed. "Assholes have got a better intelligence network than we do," he said bitterly. "I've already had two calls from them urging restraint, moderation, some sort of nonsense that sounds like healing the wounded bastard child of Turkey's psyche." Fury rose in the admiral's face, transforming his normally impassive expression into a mask of anger. "*Those assholes shot at my ship!* And they're going to pay for it."

"As they ought to," Tombstone said crisply, uncomfortable immediately with the strong ebb and flow of emotion in the room. "How can I help?"

"Tombstone, what I'm about to tell you—you can decline if you want to, son. I'm hoping you won't, but I'll leave you that option. I've got to have somebody on the scene whom I trust absolutely, an officer in command whose view of the situation mirrors mine exactly. If Turkey is committed to using tactical nuclear weapons, we could lose communications with our forces there at any point. At the very least, we're going to lose ground-support capabilities from our base in Turkey." He shook his head. "I can't risk putting an unknown quantity on the front line. Hell, if I could get away from this desk, I'd go myself. But I can't. Unless you have some objection, as of this second, you're Sixth Fleet."

The CNO fell silent and waited for his nephew's response.

"Sixth Fleet? Admiral, I'm flattered at your confidence, but—"

"Don't give me any crap, Stoney," the CNO said quietly. "I want you there, partially for reasons I can't even tell you about. The only question is, how fast and for how long? I know you're due to turn over with SouthCom in a couple of weeks, and you've got a full plate waiting for you down there. That can wait. There's no other admiral in this Navy with as much actual combat experience as you've got, and nobody I trust more. So cut the modesty and give me a simple yes or no, will you?"

"Yes. Of course I'll go. Did you really have any doubt?"

"No." A ghost of a smile tugged at the corners of the admiral's mouth. "But I thought I'd give you an out if you wanted one. You and that young lady of yours. Hell, Stoney, we've got to start producing Magruders for the next century sometime, don't you think? I thought maybe—"

It was Tombstone's turn to interrupt. "With all due respect, you thought wrong, Admiral," he shot back quickly. "My young lady, as you put it, is a combat-blooded Naval aviator. If she thought I'd turned down this assignment just to stay with her, she'd kick my ass from here to Honolulu."

A silence settled over the room, not an uncomfortable one. It was the feeling between two men who trust each other absolutely, who were related not only by blood, but by the even more binding ties of honor, loyalty, and duty. "You'll leave immediately," the CNO said finally. He stared at Tombstone as if trying to memorize his features. "Old stomping grounds for you, Stoney. Since *La Salle* is completely non-mission-capable, you'll have to park your flag on *Jefferson*. Any problem with that?"

A sudden fierce joy shook Tombstone, surprising in its intensity. To be back at sea, just when he thought he was going to be deskbound at SouthCom for a two-year tour. Not in command of the carrier, of course—that honor would remain with his old wingman, Rear Admiral Edward Everett "Batman" Wayne, the man who'd relieved him only a year earlier as Commander, Carrier Battle Group 14.

Tombstone stood. "If there's nothing else, Admiral, I need to make some preparations to get underway."

The CNO stood and extended his right hand. Tombstone grasped it, the warm configurations so like the flesh of his own hand, a pulse that was more than a physiological function beating in unison in the two hands. Tombstone held the handshake a moment longer than was necessary, then released his uncle's hand reluctantly. "I'd best get going."

"The Chief of Staff will type up your orders." The CNO regarded him gravely. "I don't have to tell you how important this is, Admiral."

"I know, Admiral."

0435 Local
State Department
Washington, D.C.

Bradley Tiltfelt glared at the man fidgeting before his desk. "Whose side are you on?" As Deputy Assistant Director for Eastern European Affairs, he had every right to ask the question. Ask it, and expect the appropriate answer from his subordinates. If the man standing in front of him didn't understand that, it was time Bradley knew that now.

The Section Chief for Turkey appeared to be giving the matter some thought, which Bradley deemed entirely inappropriate. The answer was obvious, or should be. That there might be other concerns than the political standing of his office—and more importantly, of himself—never even entered Tiltfelt's mind.

"I'm in favor of peaceful resolution of this matter before the military knee-jerk reaction escalates it into a full-scale war," the man offered tentatively.

Bradley leaned back in his chair, caressed the leather arm, and stared pointedly at the Chief. "What manual did you plagiarize that from? When I want politically correct jargon out of you, I'll tell you. Now answer the question."

The Chief's face reddened, and his fidgeting stopped. Bradley could see the anger rising in the man's eyes, felt the tension in the room build. It was unfortunate that he had to rely on individuals such as this in conducting foreign policy—extremely unfortunate. Where were the cadres of loyal subordinates that he saw staffing the offices of the other Assistant Deputies? He shook his head, feeling vaguely bitter. The State Department was supposed to be a haven for a better sort of human being, the ones that understood the intricacies of world affairs and that such matters could not be entrusted to men whose only idea of an appropriate response to turmoil was an explosive device.

His Chief started to speak, choked back a few words, and then remained silent.

"Well?" Bradley demanded. "Whose side are you on?"

"Yours, of course, sir," the Chief finally muttered. He looked down at the carpet, finding something incredibly intriguing just in front of his feet.

Well, it was less than the wholehearted support to which he was entitled, but it would have to do, Bradley decided. Indeed, the care and feeding of his subordinates had become of increasingly little significance to him. They were there to do a job, to feed him the information he required in order to make the appropriate decisions, and they'd damned well better understand that. It wasn't as though he could trust them with anything more than mechanical tasks, not after their conduct during the last flare-up with China.[3]

He let the man squirm for a few minutes more while he studied his fingernails. Finally, when he deemed that the full weight of his dissatisfaction had settled in on the man, he spoke. "Turkey is an old and valued ally of the United States," he said slowly and distinctly. "During the decades of the Cold War and even before that, there has never been an incident of this kind. Therefore, our first priority is to determine exactly what provoked this reaction from her."

"Provoked?" his section chief said wonderingly. "Sir, with all due respect—there has been an attack on American forces. A *nuclear* attack. Regardless of any supposed justification, I cannot see any possible rationale for such an egregious breach of international protocol. It's simply—"

"You've just demonstrated why you'll never be anything more than a Section Chief," Bradley interrupted. He pointed an accusing finger at his area expert. "The inability to see beyond the obvious. Of course this is an egregious act. That's obvious. I don't need you to tell me what I can hear on ACN every morning."

Bradley sighed, contemplating for perhaps the thousandth time the difficulty of working with lesser minds. If only at least a few of them had possessed a degree of class, he might have been able to live with the lack of intellectual capacity. But the buffoonish, crass man standing in front of him was all too typical of the minions that inhabited the State Department. "What we need," Bradley continued, enunciating each word carefully, "is a

---

[3]*Carrier 8: Alpha Strike*

reason. And a solution. If you can't supply it, I'll find someone who can."

"With your permission, then," the Chief said, his voice a tightly controlled filament of rage, "I'll be getting back to my desk. We'll see if we can produce the *answers* you seem to think exist." Without waiting to be excused, the Chief turned sharply and left the office, pulling the door shut behind him with a bit more force than perhaps was necessary.

Bradley dampened down his own annoyance, and pulled a legal pad toward him to outline his thoughts. The situation had the potential to be an absolute disaster. Not for the United States—the nation would survive, as she had for centuries. He had an unshakable, inchoate belief in the divine immortality of his country. No, there was a much more serious danger before him—the damage that any mishandling of this affair could do to his own career.

He laid the Mont Blanc pen on the pad, carefully centering it in the middle of the page. "I'll have to go myself," he said thoughtfully. "If I don't, something's bound to go wrong. Any mishandling of this incident, and we could end up with another war on our hands."

A vision formed in his mind, one that he found pleasing. He promptly embellished the appropriate details. It was based on a photo taken in Tiananmen Square, of the single Chinese student who'd stood in front of an oncoming tank and held Chinese military forces at bay during the student protests there. Yes, the Chinese student—and Bradley Tiltfelt. He alone could stand in front of the United States military and prevent an entirely inappropriate reaction from occurring.

A sense of duty, of destiny and historic import, settled

over him. Yes, that was what he'd do. Stop the war before it started.

And what better place to serve as a base for his operations for implementing a true solution to this conflict than aboard the potentially aggressive American warships that were undoubtedly steaming toward Turkey at this very moment?

Bradley reached down and punched the intercom button that would summon his administrative assistant. When the attractive young woman appeared at his door, he barked, "Call my wife. Have her pack me a bag— casual, yet formal. She'll understand what that means. And have the Travel Section arrange transport and passports. Get Military Liaison to send out the appropriate messages for embarkation on board the USS *Jefferson*."

0900 Local
Naval War College
Newport, Rhode Island

Bird Dog was only half awake when he felt the unmistakable touch of a small female hand trail softly across the hard ridges of his gut, lightly tickle the thin band of dark hair that ran between his groin and his navel, and descend unerringly and relentlessly toward its objective. He groaned, stretched hard to release the sleep kinks in his shoulders and hips, and rolled over on his right side. Morning had never been one of his favorite times of the day, but over the past two months, Callie Lazure had been doing her best to change his mind.

"You're awake?" a soft voice said in his ear. Her hand

closed around him, tightened. He could feel his pulse pounding against her delicate skin. "Part of you is, at least." There was a warm, affectionate note in her voice.

Bird Dog groaned, threw one arm around her waist, and pulled her close. "The best part of me is." He moved his hips forward, and felt an answering surge of her hips.

"It's not your mind I'm interested in, sweetheart." She shoved him slightly, rolling him back over on his back. A few seconds later she was astride him. "Just this." Bird Dog drove deep into her, marveling at the incredible hard wetness that engulfed him. The sensation was all-encompassing, literally driving every coherent thought from his head. He reached up, caressed the outsides of her breasts with the palms of his hands, his thumb and forefinger tracing out the rock-hard nipples. Callie planted her hands on his chest and settled back, driving him even deeper into her.

Time dissolved into the rhythmic motion, minutes and hours now counted by the slow surge and beat of the motion between them. It seemed to take hours, weeks, for the steadily rhythmic rocking to pick up speed, accelerating until it drove him almost insane from the sheer relentlessness of it. He groaned, pulled her down to him so that her face was nestled against his, and exploded inside her. He heard her answering cries, soft and insistent, as she came herself.

As his sanity returned, and he began to be able to distinguish the contours of her body from his own, he had but one thought. God, he loved shore duty.

"I'll be damned if I will," Tombstone said, his voice cold level menace. "Not on this operation."

"You've got no choice, Stoney," his uncle said quietly. "Neither do I."

The call from the State Department had come just minutes after his nephew had left the CNO's office, and had carried with it an ominous feeling like the first clouds on a storm front. JCS had approved replacing the current Sixth Fleet commander with Admiral Matthew Magruder, but it had added a complicating factor to the entire strategic scenario. Given the delicate long-standing relationship between Turkey and the United States, the president was insisting that the answer to this potentially explosive conflict be thought of in the broader spectrum—as an entire political and national response rather than purely a military one. As a result, the USS *Jefferson* would be entering the operating area carrying a senior State Department official, a supposed expert in the area.

There wasn't a damned thing about this the CNO liked, and he couldn't blame his nephew for sharing his opinions. After all, wasn't that why he was sending Stoney? To have someone whose judgment so mirrored his own on scene?

But the higher you got in rank, he reflected, the tougher the answers got. There were political trade-offs, power plays and rice bowls, not the least of those was in Central Asia. It was already evident that the State

Department would play a role in this mission. Hell, the JCS had been unwilling to discuss potential targeting scenarios without consulting with the limp dicks over in State. It had even indicated that if the Navy couldn't work with the rest of the U.S. government, they'd put the Air Force in charge of the operation.

The Air Force. The CNO snorted. *Not on my watch.*

"He's going with you," the CNO said flatly. "Get used to it, Admiral. We pay you to act like a guy wearing two stars, not like some hotshot fighter pilot." He hated the words the moment they left his mouth.

Stoney seemed to withdraw into himself, a trait the CNO had noticed all too often in the last several years. He sighed, wishing life had dealt Stoney a better hand. To lose his father so young, especially when the full details of his father's mission had never been made public—damn, it had to affect the man, no matter that he had a father-figure substitute in the form of an older uncle who loved him dearly.

"Yes, Admiral," Tombstone said finally. He shot his uncle an accusing look. "You'll get my best efforts, sir. Have no doubt about that. If there's one thing I understand, it's the concept of taking orders."

"Stoney, I—" The CNO broke off. What could he say now that would bridge this gap between uncle and nephew, that could soften the iron dictates of duty that bound them both? Nothing, he realized. In circumstances such as these, duty superseded all blood relationships. And as much as he disliked it, the admiral had his orders. "Good luck," the CNO said finally, wishing desperately there was some way to break through the new wall he felt between himself and the younger admiral. "Not that you'll need it."

Tombstone stared at his uncle for a moment, and his

glare finally softened into something that held twinges of regret. "If we have to depend on luck, Uncle Thomas, we're in a world of shit. Who am I taking anyway?"

"His name is Bradley Tiltfelt," the admiral said, relieved to be back on less treacherous ground than the emotional health of a family. "I don't know much about him—he's a political appointee. They all are," he added with some degree of bitterness. It was one of the trends that had bothered him most, especially seeing it in his own service. Appointing those who were politically correct and in favor after years of D.C. tours instead of true, operationally hardened warriors with extensive time at sea. Luckily, his nephew was an exception to that trend.

"Well." Tombstone seemed at a loss for words. Suddenly, without warning, he thrust out his hand at the man standing across the desk from him. "I'll see you when I get back."

The CNO surprised himself by walking around the desk, taking the hand, and drawing his nephew in toward him for a brief, hard embrace. "Take care of yourself, Stoney."

1000 Local
ACN News Bureau
Istanbul, Turkey

Bleating goats competed with the sharp staccato of automobile horns to drown out the continual underlying roar of crowds and machinery that was a constant background in Istanbul. The ancient city crowded down to the water, fronting on the Bosphorus Strait. From the earliest times, it had provided a demarcation between Eastern and Western worlds, cosmopolitan and tolerant of almost every culture and religion.

Pamela Drake, combat reporter for the prestigious ACN news network, studied the crowds flowing and eddying around her. Usually, she could pick up vital country details from her studies of the crowds, details that lent her reports an air of authenticity that few others could rival. It was almost a sixth sense, one anchor had once commented, the ability to be on scene at the most godforsaken and remote areas of the world just as all hell was breaking loose. It was also the reason her salary had edged up steadily toward the seven-figure mark, making her the highest-paid foreign correspondent at any network.

Istanbul was hardly a backwater, however. As the world grew increasingly smaller, major metropolitan centers started to look more and more alike, she thought, studying the cars streaming down streets originally built for goat herds. The past slowly faded out, replaced by electrons and tarmac and concrete. Yet for all the modern progress it had made, Istanbul had managed to retain the flavor of an exotic, foreign port.

The crowds today were quiet, and felt puzzled and frightened. She couldn't quantify it exactly—it was less a data-point than a personal observation born of long experience in combat theaters. And Lord knows she had experience—from the Arctic to the South China Sea and all points in between, she'd chased the vagaries of geopolitical eruptions across the globe.

At least here she wouldn't have to rely on portable satellite uplinks with their mysterious grumblings and dependence on atmospheric conditions. Istanbul boasted a fully staffed ACN office, complete with dedicated satellite dishes bristling across the roof and enough telephone line to satisfy any reporter. Sometimes too much technology was more of a pain in the ass than a help. The main bureau in Memphis tended to clamp down during breaking stories, trying to micromanage the stories pouring out of a war.

If they could just get the politics out of the way, the interminable ACN maneuverings for status and position, she thought wearily, she might even be able to figure out what the hell was going on.

She strode into the office, chin high and carriage erect, quickly scanning the crowded room for the man she wanted. There he was, encased in his glass cubicle at the back, talking on the telephone while waving a rancid Turkish cigarette in the air. She grimaced, wishing the health-conscious mandates of the ACN Stateside offices had made it out this far. Still, his disgusting personal habits were of less concern than his approach to the current crisis.

Without asking permission, she strode to the back of the room and shoved open his door. "Mike," she said warmly, "how good to see you again."

The man waved one hand at her, and motioned toward a seat. He finished off a conversation in clipped, guttural Turkish, then replaced the receiver and turned to greet her. "Pamela, I wondered how long it would be till you turned up." He made a vague gesture toward the rest of the newsroom. "We've been taking bets on it, as a matter of fact. If you'd waited another two hours, I'd be eighty bucks richer."

Pamela laughed. "It's your own fault, Mike. You should have known better after all the times we've worked together."

And he should have, she thought, studying him carefully. If not from personal experience, at least from her legendary reputation within ACN. Anyone who bet on Pamela Drake being late to the fight was sorely misguided.

The years had been harder on Mike than they had on her, she was pleased to note. Deep furrows creased his forehead, and the curly dark hair was streaked with gray in an oddly puzzling pattern: random patches of white frost in between stretches of glossy dark hair, giving him a harlequin look.

It would be a mistake to let that mislead you, though, she thought. His eyes were the same sharp, peculiar shade of light brown, piercing and knowing. He smiled, revealing perfectly formed teeth slightly stained with nicotine.

The ACN Istanbul office, while fully staffed, was a small operation. There were five reporters, a handful of mutitalented technicians, and Mike. He was double-hatted as both the bureau chief and the producer, overseeing all aspects of the operations in the area.

"How can we help you?" he queried, holding out his hand. "Always delighted to have you grace us with your presence, of course."

She slipped into the chair, relieved that at least initially there wouldn't be any wearying battles over who she worked for—or who worked for her. "I got here as fast as I could. What do you know about this nuclear detonation?"

His face looked somber. "None of us knows very much at all. I swear to God, Pamela, it's the damnedest thing. There's been no real hint of a change in Turkish position vis-à-vis the United States. No underground rumblings, no petty sniping from our sources, nothing. Not even any unexpected military movements or 'war games,' like there usually are." He spread his hands and shrugged. "Quite frankly, we're at a loss."

"What's the official reaction?" Pamela asked.

"Complete denial. In fact, if I didn't know what the U.S. military was reporting, I'd say the Turks are as puzzled by the whole thing as we are. Worried too. We're too close to Chernobyl for comfort. These people know what effect a nuclear problem can have on their country. We talked to the Minister of Health earlier today, and he was damned near in a panic."

"Strange." More than strange, Pamela thought, downright inexplicable. Her experience, like Mike's, had been that every unexpected conflict was not really that unexpected. There were always murmurings, traces of political unrest, the first few harbingers of war floating around the countryside. If you knew what you were doing, had enough sources in enough countries, you could keep track of them. Keep track of them, and beat every other reporter to the story. It was one of her specialties.

"More than strange," Mike Packmeyer said. He paused, making sure he had her full attention. "More than strange," he repeated slowly. "There's something going on here, Pamela, and I don't mind telling you it scares the hell out of me. Something's very wrong."

Pamela stood abruptly. "I'll need the standard support package, Mike," she began. "Satellite time, uplink resources, and somebody to get my material out of here. With the way this thing is breaking, I don't have time to dick around. Let me be blunt about it—are we on the same team or not?" She fixed him with a cold look.

Packmeyer shook his head. "Always the same Pamela. Listen, I live here—have for the last ten years. What I want right now is to figure out what the hell is going on." He paused and shot her a significant look. "You're the person to do it, Pamela. You'll have every bit of support that you need and more."

Pamela nodded, satisfied. "I appreciate that, Mike." And indeed she did. Now she could concentrate on the one thing that drew her on professionally, a source of endless fascination and intrigue for her—the real story.

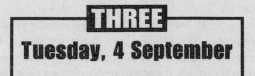

THREE
Tuesday, 4 September

The carrier was little more than a gray smudge on the horizon as seen from the cockpit of the approaching F-14. Tombstone squinted, craning his head around to see forward from the backseat of the Tomcat. Dear Lord, he hated riding backseat—but there was no way around it this time. As sharp as he still felt, he wasn't current in the F-14 cockpit. It was hard to stay in specs flying a desk, but most of the time he managed it. It was only during the last two weeks at D.C., following his assignment at ALASKCOM, that he'd managed to get out of proficiency. So here he was, an aviator en route to fleet command, riding in the backseat. And from what he'd been briefed on the situation, it wasn't likely he was going to get any stick time in the near future.

Maybe after this was resolved he could steal a few hours in the flight schedule. Just a few. Just long enough to feel a throbbing engine strapped on his ass, to satisfy the need for speed. It was why he'd joined the Navy some twenty-five years ago, and only an overriding sense of duty to his country and the off chance that an opportunity just such as this would arise had kept him in the service.

Sitting in the backseat with his hand itching to take the controls was like kissing your sister. Or worse, being interrupted on a couch by an irate father just as you were about to score. He longed to reach out and take control, to feel the stick in his hand and the rudder controls under his feet, to feel how the sheer raw power of the aircraft changed in response to his decisions, his control.

Being Sixth Fleet ought to be enough for any officer. It wasn't.

"On final now," the pilot in the front seat said. "I'll be a little bit busy for the next couple of minutes." And there it was again, that classic sense of understated irony that underlay the bravado of a fighter pilot. Busy was hardly accurate—totally focused and concentrating on the pitching carrier in the sea was more like it. Studies had shown that a pilot's pulse during a carrier-landing evolution could easily reach 160 during final approach.

"I'm all right back here, son," Tombstone said. "Like to see a three-wire trap out of you, though," he continued, referring to the model method of getting aboard an airfield moving at thirty knots. Two short clicks acknowledged his transmission.

The carrier was resolving itself into its shape, the familiar island jutting above the flight deck, the Fresnel lens now a pinprick of light off to his left. If his pilot stayed on flight path, the Fresnel would continue to glow green. Too high or too low, and it would look red to the incoming aircraft. As a final sanity check, a Landing Signals Officer—LSO—was stationed on a small platform that jutted out from the side of the carrier just below the level of the flight deck. The LSO would be an experienced F-14 pilot. As the approaching pilot "called the ball," the LSO would take over direction of his approach, coaching him into the proper lineup, neither too far right nor too far left, and gently wheedling him into the proper attitude in relationship to the deck.

If he or she were dissatisfied with the pilot's approach, the LSO could call a wave-off—an order to the pilot to cease the approach, maintain airspeed, and circle around the aft end of the carrier for another try. It wasn't a permanent black mark on a perfect pilot's record—even the most experienced aviators sometimes got waved off by either the LSO or the Air Boss for a variety of reasons. Gear or personnel fouling the flight deck—inside the yellow lines that delineated the actual airstrip, an unacceptable degree of pitch on the ship, or simply because an experienced aviator was having an off day and was a bit off glide path. It happened. You learned from it and went on from there. Too many wave-offs, though, might warrant a close look by a FNEAB—a Fleet Naval Evaluation Aviation Board. The FNEAB could recommend that a pilot be stripped of his wings if his airmanship weren't up to snuff.

They were a mile off now and descending rapidly. The air was increasingly turbulent as the massive ship plowed its way not only through sea but air as well, creating eddies and ripples that disturbed the atmosphere that buffeted the jet. The Tomcat lurched and bobbled, found its glide path, and settled firmly into it. Tombstone kept up the scan by reflex, glancing from the Fresnel lens to the needles—the crosshairs on the panel that indicated his position relative to glide path—and the airspeed indicator. So far, the kid was doing a good job.

Kid, hell. Tombstone snorted at his own description. The "kid" was probably thirty-five years old, a commander, and in command of one of the squadrons on board *Jefferson*. A two-star passenger rated no less.

The landing was, as always, a violent, controlled crash. Tombstone could feel the tailhook grab hold of the arresting wire—the three wire, if he wasn't mistaken. It spun out eighty feet down the deck, dragging the Tomcat to a screeching halt. The nosewheel slammed down, jarring both pilot and passenger.

As soon as the aircraft touched the deck, the pilot slammed the throttles forward to full military power. If he missed the wire, or if the Tomcat did a kiddy trap where its tailhook skipped over the wire or otherwise failed to be restrained by it, the Tomcat engines would be turning sufficiently to get them airborne again off the forward end of the ship. Not a pleasant maneuver—it was called a bolter, and was far more embarrassing than a wave-off. It meant you were close, too close, but just couldn't manage that final bit of effort required of a Naval aviator to get his aircraft on deck.

Finally, the yellow-shirts jumped out in front of the aircraft, and made the looping right-arm-under-left motion that indicated that the pilot was to raise his tailhook. The pilot eased back on the power, disengaged from the arresting wire, and taxied forward in response to hand signals from the yellow-shirt directing them to a station near the island.

"Good trap," Tombstone said as he unbuckled his ejection harness.

"Thank you, Admiral." The pilot's breath was still coming in hard gasps as he let the adrenaline bleed out of his system. "Good day for flying."

"Any day's a good day for flying, Commander. You'll understand that once you get parked at a desk."

The commander looked startled, as though the prospect of getting promoted to admiral and never getting to fly again was a new thought. "Don't know that I'd like that much, Admiral," he said neutrally. He gestured out toward the flight deck, toward the brown-shirts teeming around the aircraft and the green-shirted technicians darting from problem to problem. "This is what it's about, I mean. No disrespect intended."

Tombstone clambered out of the cockpit, stopping on the middle step to turn and look back at the pilot. "No offense taken, Commander. You enjoy it while you can." He eased on down the side of the aircraft, feeling stiff leg muscles slowly stretch out.

On the deck, a khaki-clad aviator sporting captain's eagles saluted smartly. "Welcome aboard, Admiral Magruder. Admiral Wayne is tied up in TFCC right now, but he asked me to be on deck to greet you. I'm Captain Leary, the Chief of Staff. This way, sir." He motioned toward the door into the island.

"I think I can still find my way around," Tombstone said gruffly. "It hasn't been that long."

"Of course not, Admiral."

Three decks later, Tombstone stepped out into the flag passageway, the blue linoleum demarcating the admiral's quarters and staff areas from the rest of the ship. Each end was hung with fireproof blue plastic curtains. Tombstone dismissed the Chief of Staff, and headed for TFCC. He walked through the conference room, then on into the space itself. So familiar—how long had it been? Less than two months, he realized.

"Welcome aboard, Admiral." Admiral Edward Everett "Batman" Wayne extended his hand. "Good to see you again, sir."

"And you as well, Batman," Tombstone said easily. He gestured toward the large-screen display. "What's up?"

Batman shrugged. "That's the question of the day, isn't it? The only thing flying out there is hot and heavy messages between the embassy and the State Department. Everything's grounded, even commercial flights. And not so much as a peep out of our liaison in Turkey. The Air Force is even laying low at Incirclik."

Tombstone frowned. "What ROE are you operating under?" he asked, referring to the Rules of Engagement that governed peacetime and armed conflict. "Any special modifications?"

Batman shook his head. "If it were up to me, I'd have a squadron airborne and inbound on Turkey right now, max load of bombs," he said bluntly. "You know that. But according to my orders—here, let me show you," he said, handing Tombstone the message. "I'm to maintain a neutral but forceful posture off the coast of Turkey. Would you like to explain that to me? A neutral but forceful posture?"

Tombstone took the message and read the details of the Rules of Engagement. It was as Batman had said, the weaseling sort of message that provided little guidance and less exculpation for the commander in the field. In essence, Batman was ordered to keep anything else from happening, but was to maintain a reactive posture only, except for matters that affected the safety of the ships under his command. "Typical Washington bullshit," Tombstone concluded, and handed the message back.

"What do you want to do first, Admiral?" Batman asked. "I can have a full-scale briefing ready in about half an hour if you wish."

"The first thing I want is for you to call me Stoney," Admiral Magruder said. "Shit, Batman, I keep ending up on your boat—and I'm sure as hell sick of Ruffles and Flourishes."

"As the Stoney One desires, oh, Flight Leader," Batman said.

"The first thing I want to do is see the *La Salle*," Tombstone said. "I've read the reports, but I want to see the damage myself. Got a helo I can borrow?"

Batman smiled. "Lots of 'em—even got some people who know how to drive 'em. When do you want to leave?"

"As soon as possible."

Batman smirked. "Somehow, I thought you might say that. Got a crew standing by for you right now."

Tombstone nodded curtly. "The sooner I see what happened, the faster we can get to work on a solution." He shot Batman a somber glance. "This one isn't going to be easy."

0900 Local
Naval War College
Newport, Rhode Island

"An unusual request, Commander." The Dean of Academics sounded thoughtful. "I'm not prepared to approve it immediately, but I certainly see the merit in your position."

Bird Dog tried again. "Captain, the entire focus of my studies here, including my Advanced Research Project— my ARP—has been on crisis response. What could be better than marrying up the academic with the practical, with basing my final paper on an actual honest-to-God crisis?"

The Dean nodded. "As I said, it's a good point. We're always in favor of kicking our students out of the ivory tower and exposing them to the real world. But truthfully, haven't you already had quite a bit of that?"

Bird Dog had to admit that was true. On his first cruise, he'd been on the pointy end of the spear in the Spratly Islands when the Chinese made a grab for the oil-rich islands off the coast of Vietnam. Later, he'd taken part in ejecting Ukrainian Cossacks from the Aleutian Islands, and had started to learn some of the harder realities of war. And there had been more confrontations after that.

This tour at the War College was supposed to be a time of decompression, a reward for a job well done. Even though he was drawing flight pay, it didn't feel like it. It had been months since he'd flown anything other than the single-engine owned by the local flying club. And as crazily gratifying as he found his relationship with Callie, he felt part of his soul was missing without access to the cockpit of a Tomcat. Maybe, just maybe, if he could get back aboard *Jeff*—no, don't let the Dean even guess that was what he was thinking of. Concentrate on the academic benefit, not the chance that he might get to do a little bit of flying.

"I'll discuss it with the admiral," the captain said. "We can let you know in another day or so. That okay?"

Bird Dog nodded. "Thank you, sir. I promise you, you won't be disappointed with the final result." As he left the Dean's office and headed back to the parking lot, a sudden conviction hit him. The Dean would approve him—he knew he would. He couldn't wait to tell Callie.

Unfortunately, Callie was not as excited about his taking part in the Turkish conflict as he'd thought she'd be. Surely she could see what an opportunity it was! After all, if she'd had a chance to get on board *Shiloh*, she would have jumped at it and he wouldn't have begrudged her that opportunity.

Would he? Suddenly, the full implications of his deepening relationship with a hot-running surface-warfare officer in the United States Navy started to hit him. How would he feel if it were Callie who was out on the front lines, if she were the one in the middle when missiles started flying? The thought was a sobering one. Bird Dog considered himself a model of equal opportunity, and certainly he'd flown with women in his squadron. Commander Flynn, for instance—Tomboy to her squadron mates. One of the finest RIOs he'd ever met, and an aviator he'd be proud to have in his backseat.

But that was different, wasn't it? He wasn't dating Tomboy Flynn—Admiral Magruder was, although that particular fact was a well-kept secret within the Tomcat community. But if it were Callie instead of Tomboy—all at once he wasn't so certain.

"You'd just walk away from us?" Callie asked acerbically. She tossed her notebook and a few reference sources down on the couch. "I guess I shouldn't be surprised."

"What's that supposed to mean?" Bird Dog felt himself go on the defensive, although for the life of him he couldn't figure out exactly why.

"It's the C word, isn't it? Commitment." Callie spat the word out as though it tasted foul in her mouth. "We start getting serious, and all at once you're afraid I'm going to tie you down. Well, hell, buddy, you can just forget it."

She stormed out of the room, leaving a puzzled and confused Bird Dog in her wake. Just what the hell had he said?

1200 Local
Istanbul, Turkey

"The American embassy," Pamela ordered. She leaned back against the rich leather cushions, keeping a tight grip on the center console as the car darted and weaved through Istanbul traffic. Mike had provided her with the car, as well as a driver and a cameraman. He'd tentatively broached the possibility of occasional updates, but had quickly shut down that line of inquiry when he saw the cold gleam in her eyes.

"We talk to the embassy every hour or so," the cameraman offered hesitantly. "Do you really think we'll learn anything there?"

Pamela turned slowly toward him and impaled him against the seat with a cold glare. "What are you, some sort of cub reporter? Or a spy for Mike?"

The cameraman stuttered and stammered, "No, not at all, Miss Drake. I was just—I mean sometimes it's—we know the way things work around here, you know. I was just trying to be helpful."

She held the glare until he looked away. "Thank you. When I need some help, I'll let you know." She turned to face forward again, and was quickly lost in her own thoughts.

Of course, the cameraman was right. There would be nothing new to be learned at the American embassy, not without some personal contacts who would be willing to work off the record with her. But it had been too long since she had been in this area of the world, and she tried to summon up the faces and names of the last two men

she'd known at the embassy. How long had it been—
eight, maybe nine years? There was little chance they
would still be there.

Nevertheless, she resolved to at least ask if they were.
Hell, they'd remember her. Who wouldn't?

"Where is the USS *La Salle* headed?" she asked
suddenly. She turned to the cameraman. "Do you know?"

Sensing a chance to redeem himself, the cameraman
said, "I heard it was Gaeta. There's no official word, but
that would make sense."

Pamela nodded. "It does make sense." She filed this
bit of information away as a potential lead, or as possibly
a sidebar assignment for one of the lesser lights with
ACN.

How to cut to the heart of this conflict? When
Ukrainian Cossacks had seized the Aleutian Islands,
she'd hired a commercial helicopter pilot to ferry her out
from Alaska to the location of the USS *Jefferson*, then
convinced him to simulate engine problems. The *Jefferson* had been forced to let her land, and she'd been privy
to a good firsthand look at the United States Navy's
operations. It hadn't hurt any—nor, now that she'd
reflected on it, helped—that her old fiancé, Tombstone
Magruder, had been in command of the carrier battle
group.

Tombstone. Now there was a subject best left un-
touched. If she'd had the slightest doubts that their
engagement was fully and finally terminated, they'd
been dispelled in the Aleutians. Never had she seen him
so cold, so completely focused on his job to the exclusion
of even her best efforts to distract him. In a way, she'd
come to admire him more during those days than she had
at any time in the past. Admire him, and realize he was
lost to her.

No matter. Rumor had it that he'd taken up with some female chippy off the ship, an aviator at that. She mulled that over for a few moments, contemplating with some satisfaction the thought of Tombstone hitched up with someone just as driven and career-oriented as he was himself.

"Take me to the airport," she said suddenly. In thinking about Tombstone and his new chick, an idea had occurred to her. A relationship with two people so alike could lead to bitter battles. Who, then, was Turkey's equivalent in international politics? The Islamic nations to the east? Possible, but she had her doubts. Turkey had spent too many centuries as an open, internationalized society with close ties to the United States to revert so easily to the social tenets of fundamentalist Islam. And certainly not Greece to the west. No, the border skirmishes between the two countries had created too much permanent ill will. But there was one other option, one she hadn't heard discussed publicly yet, though certainly some think-tank pundit had floated it in closed meetings. The north—Ukraine, the fertile breadbasket of both Eastern Europe and Asia. For centuries battles had been fought over Ukraine and her resources, and since the fragmentation of the Soviet Union, Ukraine had been increasingly vulnerable to outside influences.

But what could an attack by Turkey on U.S. forces have to do with Ukraine? She didn't know—not yet. But something was niggling at her, insisting that she look at the relationship between Turkey and Ukraine more closely. There was no rhyme or reason for it, not really—yet some of her most insightful forays into investigative reporting had come from just such strange connections as the one she'd just made.

She quelled the questioning look the cameraman shot

her with a glance. The cameraman repeated her request to the driver.

Twenty minutes later, the car pulled up outside the Istanbul International Airport. Guards ringed the perimeter—set every two hundred yards or so, she estimated. There was no traffic, none, and the parking lot surrounding the airport held only a few civilian cars, scattered amongst several platoons of drab official-looking cars and police vehicles.

"Nothing comes in or goes out," the cameraman said finally. "The Prime Minister announced that yesterday."

"Oh, really?" Pamela said scathingly. "Then what's that?" She pointed at the horizon, at the commercial cargo ship now on final approach. As it swept by them, touching down lightly on the runway into its roll-off, she noted the name emblazoned in Cyrillic letters on the tail fin—Aeroflot.

1300 Local
Kiev, Ukraine

"A good job, Yuri." The Naval Aviation commander gave him an approving look. "Superb flying in a difficult platform. Your tactical decisions were entirely appropriate."

"Thank you, sir." Yuri tried to relish the compliment, but felt only a sense of mounting frustration. The endless hours and days of familiarization flights, tactical drills, and training for the mission were over. Consequently, with fuel always in short supply in Ukraine, he was grounded. There was no longer any need for him to maintain flight proficiency, so scarce resources were allocated to other units. The possibility that he might be given another mission to fly was almost nonexistent— not until his superiors decided they needed his special talents again. Then, and only then, would they waste fuel bringing him back into currency.

"You have proven most reliable," his commander continued. He gave him a long, appraising look. "You are that, are you not, Yuri?"

Yuri stiffened. "Of course, sir. Is there any question?"

The commander shook his head. "None. That is why you have been selected for another mission. One that requires a good deal of skill of perhaps a different type than you demonstrated in the air."

The feeling of freedom he'd felt in the air flooded him. To have that back for just a while, to escape the drab walls and shoddy construction of this office building— to go anywhere, to just be outside again. And if at all possible, to be airborne—he'd do anything.

"What mission is that, sir?" he said, forcing his voice into a calm, professional tone.

His commander extended a set of orders. "You're going to Turkey. Again."

"To Turkey? But—" A frisson of fear scampered up his spine. If they ever found out what he had done . . .

"As part of an assistance mission," his commander continued calmly. "We have, as Turkey knows, a degree of experience in dealing with nuclear matters." He grimaced slightly. "The Chernobyl affair—a prime example of Russian engineering if anything is. Those bastards—well, no matter. In any event, the tragedy makes us all experts, does it not?"

"But what does Chernobyl have to do with—ah." Finally, comprehension dawned. With the prevailing winds in this part of the world running west to east, Turkey would be worried about the aftereffects of a nuclear detonation that occurred off her west coast. While the Americans could provide technical support, it was unlikely that they would be willing to extend much assistance given the attack on their forces. The next logical source of assistance would be Ukraine herself, rife with hard-won lessons born out of desperation. In the early days of Chernobyl, they'd all become experts, learning about the pituitary uptake of strontium, the basic sanitary precautions to make sure that nuclear fallout was not ingested—too many hard changes in a daily routine that was defined by poverty and deprivation.

"I am primarily an aviator, of course," Yuri began carefully. "However, if the State believes I can be of assistance, I would like to do so."

1315 Local
Seahawk 101

Immediately, thought Tombstone. Back when he'd been a lieutenant, that meant as fast as you could get your ass up the ladder into your aircraft for launch. But when you got to be an admiral, life got more complicated. Even given Tombstone's best intentions and Batman's willing support, getting off the carrier had taken longer than he'd planned on. It hadn't been Batman's fault, nor the aircrew's, but simply that the life of a two-star admiral who was heading for command of Sixth Fleet was so much more amazingly complicated than anyone thought.

In the time that he'd been en route from Gaeta to *Jefferson,* the carrier had fielded six op-immediate calls

for him, two P4—personal for—messages addressed
eyes-only to him, and six inquiries from the news media
requesting either embarkation on *Jefferson* or *La Salle,*
or in-depth personal interviews. He'd tossed those to
Jefferson's public-affairs office and turned his attention
to other matters.

Nothing, he determined, that couldn't wait a little
while. But advising the centers of those messages took a
little time, as did ironing out the chain of command and
operational responsibilities between his new staff, still on
board the *La Salle,* and the *Jefferson.* Most of the Sixth
Fleet staff would have to transfer to *Jefferson,* and
finding everything from working spaces and technical
consoles to staterooms and quarters took time.

Tombstone scribed his initials on the last op-
immediate response and tossed it toward the waiting
communications officer. "Anything else comes in, hold it
for me until I return."

The communications officer nodded. "I've got one
circuit up with *La Salle,* and if anything truly immediately comes in, I'll see that it's relayed to you."

Tombstone nodded sharply. "Stay in touch with
CVIC," he said, referring to the Carrier Intelligence
Center. "I'm more interested in information coming into
the carrier than demands that we send data out. There's
too much we don't understand about this situation, and I
need to know immediately if there's the slightest indication of another attack."

And that, Tombstone thought as he strode down the
passageway, was the six-million-dollar question. Not
only was there going to be an attack, but why did the first
one happen? Maybe there would be some answers
aboard *La Salle.*

Three ladders later, he pushed through the hatch and

out onto the flight deck. Bright autumn sun beat down on him, the sky radiant blue. He took just a second to look around him, breathe in the familiar salt air, linger in the feel of hot tarmac under his boot and the familiar weight of his cranial on his head. He pulled his goggles down from their position on the headgear, and settled them over his eyes.

Now, two hours later, USS *La Salle*'s ungainly profile loomed on the horizon. She was underway, steaming slowly toward him, generating favorable winds for the helicopter across her deck.

The helicopter's pilot brought the Seahawk around smartly, and settled neatly onto the flight deck at the direction of the LSO. Before the rotors had even stopped turning, two officers in flight suits darted across the flight deck to greet him. Salutes were foregone since they weren't wearing headgear, and introductions were postponed until they were inside the skin of the ship. Tombstone stood in the narrow compartment and waited for the door to the flight deck to close. He peeled off his cranial and goggles while the officers waited.

There was an awkward moment. Then the senior officer said, "Welcome aboard, Admiral. I'm Charlie Baker, Chief of Staff. The admiral's expecting you."

"I wish the circumstances could be better, Captain," Tombstone said. "How's the ship?"

"Still steaming, sir. Just barely. We have tugs alongside. We think we may have one of the radars operational by this evening. The technicians are working miracles with it." He gestured toward the other officer. "Lieutenant (j.g.) Harmon, Admiral. He was on watch when we took the shot. The admiral thought you would want to speak with him immediately."

Tombstone turned to the very junior aviator standing before him, and let his eyes run over him. A pilot—he could see that by the wings on the man's flight suit—and not a very experienced one at that. Probably straight out of the RAG—what the hell had he been doing on watch here by himself?

I've got more time in the chow line than this young-ster's got in the cockpit. And they sent him down like a sacrificial lamb for me to devour the moment I step on board? Maybe they're hoping I'll chew him up and spit him out and calm down before I reach the admiral's quarters. Sort of a symbolic bloodletting, if you will.

"Good afternoon, Lieutenant. I'm sure we'll have time to talk later." He turned back to the captain. "I'd like to see the admiral—immediately."

The captain appeared slightly taken aback at the lack of response to his introduction of Skeeter. He nodded uncertainly and led the way forward to the admiral's cabin.

1400 Local
Rome, Italy

"What do you mean the transport's not arranged?" Tiltfelt demanded. "God, man—I believe our message was quite specific."

The attaché nodded uncomfortably. "We received the message, of course, sir, but no clearance from the Navy yet." He glanced at his watch. "It's only been eight hours, sir. I imagine they're a little busy out there right now."

"We're all busy, mister. And one of the things you're supposed to be busy with is assuring that requests from senior State Department officials are acted upon in a somewhat timely and occasionally correct fashion. It appears that neither has happened in this instance, Mr.—Mr. Peals. I take it this is typical of your performance in your post here?"

"No, not at all. It's just that—if you could excuse me for a few moments, sir, I'll follow up on that request."

Tiltfelt turned to his aide. "This is just the sort of thing you must expect from the military. Delays, excuses— any reason to run amok on their own rather than working as part of a coherent national strategy." Tiltfelt was pleased to note that the aide looked suitably attentive.

Ten minutes later, the attaché returned. "Sir, the last flight cleared out to the carrier left eight hours ago from Gaeta."

"Why didn't you have it held? You knew when I was arriving."

"We couldn't, sir. The new Sixth Fleet, Admiral Magruder, was manifested on the flight. And the Navy owns the aircraft—I'm sure you understand that."

"What I don't understand is why you appear to be taking the Navy's part in this, young man," Tiltfelt said acidly. "I will give you ten minutes to make alternate arrangements and obtain the appropriate clearances. After that point, you will find that a permanent reprimand will be placed in your file. Unless you are quite eager to participate in the demanding professional duties at an embassy in some southern African country, I suggest you try to impress me in the next few moments."

1400 Local
Istanbul, Turkey

"Well, well, well," Pamela said, holding her binoculars steady to her eyes. "Isn't it nice of them to commence the off-load out in the open like this?"

The cameraman didn't respond, she noted with satisfaction. Evidently, she'd managed to appropriately convince him of his place on the food chain for this assignment. "You're getting all this?" she asked.

"Getting it," he replied shortly. And she was. The telescopic lens zeroed in on the figures swarming around the Aeroflot flight. He panned slowly away from them, and focused on the tail insignia. "Did you notice that?" he said as Pamela looked at the monitor.

"Notice what—that it's Aeroflot?"

The cameraman experienced a brief moment of satisfaction, then shuddered at the prospect of being permanently assigned to this woman for the duration of her stay in Turkey. Reluctantly, he divulged the one bit of information he had that she needed. "It's not Russian. It's Ukrainian."

"You're certain?"

He nodded.

"Even more interesting," she said softly, speaking more to herself than to him. "Ukraine—now what did they—of course." She immediately made the connection between the nuclear weapon fired in the proximity of the USS *La Salle* and the Ukraine's own experience in Chernobyl. "It takes a thief to catch a thief."

"What? Was something stolen?" The cameraman subsided into silence at her glare.

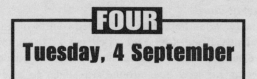

FOUR
Tuesday, 4 September

1400 Local
USS La Salle

Tombstone went immediately to TFCC, the nerve center of the flagship. No matter that the admiral's cabin was merely fifteen or twenty paces down the passageway. With the eastern Mediterranean in an uproar, his first priority was maintaining a complete tactical picture.

There were other reasons to delay his meeting with the current Sixth Fleet as well, not the least of which was to give his own temper time to cool. While many of the officers who served under him would not have believed it, Tombstone Magruder possessed an incendiary temper, not often ignited, but an almost overwhelming force when it did. Sixth Fleet had tripped that trigger by sending the young Naval aviator down to take the full brunt of the relieving admiral's displeasure.

We tell them that people are our most important asset, but do we really believe it? A surface guy eating his young like that—I can believe it. But a pilot—he should know better. It was his call, his watch—and he blew it by putting this youngster on the console by himself. I'll be damned if I'll validate that mistake by executing this nugget at dawn.

Finally, when he felt he'd regained control of himself sufficiently, Tombstone said, "Let's go see the admiral." The Chief of Staff nodded, relieved that the burden of following his new boss around was about to be lifted. The new Sixth Fleet was pissed—that much was clear. But at whom? Ascertaining that at the very earliest opportunity was essential.

"This way, sir." The Chief of Staff led the way out into the flag passageway and down toward the admiral's cabin. At the door, he knocked once, opened it, and stepped aside to let Admiral Magruder precede him. The Chief of Staff hesitated at the door frame, wondering whether or not his presence was required in the compartment, desperately hoping it was not. *When elephants dance, captains get out of the way.*

Vice Admiral Dan Latterly was seated behind his desk, contemplating a stack of folders poised uneasily at the edge of it. He looked up at Tombstone, his face set in a hard mask of outrage. "Military courtesy is a dying tradition."

He's older than me—but not by that much. That gut, those bags under his eyes—he looks greasy, unkempt, like a junior officer coming off a three-day drunk. No senior aviator should look like that. And this ship looks worse than he does. Grimy—and it smells.

The anger Tombstone had struggled to get under control flashed into fiery incandescence. He stood at attention, snapped his hand up to the brim of his cover, and said, "I relieve you, sir."

The abrupt entry into the traditional words of change of command startled Latterly out of his truculence. His scowl faded into dismay, then down a new path to annoyance. "Just like that? I'm aware of your reputation, Admiral, but even you might find it useful to have a brief turnover period. I had thought perhaps tomorrow—"

"Not acceptable," Tombstone snapped, still holding the salute. "Get your ass up and do one thing right before I call the Master of Arms to remove you from this cabin."

"Just who the hell do you think you are, mister?" Latterly shouted, surging to his feet. "You can't come onto my ship and threaten me like this!"

"It's not your ship anymore, Admiral," Tombstone responded coldly. "I'm not sure it ever was, considering what you've done to her."

"This attack—"

"Was unacceptable. As is your attempt to blame it on a nugget who should never have been left alone by himself on a console, not even for a moment."

"This change of command—"

"Will take place right now. The only choice you have in the matter is whether you reach deep down inside of yourself and find some shred of military honor and do this gracefully, or whether you force me to use stronger measures. Now which is it?"

Latterly deflated like a target-practice balloon taking a direct hit from a five-inch fifty-four Naval gun. The hard angry mask of his face sagged into despair. He reached behind him, retrieved his hat from its place on the credenza, and placed it slowly on his head, pausing to adjust it so that it was straight. His hand came up slowly to the brim. "I stand relieved."

Tombstone dropped his salute, as did Latterly.

"Under the circumstances, I'm sure you'll excuse me if I make immediate preparations to depart the ship," Latterly said. "If that meets with your approval, Admiral."

The man was beaten, no doubt about it. Normally, Tombstone would have granted him some final shred of dignity with which to leave the scene. Even now, he sought a reason to do so, wondering if he was really lacking in compassion, as Pamela had always said.

But this was a matter beyond emotion, beyond the normal rules of relationships that governed human beings. Tombstone hadn't beaten him—Latterly had done it to himself. He had endangered his ship, his crew. Had Sixth Fleet had any claim to honor—the former Sixth Fleet, Tombstone corrected himself—it might have been different. But by abdicating his responsibility, by taking incoming fire in a way that never should have happened, he'd voluntarily set himself outside military traditions. "I don't object, Admiral," Tombstone said slowly. "Under the circumstances, it's best for all concerned. I consider you a hazard to navigation, no different from undetected reefs or shoal waters. The sooner you're off my ship, the better."

The now-relieved Latterly nodded once. "Easy words, Admiral." He pointed to the high-backed leather chair sitting behind a solid wood desk. "I hope they come as easily to you when you're sitting in that chair instead of standing in front of it."

1415 Local
Tomcat 301
Eight Thousand Feet

Lieutenant Commander Jake "Snake" Wells found his imaginary point in the sky and put the Tomcat into a lazy, economical orbit around it. In the backseat, Lieutenant

Tom "Kraut" Germany fiddled with knobs, refining his radar picture and tweaking the data link with the carrier.

Keeping on station allowed a pilot some degree of latitude, and Snake generally chose fuel efficiency over fun. Not as compulsively as the Marines, however—give them a CAP station and they damn near stood their Hornets on wing tip in tight, anal-compulsive circles.

The Tomcat was one of two F-14s assigned for carrier air patrol—CAP—over the *La Salle*. The other Tomcat was far to the north, controlling the approaches from Istanbul and the Black Sea. Tomcat 301 took station between the crippled flagship and Turkey's western coast.

The Tomcat carried a standard antiair missile load—two Phoenixes, two Sidewinders, and two Sparrows—along with a full load of rounds for its nose gun. The fever-pitch tensions generated by the Turkish attack the previous day were already starting to dissipate as the routine and monotony of guarding the air approaches to his ship displaced the initial shock.

"Got one of those insects departing in ten mikes," Snake reported. The enlisted air intercept coordinator on board Jefferson had just notified him that Admiral Latterly would be departing *La Salle* shortly. "Wanna go in closer and take a look?"

"Negative," Kraut answered. "I lose too much radar horizon if you go any lower. Besides, we know what those ugly little bastards look like," he said, referring to the CH-46 that would be ferrying Admiral Latterly to Gaeta. "One million parts flying in close proximity to each other. It's a crime against nature if you ask me."

The pilot chuckled. "Yeah, but the guys at the bottom of the class out of flight basic have to fly something, don't they?" He curled his fingers appreciatively around the Tomcat's controls. It was well known that the top officers graduating out of basic flight school received priority slotting to the most demanding airframes, and were often given their choice of which aircraft they wanted to fly. Nobody ever chose helos. Not if they could help it.

Besides, who wants to ferry the big dogs around? That or fly cargo back and forth during UNREP. Snake shuddered, as much from the possibility that he might have to someday execute an UNREP maneuver in one of the ungainly workhorse helicopters as from the prospects of being a helicopter pilot at all. During UNREP, the CH-46 would drop down low over the deck of the replenishment ship, snag a load of pallets with a hook-and-wire contraption, and then ferry the dangling cargo back over to the receiving ship. It was tedious, monotonous work that was likely to get you killed quickly if your attention wavered.

"What else is in the area?" the pilot asked, glancing at his own heads-up display.

"Nothing much on the schedule. A COD flight due out from Gaeta. Old friend of ours on it. Remember Bird Dog Robinson?"

"Hell, yes, I remember Bird Dog! That crazy motherfucker, I thought he was safely stashed away in Newport for a year," Snake said.

"I don't know how he did it, but he's on his way out here. I saw his name on tomorrow's manifest."

"You want to fly with him?"

"Not on your life. I don't know how the hell Gator puts up with him."

"I think Gator deserves—what's that?" Snake broke off his running commentary on the reputations and foibles of Bird Dog's RIO as a new blip popped into being on his scope. "Contact?"

"One of the interesting kind," Kraut said tightly, his fingers flying over the differently shaped knobs that comprised the Tomcat's radar controls. "Based on its radar, I'd call it an F-16. And not one of ours."

"Turkish?" the pilot asked.

"I'd say so, based on where it's coming from. Other than that . . ." The RIO let the sentence trail off.

Both men knew that an aggressive manufacturing program by General Dynamics had equipped more than sixteen nations with the versatile lightweight fighter. Turkey had been a leading proponent of the program, and had an inventory of over 140 F-16 Falcons that were manufactured at its plant in Ankara. Peace Onyx, the program was called. The coproduction agreements had made the F-16 Falcon a mainstay of military aviation in countries ranging from Israel, Bahrain, Egypt, and South Korea to Venezuela.

"Definitely a Falcon," the RIO said. "I'm getting APG-68 radar off it."

"What's she doing out here? They haven't been flying for a day and a half now, and all at once they put a fighter up just as Admiral Latterly is leaving the ship? I don't like the sound of this."

"Neither do I," Kraut said uneasily. "Talk to Homeplate, see what they want us to do."

1417 Local
TFCC
USS **Jefferson**

"Admiral, Intel confirms the launch of one Turkish F-16. It's currently on an intercept course with USS *La Salle* at seven hundred knots."

"What's her altitude?"

"Thirty-one thousand feet. Admiral, she made a high-speed run up to that altitude. It's an unusual flight profile." Lab Rat's pale eyebrows beetled together.

Batman took in a deep breath, and felt the beginnings of an adrenaline surge. That altitude was reserved for commercial flights, but since all traffic in and out of Turkey had ceased since yesterday, it wasn't out of the question for a military aircraft to use Angels 31. But given the prior attack, with the enemy aircraft evidently hiding itself as a commercial flight, the profile was more than unsettling. It was downright dangerous.

Tombstone turned to the TAO in TFCC. "Get that Tomcat on its ass. Weapons free if he sees any hostile intent, but for now just VID—visual identification—and escort. I want to know the second he can tell whether or not the wings are dirty."

If the Turkish Falcon wings were clean, devoid of the Sidewinders, AAMRAM, and Sparrow missiles that made it a deadly air-to-air adversary, he would feel a good deal more comfortable than he felt now. However, until CAP got a good look at it, the only safe tactic was to assume that the Falcon was armed—and deadly.

1418 Local
Falcon 101
31,000 Feet, Four Hundred Miles East of USS La Salle

"Tomcats," the Falcon pilot reported back to his base in Ankara. "Two of them—one to the north, one directly ahead. Instructions?"

"Continue mission as briefed. You are merely to assert our right to use international airways, not to challenge or otherwise provoke the American forces. Is that clear?"

The pilot sighed and kicked the nimble single-seater F-16C in the ass. The single General Electric turbofan responded immediately, the muted growl that was a continual background noise in the small cockpit climbing up into a higher octave and increasing the vibration slightly.

These freedom-of-aviation operations were a pain but a necessity. The attack on the American flagship had horrified him, along with most of his colleagues. Rumors were exploding around the base, ranging from one story claiming that the Americans had taken the first shot at a Turkish commercial flight to a barely credible fantasy centering around Kurdish rebels gaining control of Turkey's nuclear arsenal. It seemed highly unlikely, if not absolutely impossible, that the Turkish government would have authorized such an attack. That fact alone gave credence to some of the more mythical rumors abounding.

On the other hand, the fundamentalist Islamic government certainly had less use for their American protectors than did their predecessors. While such political maneuverings might be far out of his scope of responsibility, the pilot was worried about the consequences of such a trend. Fewer spare parts, perhaps even an end to the coproduction facility with General Dynamics that had done so much to improve his country's military aircraft inventory. After three years flying Falcons, he dreaded the possibility of being forced to fly an older aircraft. And the Falcon was, without a doubt, one of the finest, most versatile all-weather night-and-day military aircraft in the world.

"He's turning toward me," he radioed back to his ground control intercept, or GCI.

"Maintain level flight." The order was curt, abrupt.

At least he was flying, not sitting in a classroom listening to interminable lectures on wars they'd never see. Or safety lectures—God, he hated those worst of all. It was bad enough that you had nightmares about punching out, but to see the realities of shark attacks during experiments, the effect that blood in the water had on the predators, was enough to distract you. And that was the last thing he needed, distractions—not while flying the Falcon.

Best to be very unthreatening then. The pilot double-checked his radar, making sure that it was in a simple search mode rather than fire-control-targeting. The latter mode would have given the Americans ample provocation to fire on him. Particularly under the circumstances.

1425 Local
Tomcat 301
180 Miles East of USS **La Salle**

"I need some altitude." Snake selected afterburners, yanked the Tomcat into a steep climb, and headed for altitude. Against a dissimilar aircraft such as this, the key to tactical superiority lay in exploiting the Tomcat's greater thrust-to-weight ratio. The Falcon, a lighter, more maneuverable aircraft, would prefer to stay in a flat plane of engagement. With its smaller turning radius, it would try to force the Tomcat into a scissors maneuver, exploiting its own capabilities to turn inside the Tomcat's maneuvers and obtain a favorable position on his tail.

Or at least, that was what they'd practiced back in Top Gun school. The pilot swallowed nervously, praying that he had enough experience to take on the Falcon.

"Got a visual," the RIO reported. "Seven o'clock."

Snake caught it then, the tiny smudge on the horizon. With a combined closure speed of over 1600 knots, the shape rapidly resolved into the sky-gray form of a Delta-wing fighter.

"Get under him," Kraut suggested. "Homeplate wants to know if his wings are dirty."

Snake obliged, descending to an altitude five hundred feet lower than that of the Falcon. This particular AOA—angle of attack—would give him a perfect view of the wings and fuselage. That would determine the next move.

1426 Local
Falcon 101

"He's maneuvering," the pilot said excitedly into the microphone. "Descending—Control, he's moving slower than I am. He's going to have an advantage on me if he gets on my tail."

"Evade as necessary, but make no threatening maneuvers," was the response.

Great—evade without looking suspicious. Just how the hell was he supposed to do that? For just a second, he wished he had the GCI operator in the cockpit with him so that he could strangle the man.

Whose idea was it to carry a standard practice load of dummy missiles on the wings during FON ops? At this point, what his superiors had glossed over during his brief was beginning to seem like a very, very bad idea.

In all probability, the Tomcats were simply on a VID and escort mission. In all probability. But given the Americans' claim of a Turkish attack on a flagship, how likely was it that the Tomcats were prepared to be reasonable? By the time he could answer that question with any degree of certainty, it would be too late. The Tomcat would be firmly on his tail in perfect firing position. It would be too late then to second-guess the GCI.

Better safe than sorry. He stomped the Falcon into a hard right-hand turn.

1427 Local
Tomcat 301

"He's maneuvering," Kraut snapped. "Jesus, Snake, he's on our tail."

"Not for long." The Tomcat pilot put his aircraft into another steep climb, grabbing for altitude. The more powerful F-14 had to force the more maneuverable aircraft into an altitude game, one that the Tomcat would probably win.

"Did you see his wings?" Snake asked. He had been too busy maintaining safe separation between the two aircraft during their approach to get a good look. But the one glance he had gotten was enough to worry him.

"Roger that. Full combat load, it looked like."

"You're certain?"

"As certain as I can be at sixteen hundred knots of closure," the RIO retorted. "You wanna go back that close for another look?"

"Tell Homeplate."

The RIO flipped the toggle switch to tactical circuit. "Homeplate, I think we've got a problem."

1428 Local
Falcon 101

"He's gaining altitude," the Turkish Falcon pilot reported. "Instructions?"

"Continue the mission as briefed. Approach to within sixty nautical miles of the USS *La Salle,* then turn back."

"But he's—"

"Do it."

The Turkish Falcon broke off from the preliminary engagement maneuvering and corrected his heading back toward USS *La Salle*.

1429 Local
Tomcat 301

"What the hell is he doing?" Snake wondered. "I thought we were—hell, where is he going?"

"Admiral Latterly's helo!"

Suddenly, it all made sense to the pilot. They were about to be sucker-punched. Who knows what sort of fanatical kamikaze mission the Turkish pilot might be on. After all, they'd launched nuclear weapons, hadn't they? Given that and the odd timing of the Falcon's launch, this had to be more than a routine patrol.

"Tell Homeplate—I'm going in."

1430 Local
Falcon 101

"They're turning back on me," the pilot reported tersely. "Control, I don't like this."

1431 Local
Tomcat 301

"Homeplate, he's inbound on *La Salle*. Admiral Latter-ly's helo just launched. I'm in a tail chase, and he's accelerating to Mach 1.5." Snake's voice rasped as he spouted off the pertinent tactical details.

He did the time-distance calculations quickly in his head. More speed—he slammed back into afterburner and gave chase. The Falcon was almost within missile range of the helicopter now.

"Tomcat 301, Homeplate. You are to prevent the Falcon from approaching within weapons range the helicopter. Is that clear? They've already taken a shot at his ship. They're not going to get him too."

The pilot recognized the voice. He smiled slightly—thank God they had an admiral with some balls on board USS *Jefferson*. "Roger—copy." He toggled to ICS. "Can't get much clearer than that, can you? Lock him up."

1432 Local
Falcon 101

The ALR-56M advance-radar-warning system began its insistent beep, warning that he'd been illuminated by enemy fire-control radar. The Turkish pilot swore, and jerked the Falcon away off its base course. To hell with GCI—no way was he getting caught in the middle of this. No way.

1432 Local
Tomcat 301

"Fox Three." The Tomcat jolted to the left as a Phoenix missile dropped off its right wing. The AIM-54 missile was the most sophisticated and longest-range air-to-air missile in service with any nation. Equipped with an expanding continuous-rod or controlled-fragmentation warhead, the missile had a range of up to 110 miles at Mach 5. Guided by the AWG-9 pulse-doppler radar in the Tomcat, it used semiactive radar homing for initial guidance. The final phase of the attack was carried out with its own pulse-doppler-radar terminal homing.

Although the Phoenix had a history of some unreliability problems in combat, its primary mission in a Naval engagement was to force the adversary on the defensive. While the Phoenix was susceptible to IR and chaff tactics, detecting an inbound Phoenix missile at least forced the adversary to abort any immediate thought of offensive maneuvers and concentrate on its own defense. This would allow the Tomcat to close within range of more accurate missiles.

"Got him—he's jinking," the RIO crowed. "Looks like we might get a nice shot up his tailpipes."

"Fox Three now," Snake answered in agreement. The Falcon's turn had closed the range between the two aircraft from sixty miles to less than thirty miles, well within the capabilities of a Sparrow missile, but still too far away for the deadly Sidewinder.

The Tomcat shuddered again as the Sparrow shot off the weapon's station.

At ten miles, the pilot said, "And now—as a finale—Fox Two. I'm countin' on this one," he said as he toggled off a Sidewinder. "Should be a dead kill at this aspect."

The AIM-9 Sidewinder was equipped with infrared homing. As the Tomcat followed the Falcon out of its turn, rolling in behind it, the tail aspect provided an exceptionally good angle of attack. The heat spewing out of the smaller fighter's tailpipes would draw the missile in as inevitably as a tidal wave, unless it—

"Damn it—he's got the flares. And look at the sun." The RIO swore quietly in the backseat.

As they watched, the Phoenix Sparrow lost radar lock on its target and abandoned the pursuit. The nimble Sidewinder made it through the turn, but became distracted by the chaff clouds and bright sun, a formidable heat source.

"The sun," the RIO breathed. "Damn it, Jake, why didn't you—?"

"What? Wait until he took a shot at the helo?" the pilot demanded. "Not likely. I've got a couple of other surprises in line for this guy. No one shoots at my helicopters and gets away with it. No one."

Kraut prudently declined to note that the Falcon had yet to fire a single shot.

1433 Local
Falcon 101

"GCI, I'm under attack," the pilot screamed. "Get me some help up here—I've got missiles inbound, missiles inbound!"

"Scrambling Alert Five aircraft—101, help's on the way."

For the first time, the GCI actually sounded like a person instead of a mechanical voice at the other end of a radio circuit.

1434 Local
Tomcat 301

"Snake, he's an angles fighter," Kraut reminded the pilot. "You don't want to get into a level knife fight with him."

"I know that," Snake snapped back. "I'm going to close him and then go high."

"He's not doing anything," the RIO remarked worriedly. "No turns yet for a scissors movement—just hauling ass back to base. Jake, maybe—"

"He's not, is he." The anger started to bleed out of the pilot's voice. "Breaking off," he said finally. "Tell Homeplate."

1440 Local
TFCC
USS Jefferson

"Now just what the hell was that all about?" Batman asked of the room in general. "A dirty-winged aircraft makes an attack run on a helicopter, then breaks off and turns away after a missile shot?"

"Better safe than sorry," Lab Rat said.

1449 Local
Tomcat 301

Fifteen minutes later, the airspace around them was cluttered with Tomcats looking for a fight. A few of the more nimble F/A-18 Hornets had also been scrambled, with the thought that the more maneuverable Hornet might prove a more potent adversary for the Falcon. Fifty miles back, two tankers orbited, ready to take all thirsty comers. The E-3C Hawkeye sat turning on *Jefferson*'s deck, waiting for a last-minute repair of a faulty control circuit.

The Tomcat pilot broke off with some regret, eager to try his skill again against the Falcon, but all too aware that his high-speed maneuvers had left his fuel state uncomfortably low. After a quick plug-and-suck on the tanker, he headed back into the fighter sponge. With all of the rapid tactical launches, Alert Five scrambles, and airborne support, there was just one major drawback to the entire air battle —the enemy was still buster back to shore.

1530 Local
Ground Control Intercept Site
Ankara, Turkey

"They fired on our aircraft," the GCI operator said. "There was no provocation—none. He was under close control at all times."

Yuri shook his head sadly. "The Americans—so

impulsive, so insistent on dominating the oceans of the world. It is like dealing with the Russians and the Soviets, yes?" He proffered a comradely smile to the distraught GCI operator.

"What is absolutely inconceivable is how this entire affair began," the GCI said slowly. He looked up at Yuri, a pleading expression on his face. "We did not launch that missile—it would make no sense at all for us to do so. The General Dynamics plant, the military assistance and foreign aid that we receive from the United States—we would not throw that all away."

Yuri held up his hands as if to forestall all further protests. "We have no doubts about that. That is why Ukraine is here, ready to assist our good neighbor in any way possible. If this weapon was of Turkish origin—and let me say that we have doubts about that—then the attack was surely executed without the consent or permission of your government."

"What do you mean?" The GCI operator's eyes narrowed.

Yuri shrugged. "The possible explanations are obvious. One merely has to ask the question: Who would benefit from a conflict between Turkey and the United States? And I believe the answer lies to the east."

"Iraq?"

"Who else?"

The GCI operator appeared to give it some thought. "I had heard the theory discussed, but never completely analyzed. It does make some sense, though. If the United States abandons us, we would have no choice but to look for other sources of support for our national security objectives." He shuddered slightly. "But the mad dogs who inhabit Iraq—I am Muslim, of course, but I am

Sunni, not a Shiite. The differences between the two have never really been understood by the United States."

Yuri touched the man soothingly on the shoulder. "We understand, of course. Ukraine possesses a large, peaceful population of Sunni Moslems, all good citizens of our nation."

"Perhaps it is time for Turkey and Ukraine to pursue a closer relationship," the GCI operator said slowly. "Of course, this is hardly my decision—I simply control aircraft. But I think that it might make much sense to many of my fellow countrymen." A sour look crossed his face. "Anything other than closer ties to the Shiites."

Yuri left the matter as it stood, not wanting to appear conspicuous by engaging in an extended political discussion with a mid-grade officer. It did no harm, however, to plant the seeds of thought in the man's mind. Over the last two days, he had observed that the GCI operator was well liked by his peers, a gregarious and social man who commanded a degree of respect for his thoughtful political and religious statements.

Seeds sprout slowly in this rocky country, Yuri thought, and any beginning is a good one. Let us see how this will affect matters. It cannot help but provoke discussion, and further conceal our true objectives. Every officer on the Ukrainian support mission would be pursuing similar objectives within their own pay grades. With a groundswell of junior briefing officers noting the similarities between Ukraine and Turkey's interests . . .

1545 Local
USS **La Salle**

"Stoney, you need to get your star-studded butt back over to *Jefferson*," Batman's voice snapped over the radio circuit. "It's absolutely untenable for a Sixth Fleet to remain on board that hulk any longer. There's no reason for it. After that run the Falcon made on Admiral Latterly's helo, you don't need to be taking any chances."

"I've been in command a little over two hours and you're already urging me to quit?" Tombstone asked. He held up one hand as if to ward off the angry words streaming out of the speaker.

"It's not a question of quitting at all. You should simply shift your flag back to the *Jefferson* where it's supposed to be. That was the plan originally. I know you've got complete discretion to break your flag wherever you want, but be reasonable about this. Admiral," Batman continued, switching to a more formal tone of voice, "I can provide air cover for *La Salle* as she hauls ass back to Gaeta, but if this conflict breaks open any wider, I'm going to need every airframe I have to protect the battle group. What *La Salle* needs to do is get the hell out of the way and let us run this war from the carrier. Don't you see?" Batman's voice took on an almost pleading quality. "Stoney, it's the only way."

Tombstone Magruder sighed. There was too much truth to what Batman was saying for him to so easily reject it out of hand. Still, the situation on board the *La Salle* had him deeply concerned. It was clear the material condition of the ship had been deteriorating even before the air attack, a result of lack of attention to basic maintenance practices and cleanliness. When he met with the former admiral's staff, the officers and enlisted personnel had been unwilling to meet his eyes, sullen and unwilling to speak their minds. Had he been going into combat on this ship, Tombstone would have been gravely concerned for their safety.

That's not the issue now, though, is it? This ship is not going anywhere except into port for extended repairs. It will be at least a year before she gets underway as fully mission-capable, maybe longer. Do you really want to try to run this war from a pier in Gaeta, limited to the tactical data aids that survived and a tactical link to a shore facility?

He knew the answer to that question. You lead from in front, not from behind.

Tombstone reached a decision. He turned to Captain Henry Jouett, *La Salle*'s commanding officer, a Navy surface captain with twenty-five years in the service. *La Salle* was Captain Jouett's fifth at-sea command.

Relationships between flag commanders and the captains of the ships they rode could be a source of real problems. While Sixth Fleet commanded all assets in this part of the world, the commanding officer of his flagship owned the ship on which Sixth Fleet broke his flag. Flag interference with the day-to-day details of shipboard operations was not unheard of, especially when the commanding officer was a true surface sailor instead of an aviator getting his feet wet before going on to the command of an aircraft carrier. The differences between the two warfare communities could give rise to nasty pissing contests.

Captain Jouett's face, dominated by a strong nose, was weary and lined from the tragedies of the last two days.

His expression was cold and impassive. Short, broad-shouldered, and slim-hipped, the man was built like a bulldog. His hair was cut Marine short, sunburnt scalp showing beneath copper-colored hair. Piercing blue eyes stared back.

"I want this ship squared away," Tombstone said. He watched as an expression of mixed relief and eagerness rearranged the lines in Jouett's face.

I was right about him. Based on his reputation, I'd lay odds Captain Jouett's the only man more pissed off over this ship than I am.

"Any problem with that?" Tombstone continued.

"No, Admiral. Not now." Jouett's voice was grim.

Tombstone glanced around the room, and caught a couple of sets of eyes glancing furtively his way. "In my cabin," he said abruptly.

Once inside the admiral's cabin, which still felt like alien territory to him, he turned to the ship's CO. "You had a problem with my predecessor, I take it?"

Jouett nodded. "With all due respect, Admiral—"

Tombstone cut off the preliminary and pro-forma disclaimers with a sharp gesture of his hand. "I don't have time for this now, Captain. You know what I'm up against. I have one question for this—what happens to this ship after I leave?"

"If you take your staff with you, conditions will improve one hundred percent." He stood a little taller, looking Tombstone straight in the eye. "I'm a surface sailor, Admiral. I know how to run a ship."

"I've heard that."

"I can do my job without an aviator trying to grow surface-warfare wings," the captain replied bluntly. "Admiral, I don't try to fly your aircraft—no aviator ought to be telling me how to run my ship."

Tombstone nodded sharply. "Agreed. Captain, you've got between now and the time you pull into port at Gaeta to get this ship into proper shape. I'll be back to take a look at her. You've got my support to do whatever is necessary to transform this hulk into my flagship. You run into any problems, you get on the horn to me. Other than that, I'll leave you alone. That satisfactory?"

The captain smiled. "Oh, I think that will work out quite well," he said quietly. "Admiral, I'd be honored to have you take a look at this ship in about four weeks. She might not be back up to spec by then, but I think I can show you what a warship ought to look like by then."

"Then get me the hell out of here. And while you're at it, manifest that young aviator my predecessor was trying to string up," Tombstone said. He pointed at the radio speaker. "You heard Admiral Wayne—we've got a war to fight. And if you want to be part of it, you've got to get this ship back in shape to fight."

Forty minutes later, a second CH-46 lifted off *La Salle,* with another one standing by to rotate and radiate in short order. Tombstone's Sixth Fleet staff was spread out between the two helos along with—well, what the hell was Skeeter? A little lost lamb? Tombstone shook his head, almost smiling at how the young Naval aviator would have reacted to that description. Skeeter Harmon had neither the demeanor nor the appearance to make a very good little lost lamb. Maybe a black sheep—no, that wouldn't do it either.

He looked across the fuselage at the aviator, noting that the man was already dozing in the web seat running fore and aft in the helicopter. If the young man was as good as he thought he was, then Tombstone was doing him a favor by getting him away from the black-shoe command early and onto where he belonged—on board an aircraft carrier.

"You current?" Tombstone shouted, getting Skeeter's attention.

"Yes, Admiral. I need a couple of night traps, but that's about it."

"So do I." Tombstone gazed levelly at the young man. Best to get him back in the aircraft as soon as possible, to wipe out the taste of failure that must surely linger in his mouth over the successful attack on *La Salle*.

Not that it had been his fault. But Tombstone knew that if he had been in the young man's shoes, there was nothing in the world that could have convinced him that he couldn't have prevented the attack. Nothing at all.

And the only way to well and truly get over it was to strike back. If there were any way at all to do it, Tombstone would give him the chance to do just that.

1630 Local
Flight Deck
USS Jefferson

It wasn't the gentle thump of the helicopter setting down on the flight deck that finally woke him up, but the change in vibration that radiated up through his seat as the pilot disengaged the rotor and the helicopter began to spool down. Skeeter flinched, emerging from the endlessly repetitive daydream/nightmare of the *La Salle*'s engagement. His eyes jerked open—he stared across the aisle into the somber face of Admiral Tombstone Magruder.

"We're here," Skeeter said unnecessarily, for lack of

anything better to say. He disengaged his seat harness, stood, and stretched. The admiral, he noticed, was moving with a laconic efficiency, snugging his cranial down and repositioning his goggles over his eyes. Skeeter, halfway through taking them off, decided to follow the older man's example.

"You probably haven't spent much time on the flight deck," Tombstone said. "Fly out, trap, get shot back off during CQ. That about it?"

"One hot-swap crew change," Skeeter admitted. "They kept me in the handler's office until I could get a hop back out."

Tombstone nodded. "You heard it in the RAG, but let me tell you again. The flight deck of an aircraft carrier is the most dangerous place on earth. Your head stays on a swivel, you hear? Because you can't—hear, that is." He moved toward the forward hatch in the fuselage and paused at the rim.

Skeeter moved tentatively up to stand beside him.

"You see that Tomcat turning?" Tombstone asked. "Never turn your back on an aircraft that's turning— never. Son of a bitch will suck you down and spit you out as puree faster than you can think. And listen to the yellow-shirts." He saw the skeptical look in Skeeter's eyes. "They're enlisted men, but they know what they're doing. And they've logged more hours on this deck than you've logged in a chow line. So if one of them screams at you to get the hell out of the way, you do it. Ask questions later, but don't even stop to think about disobeying."

"Aye, aye, Admiral." Skeeter tried to look appreciative over the brief refresher training. Hell, it was something—getting chewed out by an admiral before he'd even had a chance to screw up. He ought to appreciate it, the fact that the old guy cared. Still, it wasn't like he was the admiral's age. Youth and reflexes still had the advantage over age and experience. Besides, if they let the young enlisted guys hang out around the flight deck, then there was no way an officer was going to get in trouble. Not a chance.

Tombstone disembarked from the aircraft first. As soon as Skeeter took another step toward the hatch, he felt a hand grab the back of his collar. "Not so fast, youngster." He looked up into the face of a lieutenant commander. "Senior officer's always last on, first off." A look of amusement crossed the officer's face. "Seeing as you're a lieutenant j.g., I'd bet that puts you back toward the ass end of the line somewheres." He pointed back toward the rear of the fuselage. "Don't start pissing us off before you've even had a chance to check on board."

"But the admiral—"

"You fly with us, not the admiral. Now get your happy ass back to the end of the line."

Skeeter shot the older man a surly look, then did as he was told. All this seniority crap—well, when the fighting started, he'd show them what counted.

But you didn't before. You froze—hell, if you'd been thinking, you could've been a hero. A little faster reaction to what the operations specialist told you, maybe a request for air support—none of this had to happen. And it's all your fault.

Another part of his mind wailed in anguish. It was a goddamned nuclear weapon. What the hell was I supposed to do? I barely knew how to handle the buttons on the console, let alone—

Results count. That's all that matters. Even before he'd reported to his first carrier, before he'd even been assigned to a stateroom, he'd fucked up big time. And from the looks of the commander who'd just shooed him away from the hatch, nobody was going to forget it anytime soon.

Skeeter took his place at the end of the line and retraced his steps toward the front of the fuselage. It moved along quickly, and he was delayed maybe two minutes from disembarking, but that wasn't what mattered. It was the point of the thing.

Finally stepping down from the aircraft, he followed the line of officers tracking across the flight deck toward the island hatch. Lost in his own surly thoughts, he neglected to do the one thing that Tombstone had just cautioned him about—keep up his scan.

Halfway across the flight deck, the officer in front of him turned abruptly, ran back toward him, and tackled him around the waist, driving him to the deck. His cranial banged painfully against the tarmac, and Skeeter reacted instinctively. During his days at the University of Tennessee, he'd been a star member of the wrestling team. So what if he was a couple of years out of practice—the old skills so long ago memorized during his youth came back quickly. Two seconds later, he had the older officer virtually bound and gagged on the flight deck. He put a little pressure on the back of the other man's cranial, driving it down across the gritty tarmac.

Suddenly, the two men were surrounded by yellow-shirts. Two of them grabbed Skeeter by the arms and jerked him up off the officer, while a third helped Skeeter's assailant up off the deck. They lifted Skeeter's feet clear of the tarmac and carried him toward the edge of the flight deck.

Fuckers are gonna throw me over the side. Shit, what is this? Skeeter flailed violently, trying to break the grip on his arms, and succeeded only in earning himself an excruciatingly painful armlock. His original assailant, he noted, was following peaceably though quickly.

As they neared the edge of the flight deck, Skeeter saw a short flight of metal steps leading down to a catwalk that ran directly below the level of the flight deck. He heard an increasing roar, and a stiff wind fluttered the legs of his pants. He looked over to his left—the helo that had brought them in was already rotating, easing up and over the side of the deck.

Skeeter quit fighting as the two men shoved him toward the steps. He clattered down them, rage boiling in his veins now that he was finally free. He turned at the bottom of the platform to face them as they came down.

"You dumb shit! Don't you listen to the Air Boss?"

Skeeter's hand shot out and he nailed the yellow-shirt on the left side of the man's face. The blow drove him back and left him sprawled against the metal steps he had just descended. The three other yellow-shirts immediately jumped him and drove him down to the deck, reinstalling the armlock as a permanent part of his anatomy. He might have been a hell of a wrestler, but it was a one-on-one sport—no way he could take all three of them, not unless he could get free.

With his face pinned down to the metal grating, Skeeter saw a pair of brown shoes appear in front of his face. A swath of khaki cloth followed as an officer knelt next to him.

"Before I have them throw you overboard, you might want to consider listening to me for a minute," a voice said dangerously. "My money is on making you fish food right now, but the chief here thinks there might have been a misunderstanding."

Skeeter saw an arm gesture over in the direction of one of the yellow-shirts.

"Do you have any idea of what's going on?"

A slow, cold dread started to seep into Skeeter's gut. Within ten minutes of embarking on his first real aircraft carrier, he'd managed to get rousted just as though he were still back on the streets of Knoxville, Tennessee. This was the Navy, he reminded himself. It wasn't a white town that thought that all black boys were up to something they shouldn't have been, probably a couple of felonies.

Skeeter tried to shake his head, found his cranial still pinned to the deck. "No, sir." It seemed the only possible answer.

"There's a Hornet inbound that's declared an in-flight emergency," the voice continued coldly. "If you'd been paying attention, you would have seen the yellow-shirts motioning at you to clear the flight line in the fastest manner possible. They were pointing out this ladder to you, my friend. That Hornet's only two miles out, and if you'd kept going the way you were walking, you'd end up riding the engine. And," the officer added almost as an afterthought, "you'd be dead. Real dead."

The screaming shriek of a Hornet built to almost unendurable volume, and the entire ship rang as though it had just run ashore. The catwalk beneath Skeeter vibrated, and for one panicky moment he thought it might toss him off and over the side. He heard the Hornet's roar crescendo, and knew that the pilot was slamming the throttles forward to full military power in case of a bolter. The sound went on and on—for hours, it seemed—and then finally began spooling down. A harsh Klaxon sounded.

"Let him up," the officer said. "Good trap, even if it was the four wire."

There was one sharp, upward jerk on Skeeter's trapped

arm; then the pressure eased off slowly. A hand stayed on his forearm as though to maintain control in case he continued to act like an idiot.

Skeeter stood slowly and tried to regain some measure of dignity. The four yellow-shirts and one officer were staring at him with grim condemnation. "I didn't know." Skeeter tried to make the words sound believable.

The lieutenant nodded. "That was obvious. In the future, keep your head out of your ass." The officer turned to the yellow-shirt chief petty officer and said, "Find out where the hell this nugget is supposed to be, and take him there." He turned back to Skeeter. "And as soon as you check in, you go directly to your Executive Officer and explain to him or her exactly what just happened out here. If they've got any questions, they can call me."

"Yes, sir." Skeeter drew in a deep, shaky breath. God, but he'd screwed the pooch on this one. "And who shall I tell the XO to contact, sir?" He raised his chin and stared directly into the other officer's eyes, meeting their glare.

"Lieutenant Commander Bird Dog Robinson," the other officer said shortly. "I'll be assigned to the admiral's staff."

"Yes, sir." Skeeter turned as the chief tugged on his flight suit. Two other yellow-shirts fell in on either side of him and behind him.

"Aren't you forgetting something, sir?" the chief asked. He pointed back at the senior officer. "It's traditional on this ship—when somebody saves your life, a thank-you is in order."

Skeeter turned back to the other officer. "Thank you, sir."

The other officer shook his head. "Just stay the fuck

out of my way, asshole. I'm not getting killed by some nugget while I'm technically still on shore duty at the War College."

"How bad is it, Stoney?" Batman's face was almost as grave as that of his old lead. "Can she make it to Gaeta?"

Tombstone nodded. "She's got power and she's making way. She's got a couple of tugs alongside as well. If the weather will hold up, I don't see any problems. The electronics are the main problem, although the EMP damaged some of her engineering-control surfaces as well. Captain Jouett's worried about the shaft too—says he's got a bad shaft bearing he thinks may go out soon. Latterly wouldn't let him keep the ship in port long enough to get it looked at." He let loose a deep, gut-wrenching sigh. "But shipmate, the problems are worse than that."

Batman looked bitter. "Tell me about it—I've been living with that asshole for months now."

Darkness crossed Tombstone's face. "Why didn't you say something?"

Batman snorted. "Would you have, in my shoes? Whine to your old lead about having an asshole for a boss? I don't think so, Stoney. We didn't grow up that way."

"But that ship—Jesus, Batman, you should see it."

"Captain Jouett is a good man," Batman answered. "You give him a chance, he'll give you a ship that can fight."

"It's not going to be up to him. Don't you see, there's too much damage to her. She hasn't got a single combat system left intact. The only reason she has any radar at all is they had a spare Furuno stashed below the waterline. Her communications, her data link, her self-defense measures—everything gone." Tombstone's voice was bitter. "Why didn't we expect this, Batman? We've known for years how much damage an EMP blast can do—why weren't we prepared?"

"Well, the newer ships are, of course. All the Aegis platforms incorporate heavy EMP shielding."

"That's not good enough!"

Batman fell silent in the face of his old lead's rage. It was clear that the specter of the shattered, silent ship had cut deeply into Stoney, and nothing Batman could say or do would change that. As he always had, Stoney would have to puzzle things out for himself. He would, eventually. But in the meantime, he was sure as hell going to be hard to live with.

"Why don't we take a look at the things we can do something about?" Batman said to break the uneasy strain in the room. "You've brought your staff—I've got my people finding them spaces right now."

Tombstone shook his head slowly. "You're right, old friend." He gestured toward TFCC. "Want to give me a rundown?"

"Now that you mention it . . ." An odd smile quirked Batman's face. "I just happen to have a situational brief ready to go."

"Give it to me in a nutshell—how bad is it?"

Batman drew out a laser pointer and used it to highlight specific contacts on the large-screen display. "Air traffic has resumed between Turkey and Ukraine, though thus far it's all been inbound from Ukraine to

Turkey. The flight plans filed indicate they're inbound to provide relief—given their expertise after Chernobyl, that makes sense to me."

"What about that Falcon our Tomcats took a shot at? Is Turkey ready to resume regular freedom-of-navigation operations?"

Batman shook his head. "Lab Rat's not entirely certain. He's got some indications that they're moving to a higher state of readiness—one that we would have expected to see before the shot, not after. But there's nothing definitive. You know how intel is—if it's good gouge, it's too sensitive to tell us."

"Are Ukrainian flights talking to us? Anything suspicious about their transits?"

Batman looked quizzical. "Nothing out of order at all. We ask for a clearance vector, they give it, although most of their transit is just over the Black Sea. Really, absent a UN embargo of some sort, we've got no authority to regulate their commerce."

"Other than shooting them out of the air."

"We almost splashed one Falcon," Batman said. "Would have too if he'd continued inbound on Admiral Latterly's helo. And if there's any question about the decision to go weapons free on it, I'll take full responsibility. I told that pilot to keep the bird away from my carrier and away from Latterly's helo—and that's exactly what he did. I looked at the data tapes, and it looked like the Falcon was trying to put him into a scissors. You know how deadly that can be between a big bird like the Turkey and a gnat like the Falcon."

"Concur—and I would've done the same thing. There's no point in having to put the entire burden on the boys out there—we've gotta give them the tools they need to fight with. And that includes guidance from us and accepting responsibility for the consequences."

"The rest of the tactical picture is degenerating as well. Despite humanitarian aid from the Ukraine, there appears to be some tensions between the Turkish and Ukrainian militaries. Nothing specific—no shots fired—but the routine training flights are harrying each other, playing grab-ass, lighting each other up and shutting down—that sort of thing."

Tombstone frowned. "I don't like it. Why would Turkey be pissed at the one nation that stepped forward immediately to help them?"

"And there's worse news." Batman circled the laser pointer around the display. "We're in dirty water now, Tombstone. Our S-3 Vikings have been running sonobuoy barriers out along our street of advance, and yesterday they talked me into laying a pattern near *La Salle*. You're not going to like what they found."

"Submarines? Which ones?"

"Nasty ones. Ship-killers—a couple of Kilos just north of *La Salle*, and a third that's confirmed out of port but remains unlocated. All diesel boats, all black holes in the water when they're running on batteries."

"You're keeping up surface surveillance flights?"

"Of course. But you know how these guys are—they run silent and submerged all day, come up and suck down some air when it's dark. Our best detections have been off radar and flare, not off acoustics. But we'll keep trying."

"Jesus, what else?" Tombstone rolled his shoulders back, trying to relieve the tight knot gathering along his shoulder blades. The base of his head was beginning to pound, a headache creeping up his spine and circling around to clamp down on his temples.

"We've got one more COD flight inbound today. A special one, on direct orders of CNO."

"Who's flying out—God?"

Batman frowned. "Almost. It's the State Department. And there's worse news. Rumor has it that a certain reporter acquaintance of yours is prowling around Istanbul. You can guess who. We're already getting requests to on-load teams of reporters."

Tombstone swore softly. "Pamela, of course. It figures—there's shooting going on, she's in the middle of it." He looked up and glared at his friend. "No comment—nothing. As far as I'm concerned, she can watch CNN to get her updates."

FIVE
Wednesday, 5 September

"I trust your people are situated comfortably," Admiral Magruder said. He kept his voice calm and neutral, determined not to let a rocky initial meeting with the State Department influence the whole course of their relationship. When he looked at the rumpled diplomat sitting in front of him, however, it was difficult to believe that these people were anything but trouble. Particularly on a frontline warship.

"The interminable noise—how in the world do you stand it?" Bradley Tiltfelt said. "I can't believe that your own quarters are quite as noisy as mine are, Admiral." He tendered a skeptical, knowing look at the new Sixth Fleet commander.

Tombstone gestured over his shoulder. "I'm directly below the waist catapult. But I suppose it's just something you become accustomed to, Mr. Tiltfelt. After twenty years of listening to Tomcats launch, the noise makes me drowsy."

Tiltfelt's look deepened into sardonic amusement. "I find that difficult to believe."

Tombstone shrugged, suddenly tiring of the interminable pleasantries. Late yesterday Mr. Bradley Tiltfelt and five assistants had arrived on board USS *Jefferson,* proclaiming with wide smiles and firm handshakes that they were there to help. The reaction from his staff and Batman's had been guarded. They'd already been evicted from their quarters, forced to double up among themselves and with the ship's company, and otherwise inconvenienced by the arrival of the civilians.

"Admiral, if we might perhaps get some preliminaries out of the way. . . ?" Tiltfelt suggested delicately. "First, I want you to know how much I appreciate your having us on board."

It's not like I had a choice. "Glad to have any assistance possible, sir," Tombstone said, surprising himself a bit at the smooth tone in his voice. Perhaps it was something you learned when you got more senior, this ability to dissemble and mislead on command. "The sooner there's a resolution to this, the happier we'll all be."

"Yes. Of course. Which brings me to my first point. Admiral, I want you to know that the State Department takes this matter most seriously. In our view, there should be an immediate in-depth investigation into this entire incident. No holds barred, sir. And we expect some answers—at least preliminarily—along with appropriate disciplinary action within the next forty-eight hours."

Tombstone nodded pleasantly at what at first appeared to be the suggestion that the State Department was more firmly on board with his thinking than he thought possible. The last phrase jerked him out from his comfortable assumptions. "Disciplinary action? I'm afraid I don't understand. If you mean perhaps a reexamination of the relationship between Turkey and the United States, then that's hardly our province."

Tiltfelt shook his head from side to side emphatically. "Don't try to misunderstand me, Admiral. I'm talking about the unprovoked attack by your aircraft on a Turkish freedom-of-navigation operation. This sort of unchecked aggression simply cannot form a solid basis for mature international relationships."

"Mature international—you want me to put my guy in hack for taking a shot at that Falcon? Hell, they *missed*."

"Did you think that you could cover it up forever?" Tiltfelt demanded. He snorted in disgust. "I think not. Matters are at too delicate a stage of resolution for inappropriate retaliation."

"They're not in any stage of resolution as far as I know," Tombstone shot back. "The last I heard, Turkey did the unthinkable. My pilot was simply following orders."

A deep expression of sadness and disappointment crossed Tiltfelt's face. "How often have we used that expression for war crimes?" he asked the room in general. "Admiral, this situation simply must be stopped before it gets out of hand."

"It's already out of hand," Tombstone roared, forgetting his resolution to play their game with the same cold canniness the State Department was famous for. "Dammit, that was a nuclear weapon. And you expect me to let them back within tactical range of this ship?"

"I expect you to do more than that, Admiral." For the first time, Tiltfelt bared the iron hand that lay beneath his smooth, soft words. "And I think you'll find your superiors back me up on this."

"On what?"

"On an immediate diplomatic resolution of this unacceptable state of affairs. It is clear to me that Turkey has found some reason to feel extremely threatened by the American presence in the Mediterranean. Our only hope for a peaceful resolution to this conflict is to bring all parties together to uncover the underlying rot in U.S.-Turkey relationships. We must talk, Admiral, not fight. Can't you see that?"

"You want to talk to them?" Tombstone couldn't believe what he was hearing.

"Talk. And not only with Turkey. I have authority," he continued, drawing an intricately sealed and stamped document out of his briefcase, "to invite representatives from area nations on board this carrier in order to work out a lasting peace proposal."

"On my ship." Tombstone had passed from shock into sheer incredulity. "You must be joking."

"Read this." Tiltfelt thrust the document at him. "I have appropriate copies for you, of course, signed by your superiors. Including," he continued pointedly, "your uncle."

Tombstone scanned the document rapidly. It was just as the State Department official had said. Admiral Matthew Magruder was directed to provide air support, transportation, and berthing for such concerned nations as would agree to attend an Eastern Mediterranean peace conference. Moreover, it appeared that his uncle and the other Washington cohorts had been busier than he'd thought.

No wonder they wanted to get me out here so quickly. There's no way I'd sit still for this, not if I were back in D.C. They must be insane. Or maybe they weren't. Perhaps the pressure brought to bear on the Navy establishment had simply been too great. Uncle Thomas might have known that, might have even made sure that

Tombstone was on site so that at least one admiral tied to him with additional ties of loyalty and kinship would be on scene.

To ensure that I'd go along with it? Or to serve as an extra set of eyes and ears? Suddenly, Tombstone desperately needed to make a secure phone call to his uncle, to hear the words from his own mouth. He needed an explanation, some framework in which this entirely unprecedented maneuver would make sense.

"When?" Tombstone shook his head in resignation. "This will take time to arrange. Security alone will be a nightmare."

"We have nothing to hide from our allies, nor will I have you offend them by assigning Marine Corps 'escorts' to make them feel as though we don't trust them," Tiltfelt said firmly. "If you will read the last paragraph, you will find the intended commencement date."

Tombstone leafed rapidly through the document, finally coming to the last page. His eyes lingered on the paragraph, then widened in shock. He looked across the table at Tiltfelt. "You must be joking."

"I am hearing that phrase entirely too often from your mouth, Admiral," Tiltfelt snapped, evidently at the end of his patience. "What is there that you do not understand? Or is your ship simply incapable of fulfilling any mission that doesn't involve dropping ordnance on a civilian target?"

Tombstone stood, icy with rage. He glared down at the five civilians and said, "I think you'll find this ship far more capable than you ever dreamed, Mr. Tiltfelt. And as for your damned directive—*Jefferson* will be ready to receive these representatives on the scheduled date. Tomorrow."

0900 Local
Tomcat 308
Eighty Miles Southwest of USS Jefferson

"Okay, let's see an Immelman," Commander Steve Garber ordered. "So far, so good."

Skeeter obediently eased the Tomcat into a picture-perfect Immelman, completing the maneuver to settle into rock-stable level flight. He'd said barely two words to his squadron XO since they'd gotten airborne, and had no intention of changing. He'd been on the carrier less than twenty-four hours, and he was already in hack. A not-unusual experience for a nugget pilot, but still a squadron record, the XO had assured him.

As instructed by Lieutenant Commander Robinson, Skeeter had made his way directly to the VF-95 Executive Officer and shamefacedly reported his incident on the flight deck. The XO had transitioned rapidly from a relatively pleasant greeting to irritation. Ten minutes later, Skeeter had left the XO's stateroom dragging ass. In hack. And with a new set of orders—report to CAG and get himself slotted for a checkout flight with his new XO the next day.

"You look like you've got the makings of a good pilot," the XO said over the ICS.

"Thank you, XO." Skeeter's voice was polite, noncommittal.

"Were Tomcats your first choice?"

"Yes, XO."

An uncomfortable silence descended in the cockpit. Finally, the XO said, "Talkative little shit, aren't you?

Listen, mister, everybody screws up once in a while. You'd best get that chip off your shoulder most-skosh, or I'll be all over you like stink on shit? You copy?"

"Yes, sir." Skeeter's heart sunk even lower in his chest. Well, this was just fine. Now he could add giving the XO a hard-on for him to his list of sins.

How had everything gone so bad so quickly? It had all started on the *La Salle*. He'd been confident—too confident—hell, he'd barely been out of the RAG for a month before he'd screwed up big-time. No matter that some paperwork shuffle in D.C. had led to him being stashed on board *La Salle* until his orders could get straightened out. He hadn't minded it, except for the complete lack of stick time. In fact, once he'd gotten over his initial outrage, Skeeter had been rather pleased at it. Some exposure to some senior officers, a chance to get an inside look at how a fleet staff functioned—he'd been determined to make the best of it.

First Sixth Fleet, now his own XO. Where was that fabled Naval leadership he'd heard so much about in ROTC? It sure as hell hadn't worked on him so far. If it hadn't been for his completely fulfilling and insanely intoxicating passion for flying the Tomcat, for flying in absolutely anything at all if the circumstances required it, but especially in the Tomcat, he would have bailed out of this canoe club a year ago. But his first contact with the sleek, powerful fighter had been love at first sight. As soon as he'd settled into the cockpit, even in the simulator, he'd known that this was what he'd been born to do. To be the master of this nine thousand pounds of steel and hydraulics, strap it on his ass every day and become as one in the sky. It was more than he'd ever thought it could be, more completely satisfying and fulfilling than the finest lady he'd ever had a chance to spend an evening with. Given the choice between sex and flying, he was fairly sure which one he'd choose on any given day.

"Skeeter—that's your call sign, right? Let me try this one more time," the XO said, breaking into his reverie of lost dreams and stolen hopes. "You seem to have gotten off to the wrong foot around here. Do you get that feeling?"

"Oh, I don't know, XO," Skeeter said suddenly, still feeling the pangs of anticipated loss that not making it as a Naval aviator would bring. "How could you possibly say that? In the past two days, I've only gotten the Sixth Fleet flagship shot up on my watch, managed to piss off the entire aircrew on board *Jefferson,* taken a swing at a chief petty office, and landed myself in hack. That's nothing, right? Just good old Naval aviation at its best." Skeeter heard the bitterness dripping out of his voice, and wished desperately to call the words back. All he'd managed to do with his little tirade was to prove conclusively to the XO that he had no control over his temper and that he was a sullen, whiny child. He'd thought it impossible, but his spirits sank even lower.

"You were on watch when it happened?" the XO said quietly. "I didn't know that."

"Yes, *sir,* I had the watch, I was TAO, and I'm the one that made the call—I let that aircraft sucker-punch us, wiped out a whole ship. Pretty impressive, huh?"

"Boy, that's—"

"Don't call me boy." Skeeter's voice lashed over the ICS like a snapped arresting line. "Goddamn it, XO, don't you ever call me that again."

"I'm sorry—it's just an expression I use with some of the younger pilots. But you're right—I can see how it would sound patronizing."

"Anyone ever call you boy, XO? You hear any of the white pilots called boy?" Skeeter demanded.

"Yes, as a matter of fact, I have." The XO's voice turned frosty. "But for the record, I won't make that mistake again. Anything else on your mind?"

"No, sir." A tight band settled around Skeeter's throat, ratcheting a notch tighter. Jesus, he wasn't going to—he felt the hot wetness well in his eyes. He choked back a sob, turning it into a muffled throat-clearing.

"Skeeter, let's talk for a minute," the XO persisted. "This is no way to get started with the squadron. And I didn't know you were on watch on *La Salle* during the attack. Tell me what happened."

Skeeter cleared his throat noisily. With his hopes for a career in Naval aviation raining down in flames around him, the last thing he wanted to do was talk about *La Salle*. The very last thing. "I was on watch, I made a mistake. That's pretty much the whole sum of it, XO."

But it wasn't, one part of his mind insisted. There'd been other factors at work, things he could hardly explain to the XO. Not now, not under these circumstances. How proud he'd felt, selected to stand a flag watch position. How determined he'd been to appear self-confident and at ease, all the while still desperately trying to remember what each of the buttons on his TAO console did. How he'd wanted to get along with everyone, been confused by his first prolonged exposure to the enlisted men and women, uncertain as to how familiar, how friendly or how distant, to be with them. In the end, when the operations specialist had tried to focus his attention, he'd failed.

"So you were on watch by yourself," the XO persisted.

"There was an enlisted man there as well. He was running the radio circuits, for the most part." Suddenly, the story started to pour out of his mouth. Skeeter listened to himself in amazement, tried to stem the growing tide of words and couldn't. All of the pent-up rage, the hurt, the anger and frustration and disappointment came pouring out.

"He told me, you see, sir. He tried to get me to do something—but I didn't. I thought it was another routine flight. I didn't ask for CAP, didn't request that the ship maneuver to open weapons armament, didn't do any of that. I blew it. Completely, without a doubt, and through no fault of anybody's but my own—I blew it."

Skeeter felt surprisingly calm as he finished his recitation of his own failures. It felt like that moment when a Tomcat reached the highest point of an Immelman and you hung suspended in the ejection harness, free of gravity and floating more than sitting in the cockpit. It was a feeling of lightness, of an unbearable diffusion of self until the boundaries between you and your aircraft disappeared, until you were one with the hydraulics, the engine, the leading and trailing edges of the wings.

"So that's what that was about," the XO said finally.

"You mean my screwups? Yes, XO—I guess it was. By the time I got to the carrier, I wasn't even thinking straight. Not really."

"No, not that at all. I mean what Admiral Magruder said about you—he saw me before you checked in, you know. It was his first stop when he came on board."

Skeeter's head jerked up from his automatic instrument scan. "Admiral Magruder? Why? I only met him for just a minute. Flew over with him on the helo, but that hardly counts."

"There's more that counts than you know," the XO continued. "I take it you met Admiral Magruder as soon as he came aboard *La Salle*, right?"

"Yes, sir. Sixth Fleet sent me out to greet him."

"You didn't feel a little naked out there, like a Christian in the arena with lions roaming around?"

Skeeter was confused. "No, XO. They just told me to go out and escort the admiral. Besides, I figured he'd come looking for me eventually, since I'm the one who screwed up his ship. I thought it might be better to get it over right away."

"Oh, that's not the half of it," the XO mused. "Not the half of it at all. Sixth Fleet sent you out there figuring that Tombstone would have you drawn and quartered right there on the flight deck. From what Admiral Magruder said, the Sixth Fleet Chief of Staff was along as well, to make sure it happened. Didn't you notice that?"

"I thought it was just standard procedure."

"Hardly. Sixth Fleet intended to sacrifice you to preserve his own ambitions." The XO's voice was grim. "That's a nasty thing to do to a lieutenant—make him take the fall for your mistake."

Skeeter's confusion deepened. "His mistake? But the admiral wasn't even in TFCC when we were attacked."

"Exactly. It was as irresponsible an act as I've ever seen from an officer to leave you alone in that flag plot, Skeeter. You had no right to be on watch there alone— none at all. Now, I'm not saying that you're not a good aviator—I can see from the way you handle this Tomcat that you've got the moves, the reflexes. If you've got the brains to go with your nervous system, you're going to do just fine. But a couple of months out of the RAG, standing watch in a flag officer's TFCC? I don't think so. Someone was too lazy—or even worse, just didn't care—to put experienced officers on that watch bill. You may have been the actual officer on watch, but the rot in Sixth Fleet went a lot deeper than that."

Skeeter felt a new humility seep into his innermost self. He knew, at some level, that what the XO said was true. He'd wanted to believe himself that he was competent, capable—a bloodied and salty Naval aviator taking on responsibility early, just like in the commercials. But in truth, he'd never felt entirely comfortable with standing TAO watches there. Sure, he'd done it—and to even be asked was entirely flattering. But had he really been qualified to do so?

"I should have said no, shouldn't I?" he asked the XO slowly. "I just didn't think I could."

"There are ways of saying no, and there are ways of saying no. You'll learn 'em as you get some more time under your belt. But as far as the VF-95 Vipers are concerned, the only mark on your record is the stunt you pulled on the flight deck. And under the circumstances, I can almost see why that happened. That soon after the attack, you should have at least been medically cleared—mentally, I mean—before you went wandering around a flight deck for the first time on your own."

Another surprise. "Admiral Magruder was right," Skeeter said quietly. "He warned me before I stepped out on the flight deck, told me to keep my head on a swivel. I started to follow him off of the helo, but I got bumped back to the back of the line by the other senior officers. Something else I didn't know."

The XO chuckled. "I heard about that—Bird Dogs's an old shipmate of mine. He came crowing in to me about setting our newest nugget straight. But I think what Admiral Magruder had in mind was for you to follow him across the flight deck. I don't know, Skeeter, I wasn't there, but I'd bet on it. Stoney's that kind of man. He's got a sixth sense about when an aviator needs a little looking after."

"Stoney?"

"Tombstone—he got that call sign from his face. Don't you ever think about playing poker with the man, Skeeter. He can outbluff anyone I've ever seen."

Another silence settled over the cockpit, one considerably more comfortable than the one that had preceded it. Skeeter felt relieved, purged. The sense of lightness, of freedom, was growing. He put the ICS back on and ventured, "XO?"

"Yeah?"

"How about we see what this Tomcat can really do." An earsplitting smile crept across the young pilot's face.

"Roger—go for it. Impress me, Skeeter."

0915 Local
Hunter 701
Twenty Miles East of USS Jefferson

"I'm just a lonely cowboy, lonely for my baby," Lieutenant Commander Steve "Rabies" Grill sang lustily. He could hear the muttered protests from the other three crew members over the ICS, and chose to ignore them. They simply had no taste in music, and despite two cruises flying together—three for some of them—they had yet to learn to appreciate the finer nuances of country-and-western.

"Another Tomcat launch," the TACCO said, desperate for something tactical to say over the circuit to forestall a second chorus. "Should be well clear of our area, though."

"Altituuuuude separaaaaaation," Rabies sang in response, picking up the notes from the refrain.

"Come on, sir, give it a break," AW1 Harness said wearily. "I've never heard a key before that had seven flats and eight sharps." AW1 Harness was cursed with perfect pitch.

"All right, all right," Rabies said, reluctantly abandoning his newest favorite melody. "But when I retire and make it big in Nashville, you'll be telling people about back when. But as good as I'll sound at the Grand Ole Opry, I sound better at ten thousand feet."

A chorus of groans greeted the all-too-familiar beginning of his plans for his future career. "As long as I don't have to fly with you," the TACCO muttered.

"What's that?"

"Nothing, I didn't say—"

"No, down there." Rabies waved over toward the left side of the cockpit. "I saw a flash."

"Nothing on FLIR," muttered Harness. The forward-looking infrared sensor was one of the many potent avionics carried on board the S-3B Viking ASW hunter-killer.

"I saw something," Rabies insisted. "Let's go take a look."

"I'll lose contact on the more distant buoys if you get too low," the TACCO warned. "Any of those bastards have the little missile launcher on top of them that we saw in the South China Sea?"

"Not to my knowledge," the copilot said promptly. Of the four, he was the one who stayed most current on intelligence threat estimates. The crew's interest in submarine-launched antiair missiles had become almost an obsession after their first encounter with the first operational platform carrying the weapons in the South China Sea. "But it doesn't hurt to be careful."

"Careful, hell," Rabies snorted. "This here's a jet,

fellas. Any of you limp dicks want to bail out, you know where the panic button is." Rabies tipped the sturdy aircraft over into a deep dive. Of all the aircraft carried on board *Jefferson*, the S-3 Viking was arguably the most airworthy and stable of any platform. It was designed to cruise at patrol speeds for long periods of time, carrying a comprehensive set of sensors. Foremost in its arsenal were the sonobuoys tucked into its gut, each one spat out on command by a tiny explosive charge in the end. Depending on the water conditions below, a single line of sonobuoys could provide comprehensive undersea surveillance for the entire battle group.

"Rabies, take it easy. You're passing four hundred knots." The copilot's voice was annoyed.

"Ain't seen nothing yet, asshole. Max speed on this baby is four hundred and forty knots, and I figure that's going downhill." Rabies grinned insanely. "About time somebody set a new speed record in this aircraft, don't you think?"

"I've got it," Harness said suddenly. "Buoy Four—it's barely there, but I have contact on some electrical sources. Flow tones as well. I make her doing about six knots."

"Six knots? That's moving along for a submarine running off battery."

The TACCO looked puzzled. "She probably heard our sonobuoys hitting the water and wants to clear the area at all possible speed," Harness countered. "I don't know that that makes much sense—it just makes her more detectable, and it's a long time until sunset when she can snorkel in relative safety."

"Any indication of depth change?" Rabies asked, suddenly all business.

"Negative. She's headed due west, and I've got no indications of a depth change."

"How deep?" the TACCO asked.

"Deep enough—she's not shallow, if that's what you mean."

"That's what I mean," the TACCO confirmed. "As long as she stays at depth, even if she's got that Codeye installed," he said, referring to the surface-to-air-missile assembly they'd seen before, "she can't launch. Isn't that right?"

"As far as we know." The copilot sounded dubious. "I don't know that I want to bet on our intelligence estimates."

"This is the Med," Rabies chimed in. "No weird shit here—just straightforward find 'em and kill 'em."

"Sir, she's headed directly for the carrier." The TAC-CO's voice took on a formal note as his training took over. "Recommend that we set up for deliberate attack. We've got time."

"And torpedoes," Rabies responded. "You give me a fly-to point, and I'll take us there. But no weapons free until I talk to Homeplate."

"Roger." The TACCO's fingers flew over the keyboard, entering the tactical fly-points that would appear on Rabies' screen. "You've got it."

"Got it, aye." The S-3 tipped over into a steep port turn. "You want a six-buoy pattern in front of them, right?" Rabies confirmed.

"That'll do it."

The TACCO switched his radio to the tactical circuit. "Homeplate, this is Hunter 701. We hold contact on an unidentified diesel submarine," he said, continuing with range, frequency, and bearing information. "Request weapons free."

There was a long pause over the circuit, just as he'd expected. Requesting weapons free on an unidentified submarine was particularly dangerous. Of all bodies of water in the world, the Mediterranean was most crowded with allied submarines. Most littoral nations built their own or bought some variant from any one of the number of other nations exploiting submarines. Without positive identification, the submarine they were tracking could just as easily be Russian, Ukrainian, or even Israeli. Still, to hold contact and not request weapons free would label one as a bit of a pussy.

"Negative, Hunter 701. Launching two SH-60 helos in five mikes. Coordinate transfer of prosecution to Sea Lord 601. After turnover, continue to monitor forward ASW barrier as briefed."

"Well, ain't that the shits," Rabies remarked. The transfer of responsibility for the prosecution was hardly a surprise. Two dipping helos working in tandem against a submarine contact were every submariner's worst nightmare. In addition to a smaller load of sonobuoys, the SH-60 carrier variant had a dipping sonar capable of being deployed to a considerable depth. While the submarine might try to hide by shifting between the various thermal layers found in the warm, salty Mediterranean, it would be difficult to escape two determined and proficient helo crews.

The turnover went quickly, and the Sea Hawks eagerly took up prosecution of the contact. Twenty minutes later, Hunter 701 was headed back on station.

Rabies sighed. "So that's all we get for being the best around—always the bridesmaid, never the bride."

"You're forgetting about the Aleutians," Harness said. He shuddered. "A submarine with antiair missiles—it's damned unnatural if you ask me."

"Ain't that the truth," Rabies agreed readily. "Still, this
is the Med, not some weird-ass corner of the world."

The Mediterranean. He gazed down at the clear blue
waters, always looking for that unexpected flash of light
that indicated a protruding snorkel tube, an amorphous
shape just below the surface of the ocean that would
reveal a submarine running submerged and shallow. The
Mediterranean was a submarine hunter's worst nightmare for water, and Rabies loved it for that.

The enclosed sea was divided into two distinct thermal
layers, in one of the oddest arrangements of any ocean in
the world. The top layer was warm and salty, and flowed
toward the mouth of the Mediterranean. Deep beneath it,
a second layer replenished the Med, cold, less salty
ocean water rushing in to replace that lost through
evaporation and outflow. The difference between the two
vertical currents could produce odd acoustic effects, and
an inexperienced crew could easily lose their prey in the
shifting sound channels.

"Just another hour on station," Rabies said cheerfully.
"Our reliefs are probably taking a last piss call as we
speak."

"Don't talk about that," Harness groaned. "I hate those
damned piddle packs."

The rest of the crew chimed in in agreement. Of all the
hardships of flying a long-endurance ASW aircraft, the
lack of an adequate relief tube was among the most
significant. While some tactical aircraft had a tube built
directly into the airframe venting to the outside, the S-3
aviators had to be content with a device that most
resembled a hot-water bottle. The "piddle packs" had
been banned by Rabies based on an entirely understandable accident two missions earlier involving a too-
exuberant change of altitude by the pilot that was not

coordinated with Petty Officer Harness's more personal-ized maneuvers in the backseat. "I'd even take the pack right now." Harness's voice sounded strained.

He heard Rabies rooting around in the forward part of the aircraft, and moments later the dreaded clear plastic pack was passed back to him. "Don't say I never gave you anything."

0925 Local
Tomcat 308

"Tomcat 308, you have strangers inbound." The laconic voice of the TACCO in the E-2C Hawkeye orbiting ten thousand feet above them was calm. "Vector zero-four-zero to intercept and VID."

"What the—? Sentry, this is 308. We're on a checkout flight. What about on-station CAP?"

"Four aircraft inbound," the Hawkeye replied. "Both CAP currently on station are already en route. Request you break off current training operations and join them." There was no mistaking the note of command now in the E-2C TACCO's voice.

"Okay, Skeeter." The XO's voice was determinedly calm. "You want to show me what this aircraft can do—you've got your chance. Good thing you've got the best RIO in the squadron," he continued.

"We're going on an intercept?"

"Looks like it. Here, here's your fly-to point." The XO transmitted the coordinates of the station he wanted his pilot to take. "Get hot, Skeeter. Training missi⁚ ; over."

"Roger, copy." Skeeter slewed the Tomcat around into a tight port turn. They were currently at Angels 11—

eleven thousand feet—and had been drilling on a scissors maneuver, the tactic preferred by the light Falcon against a heavier aircraft. The XO had just been reviewing the breakout points and counters with him when the call from the Hawkeye came in.

"I hope you were paying attention," the XO said. "I'm going to be a little bit busy back here, but I'll coach you through it when I can."

"Not a problem, XO." Skeeter felt a surging buoyant feeling of confidence. What had Admiral Magruder said—that he'd give him a chance? Well, if more of those assholes who'd shot up the flagship were inbound, they'd find they were facing an entirely different Skeeter. This time, he was in his platform of choice, one that he knew as well as his own bedroom. The Tomcat was an extension of his skin, a natural marriage of man and machine so intimate as to defy complete description. No one who had never flown in a Tomcat could fully understand how it felt to him, how it reacted to his demands and requests almost before he could translate them into action, how he and the aircraft seemed to meld into one being—a deadly, potent, unified force.

"I'm ready," he repeated, this time out loud. "Let's go kick some Turkish ass."

Falcon 101

"Ah, there you are." The pilot glanced at the heads-up display and identified the third fighter inbound on their flight. "Four of us, three of you—yes, I think these odds will be fair."

"Red Three, break right and intercept new bogey." The

flight leader's voice cut through his contemplation of the new contact. "Stick to the Rules of Engagement—no incidents this time. But if the Americans wish to play hard, we may show them what we're truly capable of."

The pilot turned his aircraft slightly toward the south and accelerated to Mach 1.5. At that speed, he was traveling fifteen miles every minute, closing on the incoming aircraft at breakneck speed. The radar-warning receiver squealed one short alarm. He glanced at it, assessing the data instantly. "Tomcat—yes." The signature of the AWG-9 radar was unmistakable. "Are you as reckless and aggressive as your squadron mate was? Shooting at our aircraft with no provocation other than he was near your ship? We will see if you find a prepared fighter pilot as easy a prey."

He could see from the speed leader that the Tomcat was accelerating as well, quickly moving to match his speed. Their combined closure speed was now in excess of 1800 miles per hour, and the powerful Tomcat had a slight advantage. The Falcon, while lighter and more maneuverable, simply could not keep up with the sustained speed of bursts of the Tomcat if it involved an altitude change. "This time, we will fight my game."

0928 Local
Tomcat 308

"Steady, steady," the XO murmured from the backseat. "He hasn't done anything yet, Skeeter. Don't toggle one off until I tell you."

Skeeter clicked the mike twice in acknowledgment. His earlier burst of ebullience was fading. This was his second time under attack this week, and he was determined to acquit himself more honorably than he had aboard *La Salle*. Despite the XO's warning, he moved the weapons-selector switch to the Phoenix position. When the XO deemed it necessary—he would be ready.

Falcon 101

"You have not targeted me yet," the pilot said softly. "Are you afraid? Do you know what vengeance I am about to extract from you?" He adjusted the Falcon's course minutely to bring it directly head-on to the Tomcat. "Be careful, you may get more than you bargained for."

0929 Local
Tomcat 308

"Sir, he's within Phoenix range." Skeeter heard his voice skid slightly up at the end of the sentence. "Recommend we—"

"No. Not yet." The XO's voice was firm. "It's bad, we're not making it worse. They may not be out here for us."

"Not here for us?" Skeeter asked. "Sir, it's a Falcon."

"I'm aware of that. After all, I've got the ESM gear back here. But you're not paying attention—didn't you hear that last contact report? The submarine?"

"Yes, but—oh. Targeting profile."

"Exactly. These bad boys may not be here for us. They may simply be providing position updates to that submarine, vectoring it in closer to the ship. And the submarine's not our problem—the Viking's turned it over to the helos. They've got him pinned down right now, bouncing him from sonar dome to sonar dome like he's a badminton bird. Until he shakes them, he's not going to feel comfortable coming up to data-link with those fighters. Besides, we're still inside the inner missile engagement envelope."

"Sir, this is going too fast," Skeeter warned. "It was like this last time—aircraft inbound, nobody willing to take them with missiles. Look what happened then."

"Wait for the Hawkeye, Skeeter. We've got to make sure the Aegis doesn't need us to clear the area, and there's no point in wasting missiles on him yet."

I waited last time. I ended up with a dead ship. What happens this time?

0929 Local
TFCC
USS Jefferson

"You can't shoot." Bradley Tiltfelt's voice was insistent. "Admiral, you risk everything we've worked to achieve if your men take a shot now."

Tombstone wheeled around and glared at the civilian. "I can and I will if I have the slightest indication that this ship is in danger. This is not a game, Mr. Tiltfelt. People die. Ships die. And I'm not losing another one in this sea, not based on your in-depth analysis of a tactical scenario."

"They're doing freedom-of-navigation operations," Tiltfelt insisted. "You saw their message yourself."

"I know what it said." Tombstone pointed at the large screen display. "But that is not an unthreatening profile as briefed. Those bastards are inbound at Mach 1.5, and in five minutes they'll be within missile range of this ship. Unless they break off within four minutes, I'm firing."

"Admiral, " Tiltfelt wailed, "they told us they were going to do this. You can't—"

"Watch me." Tombstone settled back in his brown leatherette chair to watch the battle unfolding on the screen.

0930 Local
Falcon 101

The fighter bore down on the incoming American aircraft, eking out another few tenths of Mach and accelerating again. The fighter jittered slightly under his hands, then settled into a steady, screaming roar.

A little closer now, a little closer—that's it. Commit yourself to this profile. In level flight, you have no chance. Not one. He kept his hands away from the radar switch, careful not to toggle it into fire-control mode. At the first sniff of the tightly focused radar beam beating down on the skin of their aircraft, the Tomcat crew would be justified in retaliating with a missile. At this distance, it was not the Falcon's preferred fight. No, in close— knife-fighting, his instructors in the United States had called it. The Falcon was a knife-fighter, the Tomcat a heavyweight boxer. In close, it was no contest.

Tomcat 308

"Remember, he's an angles fighter," Garber said rapidly, back-briefing his young pilot as quickly as he could. "His first priority is going to be to keep you at the same altitude. You'll see him start to cut in on you, to turn inside your own turn, get position on you from behind. Skeeter, pay attention—it comes with experience, and you've gotta get that fast."

An angles fighter—God, how he'd studied the maneuvers at the RAG. Back then, there'd been pilots who'd flown against MiGs in Vietnam, and they were more than willing to share their experience bought at the price of their squadron mates' lives with the incoming generation of fighter pilots.

Altitude—you have to use altitude to your advantage. The Tomcat, with its higher thrust-to-weight ratio and higher wing loading, could easily outstrip and turn inside the Falcon on the vertical plane. On the horizontal, it was a turkey trying to evade a chicken hawk. A beached whale trying to writhe away from pecking seagulls. Altitude is safety—altitude and maneuverability.

"I'm taking us up to twenty-five thousand," Skeeter said firmly. "Energy fight—standard tactic while he's down this low."

"Concur." The XO's voice was slightly muffled. "I'm getting a fix—there. Solid data link with the Hawkeye. Good data, good solution. If we need to shoot—"

Skeeter's burst of acceleration turned the XO's last words into a grunt. The Tomcat accelerated rapidly, afterburners spitting unholy fire out the tailpipes, speed over ground decreasing to almost zero. The Tomcat was in a pure vertical climb, gaining altitude and, with it, kinetic energy. When the time came for forcing the Falcon into an energy fight instead of an angles one, Skeeter would be ready.

"Fuel," the XO warned. "It kills more pilots than missiles. Skeeter, easy on the afterburners. Save it for when you need it."

Cursing his impulsiveness, Skeeter eased back out of the afterburners and decreased his angle of attack. There was still enough separation between the two aircraft that afterburners had not been necessary. But his increasing sense of urgency not to be vulnerable to this second attack had overridden his professional good sense.

"I've got him—at five o'clock," the XO said.

Skeeter leaned over and gazed down outside the right side of the cockpit. He could see the flash of light on metal that had caught the XO's attention. "I've got him too."

"Something odd about this guy," the XO said tersely. "He's climbing to meet us. Skeeter, watch you ass—he's not much off your six."

"Got it. I'm going to nose over here in just a second."

Skeeter rolled over to the side opposite of the Falcon, preventing him from closing to within guns range on his tail. For just a moment, he thought he'd outflown him. Overconfidence replaced his fear.

He pulled down, pressing in for a favorable angle of attack. To his surprise, the Falcon pulled up under him, again in excellent guns position.

"Skeeter," the XO snapped, "you're getting into a rolling scissors. You can't play this game with him."

"I know, I know—but he's climbing with me. Every

time I try to outrun him, I put him in guns position on me."

"At least he hasn't shot yet—Skeeter, we need to break out of this—*now.*"

The Tomcat was descending now, bleeding off energy advantage as it lost altitude. Skeeter searched his memory, tried to remember if any of his instructors talked about an angles fighter that didn't mind fighting in the vertical. They weren't supposed to—most of the MiGs in encounters that his instructors had discussed had either kept the fight strictly to the horizontal or turned to run if they didn't have the advantage.

At eight thousand feet, with the Falcon still high above him, Skeeter put the Tomcat nose up and grabbed for altitude. The Falcon zoomed down not five hundred feet away, canopy to canopy. Skeeter resisted the impulse to job the afterburners again, lessen his angle of climb. "Watch him for me," he said to the XO. "Keep an eye on him—"

"Got it. Skeeter, he's at the bottom of his arc right now. He'll be back up on our tail again." The XO's voice was cold, professional, but Skeeter could hear the undertone of worry in it.

What was it, what was it, something he'd read somewhere, the story of a MiG and a—a Phantom—that was it. The details came flooding back. It had been Duke Cunningham, now a U.S. Representative from California. Flying his F-4 Phantom against a MiG-17, the Duke, as he was known, had run into a MiG fighter who didn't mind the vertical. They'd done the same maneuver, up and down, rolling scissors, with the MiG consistently turning inside the vertical and stitching the Duke's ass with his nose gun. And the solution was— "Where is he now?" he asked the XO sharply. "Give me a range."

"Just bottoming out at three thousand feet. We've got ten thousand feet of separation, Skeeter. Let's turn and wait for him."

"No. I think I know what—is he climbing now?"

"On afterburners," the XO confirmed. "Skeeter, he's just going to move back into perfect position on your ass. Let's get out of here—while we can."

"Hold on—I thought you wanted to see what this Tomcat could do." The note of cold glee in his voice surprised even him.

Five thousand feet—four thousand feet—Skeeter asked the XO to sing out the altitudes as the Falcon gained on them. Skeeter eased slowly back on the throttle, decreasing his speed of ascent while avoiding even the edge of the stall envelope. It was a tightrope calculation, walking the thin line between appearing to maintain a continual ascent and stalling.

"Five hundred feet—Skeeter, let's—"

Skeeter pulled hard toward the Falcon and yanked the throttle back to idle. At the same time, he disengaged the automatic control that configured the Tomcat's wings for the most efficient airspeed, driving the wings forward into their low-speed configuration. As he felt the aircraft start to turn, he kicked in the afterburners to avoid stalling.

Like a gray streak, the Falcon shot by him. Skeeter thought he saw the pilot's face, hoped there was as much fear and confusion in it as Skeeter had experienced on *La Salle*.

"Take that, you bastard," the pilot muttered. No, it wasn't a kill, but if he had been free to shoot it would have been. He held position on the Falcon, in perfect guns position. If he hadn't been so close, a Sidewinder up the tailpipe would also have been an ideal shot.

"Skeeter—he's turning out of it."

The lighter, more maneuverable aircraft turned sharply to the right, intentionally stalling as the pilot repeated Skeeter's maneuver. It swung over to point down at him, nose first.

"Lockup," the XO screamed. "There's no time for—"

Skeeter was just closing his thumb over the weapons-selector switch to select guns when his world exploded.

He woke up when he tried to breathe. The metallic tang of salt water filled his mouth, his nose, and jolted his survival instincts into action. Skeeter coughed violently, spewing out seawater before his eyes were even open. He flailed his arms, the motion driving him the last few feet up to the surface.

The paroxysm of coughing occupied his entire world for a few seconds. His eyes were open, but they were misted with tears and stinging from water. He choked, coughing up a last cup of water, then finally drawing a deep, shaky breath.

His eyes focused. Water, waves—he looked up into the blue sky. For another few minutes, his mind refused to focus, simply satisfied with the fact that he was alive.

It came back to him slowly, in bits and pieces. An explosion—the canopy bolts firing, he realized. The Falcon—it had been inbound. The rest of the encounter flooded his mind.

The XO must have gotten them out. Suddenly, he was frantic. He scanned the ocean around him, praying for a glimpse of a flotation device or a rubber raft. He started screaming, his voice raw and hoarse from the water. He tried to propel himself higher up on the waves by flailing his arms, and found new sources of pain. His groin— another throb awoke to join the growing chorus.

Finally, his training kicked in. He fumbled open the flotation device pocket, extracted the dye marker, and broke it open. A sickly yellow stain flooded the water around him, gradually spreading out. He then took out the shark repellent packet, prayed that all the studies he'd heard on its effectiveness were true, and broke it open.

The pain in his face was now a throbbing, insistent beat. He let his flotation device buoy him for a moment, leaned back in the water, and started running his hands over his body. Wetness—he held his hand out in front of him. Not just water. Blood. Evidently shards of the canopy or the sheer force of the ejection had cut his face. He looked again at the growing yellow stain and prayed that the shark repellent was just as effective.

One by one, he ran his hands over his arms, his torso, then finally his legs. Everything seemed to work, although movement was accompanied by a dull ache that promised to blossom into something fiercer later on.

So where was SAR? Dammit, the helo guys—just then the distinctive whop-whop of an SH-60 reached his ears.

Minutes later, a rescue diver plunged into the water a few feet away. He swam over to Skeeter, quickly ascertained that he was conscious and not seriously injured, and helped the pilot struggle into the horse collar. Satisfied finally, the diver lifted his hand in a thumbs-up to the crewman leaning out the open hatch of the helicopter. The downdraft from the SH-60 was explosive, generating wind speeds of up to sixty knots directly down on the water. It spread waves out in odd, flat ripples that beat a counterpart to the normal progression of waves. Skeeter fixed on that, staring at the concentric disturbances that looked like water washing out from a stone thrown in a pond, the diver situated in the middle.

Except this wasn't a pond. It was the Mediterranean, and as soon as he was hauled aboard, he asked, "Did you find my backseater?"

One look at the aircrew's faces gave him the answer. Skeeter exploded. "Dammit, he's out here somewhere. We've got to find him. We have to—"

"Just take it easy, sir," the corpsman said, gently trying to muscle him to the aft part of the helicopter. "We've done this before—just let us do our job for now. We'll find him."

He was there," Skeeter said mindlessly. "In the back-seat—he must have punched us out." He shot the corpsman an anguished look. "Just before the Falcon got us—he punched us out. How could he—?"

"Just lean back, Lieutenant." The corpsman's voice was gentle but insistent. "Need to take a look at you, sir. Your backseater's gonna be just fine."

"Where is he?" Skeeter struggled to his feet and tried to walk toward the open hatch. The rescue swimmer was just being hauled aboard. "I have to—"

A sharp prick in the left arm. Skeeter spun around, unsteady on his bruised and battered legs. "What did you . . ." The rest of the sentence faded away as a cool fog settled over his mind.

SIX
Thursday, 6 September

0300 Local
Medical Department
USS Jefferson

"How is he?" Batman asked the doctor, his voice pitched low to avoid disturbing the unconscious pilot. "The face—just normal ejection injuries, right?"

The doctor nodded. "Some bruises, a couple of lacerations. None of them even required stitches. The only reason he's still here instead of in his own rack was that he got a bit agitated with the helo crew when they pulled him out of the water. The corpsman had to jam him with some morphine to get him to calm down."

Batman let out a long, troubled sigh. "His backseater." It wasn't a question, more a statement of fact. It was the first thing you worried about, the last thing you thought of as you departed controlled flight on the rocket-powered ejection seat and headed for the deck. Your backseater, the other part of your team, who helped keep you both alive.

"Have they found him yet?" the doctor asked.

Batman shook his head. "No one saw his chute. The more time passes, the more difficult it will be to find him."

The doctor nodded, understanding the unspoken implication. No chute, no sighting, and no emergency beacon from either the sea or the portable radio each aviator carried. It didn't look good.

"But—there's always a chance." Batman straightened, then looked back at the pilot sprawled out on the bed. "How long before he's conscious?"

"That's just normal sleep," the doctor answered. "The morphine's worn off. If you need to talk to him, you can wake him up."

"I guess I should let him sleep," Batman fretted. "But I need to know what actually happened up there. We've got the radar picture, the cat-and-mouse game they were playing up there. What I don't have is a firsthand report, what the pilot on scene did and saw and thought."

"He'll have to find out about his RIO sooner or later," the doctor said. It was not something he looked forward to telling the pilot, and he could sympathize with the admiral's concerns.

"I know. I'll do it when the time comes. But for now, what he saw up there might make a difference—might save some other man's life."

The doctor walked over to the bed, and placed one hand gently on the sleeping pilot's shoulder. He tightened his hand slowly, trying not to put too much pressure on damaged muscles and tendons. He listened to the pilot's breathing change, becoming shallower and quicker, then saw his eyelids flicker open. "Good morning," the doctor said softly. "Do you remember where you are?"

Skeeter groaned, and rolled to one side as though trying to prop himself up on his elbows. The doctor placed his other hand gently on the opposite shoulder and forced him gently back down on the bed. "Don't get up yet. Your body took a beating, and it's going to hurt for a few days. You're okay other than that, though."

"What happened?" Skeeter shook his head, trying to clear out the fog. "Why am I—" The sentence went unfinished as the details came back to him. "We ejected, didn't we? My RIO—" Again he tried to struggle back up into a sitting position, even flung one foot off the edge of the bed as if he were going to jump out.

The doctor held him down more firmly. "Admiral Wayne is here. He'd like to ask you a few questions, if you're up to it."

Too weak to resist further, Skeeter lay back down on the rack. His eyes were brighter now, focusing on his surroundings. "Admiral—my RIO. How is he?"

Batman walked over to the hospital bed and laid his hand over Skeeter's. "We haven't found him yet."

Skeeter moaned. "He got out—I saw him. Heard him, at least."

"Did you see his chute?" Batman asked carefully.

Skeeter furrowed his brow, trying to think. Had he seen a chute? He shook his head, tried to force his mind to yield up the details of the ejection. Nothing came to him. "I don't know." He looked up at the admiral, his eyes blurring. "But it had to work. They always do. Don't they?" His voice begged desperately for reassurance.

"Most of the time they do," Batman said. It was tempting to offer the young airman what he wanted, reassurance that the missing man would be found eventually. But to do so would only prolong the agony. Batman was just coming to terms with it himself, the probability that the RIO's parachute had failed to deploy and the man would never be found. As painful as it was, it was better that Skeeter start facing that now.

"We're doing everything we can. We have every helo

on deck airborne during daylight, and the *Shiloh* is quartering a search pattern now. If he's out there, we'll find him."

"Daylight? What time is it?"

Batman glanced over at the doctor, who nodded. "Three o'clock in the morning. You've been out for a while."

"Unconscious?"

"Skeeter, I hate to do this, but I need to ask you about the attack," Batman said, skillfully avoiding the details surrounding Skeeter's own rescue. It troubled him in a way, although it would normally be understandable, following on the heels of Skeeter's incident on the flight deck. It made him wonder whether the young man had the temperament to make it as a fighter pilot. It took guts and passion to climb into that Tomcat every day. He wanted people who cared about flying, cared desperately. But that was only part of the equation.

To be successful, a fighter pilot had to compartmentalize his mind. When he walked out of the island and onto the flight deck, he had to drain every bit of emotional tension out of his mind, lock it away in some dark corner for the duration of the mission. Later, he could worry about his wife, fret over his kids, or generally be pissed off at the world. But while you were on the flight deck, while there were airplanes turning nearby or while you were airborne, everything ceased to exist except the mission.

"You saw the Falcon in plenty of time, didn't you?" Batman asked, focusing in on his current mission—gaining information that could save the life of another pilot. "I saw the radar picture—what really happened?"

Skeeter began detailing the encounter with the Falcon, using his hands to illustrate the relative position of the two aircraft during the rolling scissors he'd been trapped into. When he reached the part of it where he'd decided to pop his speed brakes, Batman smiled appreciatively. "Good call. Who taught you that?"

Skeeter thought for a moment. "Something I read in *Fighter Combat*, Admiral. The Duke—Duke Cunningham."

Admiral Wayne nodded. "Hell of an aviator—even a better Congressman."

"The thing is, that Falcon's not a typical Falcon. Not the way they told me, at least. He just jumped right into the vertical, didn't stick to an angles fight like he was supposed to." Skeeter frowned. "It was almost as though he didn't know what he was doing. No, but that couldn't be it—he was too damned good." Skeeter looked up at the admiral, puzzled. "It was like a Chihuahua that thinks it's a Great Dane."

"Come again?" the admiral asked, failing to follow Skeeter's analogy.

"You know how some dogs are, Admiral. They may be little, short, and not any more dangerous than a gnat. But you get some of 'em, they get sort of this complex—they yap and yell and charge at you like they were a Great Dane. I guess nobody ever bothered to tell them they were just small dogs." He chuckled, then winced at the pain in his ribs. "That's what this Falcon guy was like—nobody ever bothered to tell him he ought to be in an angles fight."

Batman frowned. "Anything else unusual about his performance?"

Skeeter's face lit up suddenly. "I know what would explain it—it's the only thing that makes sense."

Batman nodded. "We may be thinking the same thing—an equipment change-out."

"That's exactly it."

It did explain it, Batman thought. The intelligence briefing on the Turkish Falcons had made the assumption that they were outfitted with one of the two engines normally used on that airframe. But what if they weren't? What if Turkey had found a way to put a different power plant in the airframe, one with more thrust? It wouldn't take a lot, not as light as that aircraft was. Fuel would be the main problem, but Turkey's strategy probably called for fighting close to home. It wasn't like fighting from an aircraft carrier, where every gallon of fuel counted, not when you stayed close to home base and fuel support.

Batman laid a hand on Skeeter's shoulder. "The Intelligence guys will be down to talk to you soon. They'll want to follow up on this—you up to seeing them in the morning?"

Skeeter nodded. "I don't think I'm going anywhere for a while, Admiral."

On his way back to his cabin, Batman considered the possibility of a higher thrust-to-weight Falcon and what impact that would have on his tactics. Or was this just an especially canny Falcon pilot, one who knew that the American aviators would be expecting an angles fight? Wasn't that one of the first tenets of Naval warfare—do what the enemy least expects?

No matter. He stopped by CVIC on his way back to his cabin, and quickly filled the duty officer in on what he'd learned from Skeeter. The officer promised to tell Lab Rat and have a full briefing on the possibilities ready by ten o'clock that morning. As he left, Batman saw the duty officer was calling the on-watch team around him for a war conference.

There was still no sign of Skeeter's RIO, the XO of VF-95. No debris, no international air-distress beeper, nothing. While the search would continue for another twenty-four hours, Batman already knew what the final result would be. Another good pilot lost. Tomorrow he'd have to start thinking about the memorial service, about dealing with the squadron's grief and anger over losing their XO.

Tired, so tired—finally, he reached the door to his office and shoved it open. Stacks of messages spilled over on his desk. He considered taking a shot at clearing the paperwork, and finally gave up. He could hear his rack calling him.

0900 Local
Flag Mess

The representatives from the various countries filed in in a flurry of aides, position papers, and protocol. Tombstone had been briefed on their relative seniority, on how essential it was that each took exactly the correct position around the long rectangular conference room, with precisely the correct number of chairs positioned behind each for aides and assistants. Tombstone had tried to explain that there simply was not enough space in his conference room to comply with all of Tiltfelt's demands. The State Department representative had acted as though Tombstone were intentionally interposing difficulties into the negotiation process, and it was only after Tiltfelt had actually seen the arrangement of chairs crammed into the room that he'd finally subsided. Tombstone had suggested moving the proceeding into a portion of the flag mess, and Tiltfelt had reluctantly agreed.

"Good morning, ladies and gentlemen." Tiltfelt had an expression of grave sincerity on his face, thoughtful yet concerned, open and willing to talk. Tombstone tried to believe that he meant it.

"Welcome to the USS *Jefferson*. We are honored that you have chosen to participate in this process."

And just as happy when you get the hell off my boat. Tombstone watched each of the representatives carefully mirror Tiltfelt's expression. Was it something that they taught in diplomacy school? Or merely a quality of dissimulation that permitted one to rise in diplomatic circles in any country? No matter—his own poker face had served him well in the Navy. He wouldn't begrudge another department their peculiarities of custom.

"And our thanks to our host, Admiral Matthew Magruder. Admiral?" Tiltfelt yielded his place at the podium.

Tombstone rose and walked slowly to the forward part of the room. His carefully prepared remarks, already vetted by Tiltfelt and his minions, were laid out on a three-by-five card he carried in his right-hand pocket. For this occasion, he had put on his dress blues, an uncomfortable uniform he had been wearing all too often in the last three years. A flight suit would have been infinitely preferable.

"Welcome aboard. We're glad to have you here. If there is anything I can do to make your stay more comfortable or convenient, please do not hesitate to let me know personally." Tombstone slipped the card back in his pocket and prepared to depart.

"Your uncle—he is in the Navy also?" the gentleman from Ukraine asked quickly. "Thomas Magruder, yes?"

Surprised, Tombstone could only nod. "Yes, Admiral Magruder is my uncle."

The man nodded, satisfied. He shot a knowing look at the man seated behind him.

"Why?" Tombstone asked. "Do you know him?" He resisted slightly as Tiltfelt gently tried to hustle him away from the podium.

The Ukrainian shook his head in the negative. "Only by reputation," he answered, enunciating each word carefully. "A product of the Cold War, is he not? As is your father. Another fine man." The Ukrainian's eyes gleamed, secrets dancing behind them. "I met him once. More than once, perhaps."

Rage and fear in equal proportions coursed through Tombstone's body. The mention of his father, who had been shot in a bombing run over Vietnam, in so incongruent a place at so entirely inappropriate a time, stunned him. He took two steps toward the man, the import of their current location lost on him.

Tiltfelt finally asserted himself, grabbing the admiral firmly by the elbow. "Not now," he whispered sharply into Tombstone's ear. "Admiral, this is neither the time nor the place."

Tombstone shook free of the smaller man and continued his advance on the Ukrainian. "Why did you ask that question? And make that comment?" Tombstone's voice was low and deadly.

The Ukrainian shrugged. "It was simply a question, Admiral. I wished to make sure that I had my facts right."

Tombstone regained control of himself, unsure of how to proceed, but shaken to his very core. There had to be a purpose behind the questions—had to be. But as much as he hated to admit it, Tiltfelt was right. Tombstone nodded, and stepped back toward his seat. As he settled back down into the hard-backed chair, he silently let out a deep, wavering breath. Whatever Tiltfelt had intended

to accomplish at this conference, Tombstone had a
feeling that the results were going to be quite different
from what the State Department representative expected.

After almost an hour of preliminary maneuvering and
polite assurances of eternal friendship, the meeting
adjourned to the rear of the room for refreshments.
Donuts and coffee, along with more delicate pastries
provided by the flag mess cooks, disappeared at an
alarming rate.

"It's a hazard of the profession," Tiltfelt said to
Tombstone casually, delicately biting into a croissant.
"Too many diplomatic events and you gain weight every
day." He nodded toward the rest of the representatives.
"Not a skinny one amongst them."

Tiltfelt's confiding and congenial manner was almost
as confusing to him as the Ukrainian's earlier question.
Tombstone stared down at him, is arms planted firmly on
his hips. "What happened in there?"

Tiltfelt shrugged. "You were there. What do you
think?"

"I think nothing happened. Nothing at all—except for
that crack about my father."

Tiltfelt smiled. "An accurate assessment. This is the
way these things always go. It's almost an art form—the
ability to plant the little seeds and casual comments that
later grow into major issues." He then cited a couple of
examples from the members' opening comments, and
speculated on how those seemingly innocent remarks
would later turn into intransigent demands. "And as for
the question about your father—I'm not entirely certain." Tiltfelt regarded Tombstone as though he were a
specimen under a microscope. "Do you have any idea?"

Tombstone shook his head. "It was a long time ago—I

was very young." Briefly, unemotionally, he sketched in the details of how his father had been lost over Vietnam, the fact that his wingman had seen his parachute. His father had been carried as MIA—missing in action—for almost twenty years. Finally, despite the lack of a body, with his name never appearing on a POW list, he had been declared killed in action.

"Well." Tiltfelt deposited his coffee cup on a credenza and brushed his hands together lightly. "I don't know what it was about. Not really. But you can bet it will come up later on. It's either an opening ploy, or perhaps just a validation of their own in-country intelligence processes. You'd be surprised at what a complete dossier they keep on every senior American military official."

"But Ukraine—of what possible interest could it be to them?" Tombstone asked. While he neither believed nor trusted Tiltfelt's change in attitude, he would use it for what it was worth.

Tiltfelt gazed at him gravely. "I have no information, you understand—none at all. And I insist that you keep this completely between the two of us. Off the record, if you will."

"Understood. Now tell me." Tombstone was beginning to lose patience with the delicate circumlocutions that seemed an integral part of Tiltfelt.

"Just this—during the Cold War, Ukraine was part of the Soviet Union. You've heard the rumors. There's always been speculation—speculation with no basis in fact so far—that American POWs from Vietnam were transported to the Soviet Union for interrogation. That question might have been intended to get you thinking about that possibility, for some reason that we don't yet know about. Or, it could have been what I think it was—an attempt to throw us off balance, to drive a wedge into the integrity of the U.S. negotiating team. That would be entirely reasonable and certainly in keeping with Ukraine's style. I wouldn't give it much more thought than that."

"He's trying to make me think that my father might have been alive after all?" Tombstone felt the blood drain from his face as understanding dawned. "He couldn't have been."

Tiltfelt shrugged again. "Who knows?" He abruptly turned back to the delegates crowding the room, leaving Tombstone to try to interpret his last remark.

Tombstone watched Tiltfelt move about the room, glad-handing representatives with careful impartiality. Five minutes with this one, five minutes with that one, remembering each aide's name long enough to greet them and then ignore them. While it looked random, Tombstone recognized the real skill that lay behind the man's progress through the room. Recognized it, appreciated it, and had no use for it.

"Thank you for having us aboard, Admiral," a voice said just behind his left shoulder. Tombstone turned and saw the representative from Turkey.

"If your pilots came any closer to my ship, I was going to wave them in for a trap," Tombstone said. His face was pointedly neutral. Let the Turk try to decide how to take it, as a poor joke or blatant provocation. Suddenly, Tombstone didn't particularly care which.

The Turk's smile wavered for a moment, then settled firmly on his face. "This is international airspace."

Tombstone took a step closer to the man, and pitched his voice low. "We lost an aviator the other day following an encounter with one of your freedom-of-navigation flights," he said carefully. Suddenly, he wished he could retract his earlier remark. If this man could help, if he knew anything about their downed aviator, then it would be sheer folly to alienate him. Coming so soon on the heels of Tiltfelt's speculation on his own father, the possibility that he'd done anything to jeopardize another aviator's safety was unbearable. "Have you heard anything about him, by any chance? Perhaps one of your fishing vessels has seen him?"

The Turkish representative took a sip of coffee before answering him. "No, I'm quite sorry. We have heard nothing."

"Would you tell me if you did?" Tombstone asked, unable to keep a trace of bitterness out of his voice.

The Turkish representative drew away from him. "We abide by all international laws of armed conflict," he answered. "These matters that we are here to discuss— they are between nations, between states. Not between individuals. If your lost airman is found, he will be treated appropriately."

"Appropriately according to whose standards?" Tombstone asked, his voice slightly louder.

"Admiral," he heard Tiltfelt say. "Perhaps we could—"

"Answer the question," Tombstone said.

"According to international law," the Turkish representative said firmly. He put his coffee cup down on the table with slightly more force than necessary. He turned to Bradley Tiltfelt. "If you might excuse us, I have matters I need to discuss with my staff before our next meeting."

"Of course," Tiltfelt said promptly, shooting Tombstone a furious look. "May I have someone escort you back to your quarters? The ship is a maze if you're not used to it."

"Very kind." The Turkish representative bowed slightly,

carefully watching Tombstone. "We will see you at eleven o'clock."

The Turkish entourage departed, flanked by the Marines ostensibly assigned as their escorts. That had been Tiltfelt's one concession to security during a heated discussion over the dangers of having the delegations on board. The other delegations were provided with escorts only as requested to guide them through the maze of the ship's passageways as a demonstration of trust and goodwill.

As the door closed behind the Turkish entourage and the low murmur of voices rose again in the conference room, Tiltfelt turned to Tombstone, "Fuck this up, and you'll be retired within twenty-four hours. I promise it."

1000 Local
Starboard Passageway, 03 Deck

Yuri Kursk waited until the rest of the room was chuckling appreciatively at a mildly ribald joke told by the Turkish representative. He slipped quietly out of the door to the conference room, and headed aft on the ship, walking purposefully.

Six frames down, he turned left and moved over to the starboard passageway. He nodded to the sailors he met walking past, maintaining a purposeful look on his face. One stopped, hesitating as though to ask him if he were lost, but Yuri brushed quickly by. Seventy feet later, he was at his destination. This was the only dangerous portion of the mission, for he had no ready explanation for his presence outside Tombstone Magruder's quarters. He could always say he was lost, and indeed that explanation might hold up. The aircraft carrier was massive, far bigger than he had imagined it from studying its technical specs. Translating the one million square feet of living space into an actual map of this vessel was an entirely different matter.

Still, by watching the frame numbers engraved on metal strips on top of the main support members of the hull, he'd found his way to it with relatively little difficulty.

Now, if he could get his bearings . . . The diagrams had shown a separate suite for VIPs on board the carrier, and it had been their estimation that that was where Tombstone Magruder would be berthed.

He walked past his target door, and cast a quick glance at it. He smiled—the Americans made things childishly easy sometimes. Posted in the small metal frame on the doorjamb was Admiral Magruder's business card.

Yuri kept walking, careful to maintain his pace. He stepped over a knee-knocker and moved past the next frame, still looking for any hatch that showed the slightest possibility of granting him access to the compartment next to Admiral Magruder's cabin.

He found it. The metal plate indicated it was a teletype repair facility. Yuri tried the handle. It turned. He pushed the door open.

At some time, the space must have served for repairing teletypes, but those days had long since past. Now it was a miscellaneous storage area, cluttered with mops and buckets and the normal equipment used for cleaning compartments.

Perfect. In fact, it could not have been more ideal.

Yuri closed the hatch behind him before he turned on the light to the compartment. He maneuvered between the buckets and wringers to the back wall. If he could only be certain—no, this must be it. He'd seen nothing else that looked like it might do. And there was certainly not enough space between what he'd estimated to be the end of the admiral's cabin and this compartment for there to be any problem.

Yuri knelt and dug in his briefcase for a moment, then extracted a harmless-looking radio. He adjusted the dials on it, then moved aside some cleaning supplies on a shelf and placed the radio behind them.

So easy. So simple, and easy enough when the foolishly open, trusting nature of the Americans labeled each compartment so clearly.

Yuri straightened, brushed a tiny bit of lint from his pants, turned off the lights, and left the compartment.

As he stepped out into the passageway, he glanced right and left. A young sailor—a female one, he noticed bemusedly—approached him and eyed him oddly. "You need some cleaning gear, sir?" she asked politely. There was an undercurrent of suspicion in her voice.

Yuri spread his hands out in front of him as if he were harmless, deepening his accent slightly. It was odd how that always worked to his advantage. Americans instinctively believed that anyone with a foreign accent was stupid. "I am lost, I think." He pointed back toward the hatch. "Those numbers—my room?"

The expression on the young sailor's face cleared. Visitors getting lost on a carrier was a common occurrence, and the long-suffering permanent inhabitants of the aircraft carrier quickly learned to recognize the mixture of chagrin and embarrassment that went with asking for directions.

"What were those numbers, sir?"

Yuri handed her a scrawled piece of paper, the one that the admiral's Chief of Staff had given him.

"Here's the problem." She pointed to the first digit in the group. "You're on the wrong deck—the floor, I mean." She pointed down and spoke a little louder. "One floor down, you see."

"Ah, I understand." He looked up and down the passageway. "But where are the stairs?"

Her suspicions completely vanquished, the young sailor smiled. "If you'll follow me, sir, I'll take you straight there."

"You are too kind." Yuri fell into step behind her.

If the device did as its makers claimed, then the bomb would accomplish two purposes. First, since it was set to go off at three o'clock in the morning, it would undoubtedly catch Admiral Magruder in his room. The shrapnel from the shape charge should kill the man. Yuri glanced up at the overhead, smiling as he realized exactly where he was. Additionally, the upward force of the blast should cause some damage to the deck. In fact, if his estimation were correct, they were now directly below the waist catapult. It would not take much damage to sever the steam lines that ran to the catapult launch shuttle or warp it beyond immediate repair.

At any rate, sometime within the next twenty-four hours, the USS *Jefferson* would find herself decapitated and severely restricted in her ability to launch aircraft.

Yuri hoped it would be enough.

1010 Local
Admiral's Briefing Room

"Sorry I've kept you waiting—let's get on with it," Magruder said as he strode into the room. It was a relief to be back among his own kind, other sailors and officers. He felt uncomfortable in his stiff dress uniform surrounded by the other officers in their comfortable working uniforms.

Tombstone turned to the senior Intelligence Officer. "What have you got for me?"

Lab Rat looked grim. "It's possible," he said bluntly. "Based on the Falcon's flight profile, I can't rule out the possibility that it has a vastly more capable power plant than we suspect." He held up one cautionary finger. "I have no hard data to support that, Admiral, but it's worth briefing all the squadrons on the possibility. They might want to take another look at their tactics against it."

Tombstone nodded. He was sure that a wealth of technical detail underlay Lab Rat's warning, and equally certain that he didn't need to hear it. If Lab Rat said that a warning was warranted, then so be it. "Anything else I need to know?"

Lab Rat glanced around the room. "Not here, Admiral. If you will step into SCIF."

Tombstone shot him a surprised look. He followed the Intelligence Officer to the back of the conference room and into the highly secure intelligence spaces located directly off the TFCC. "What gives?"

Lab Rat took a deep breath. "More speculation, Admiral. I'm short of proof on a lot of things these days. But you might want to read this."

Tombstone stared at the message, reached out to take it, and then drew his hand back. "Give it to me short," he ordered. He glanced at his watch. "I have to get back to the goddamned diplomats in a while."

"Stealth technology," Lab Rat said. "There's a possibility that somebody besides the U.S. has it."

"Who?" Tombstone said, unable to contain his impatience.

"The former Soviet Union had the beginnings of a program at the end of the Cold War. Most of the engineers on it were Ukrainian. National intelligence estimates say they returned to Ukraine after the dissolution of the former Soviet Union, and are probably continuing their work along those same lines there." Lab Rat paused for a moment, and his frown deepened. "Admiral, if Ukraine has stealth technology—operational or capable—it changes the whole complexion of this scenario."

It took a moment for Tombstone to catch on. When he did, the implications stunned him. "Turkey—it wasn't necessarily Turkey," he said, not wanting to hear his own words. "That makes even more sense, in one way. There's not much tactical reason for Turkey to have launched on us—none, as far as I can see." He thought back to the initial briefings he'd attended in the conference room. "They certainly don't seem like they're culpable, at least in public. They even seemed—" He struggled for a moment to find exactly the right word. "Outraged," he concluded finally. "Angry at the United States, justifiably angry. And we know that Ukraine has fissionable materials taken from the long-range warheads that were left on her soil after the dissolution." He stared at Lab Rat for a moment. "God, man, I've got to have more to go on than this."

Lab Rat nodded. "I know. I've asked for a special intelligence analysis of Ukraine's nuclear capabilities as well as a complete rundown on their stealth program. I sent the query out this morning, and I've already got two very concerned intelligence officers calling on top-secret lines to talk to me. Not with answers—with more questions. Evidently, I'm not the first one to think of this possibility."

"Then why don't they tell us this out in the field?" Tombstone raged. "I have lives depending on this sort of intelligence, decisions to make—and after yesterday, if we weren't in a shooting war with Turkey, we almost are now. I've got one man injured, one still in the water somewhere, dead or alive."

"I've suggested we redirect satellite coverage to provide continual surveillance of Ukraine," Lab Rat added. "In particular, I'm looking for any unusual troop movements, anything out of the ordinary, and most particularly, any indication of nuclear material being moved around on the ground."

"If that's all we can get, that's all we can get," Tombstone answered. "It had better be enough."

SEVEN
Friday, 7 September

0200 Local
USS **Shiloh**

"Lieutenant," the starboard lookout howled. "I got it, sir—I got it!"

The officer of the deck darted across the bridge and jumped over the combing around the edge of the hatch. His foot caught on it in mid-leap, and he stumbled out onto the bridge wing, fetching up against the alidade. "What is it, Simpson? Dammit, you keep yelling—didn't anybody tell you how to make a proper contact report?" The lieutenant's tirade came to a dead stop in midstream.

The lookout grabbed the lieutenant by the left shoulder and turned him around so that he faced out toward the sea. The sky was partly cloudy, and the moon obscured by the overcast. Nevertheless, there was enough ambient light for the surface of the water to be clearly visible.

"Just look, Lieutenant." The lookout pointed.

The officer stared, his eyes slowly resolving the pattern of shape and motion into the vision that had so excited the lookout. He grabbed the sound-powered phone microphone that hung around the lookout's neck. "Combat, OOD. Set Condition Two AS. I've got a visual on a snorkel mast, range four thousand yards, bearing zero-four-zero. If sonar's not holding it, I damned well want to know why." The officer dropped the sound-powered phone and leaped back into the bridge, clearing the combing this time handily.

"Ensign Carter, set Flight Quarters. Roust those helo smart-asses out of their racks. I want that bird turning in fifteen minutes."

The ensign nodded, then turned to the boatswains mate of the watch. "You heard the lieutenant. Set Flight Quarters." As the first announcement blared out shipwide over the 1MC, the OOD called his CO, Captain Daniel Heather.

0225 Local
TFCC
USS Jefferson

"They had to come up sooner or later," Gator declared. He pointed at the small symbol now blinking red on the tactical display. "A partly cloudy night, being held down by the helos—man, he's probably running low on battery power."

"Helicopters or S-3's?" his assistant watch officer asked.

In answer, Gator picked up the Batphone that connected him with the TAO in CDC. After a brief discussion, more of a confirmation really, Gator turned back to the watch officer. "Both. This time, that little bastard's not getting away."

"I know I should have gone to the carrier," Lieutenant Commander Rando Spratley grumbled. "You fly the F bird, you go to the carrier and get a dipper. None of this two-crews-and-one-helo bullshit you get on a cruiser." He sighed, looking at his copilot for sympathy. "If we were on the carrier, we'd be pulling Alert 15 every fourth day—not every fifteen minutes."

"So you say. But you sure as hell wouldn't be officer in charge of a helo detachment. At best, you'd be the senior lieutenant commander in charge of coffee. And pulling a whole lot more duty-standing than you do now."

"Yeah, well." In truth, Rando wouldn't have traded his tour on board the cruiser for duty on the bird farm. No way. Out here, it was just the *Shiloh* and her two helos, an eight-person aircrew detachment with support personnel along. They went alone and unafraid, and were capable of killing damned near anything that was looking to paint the profile of an Aegis cruiser on its conning tower.

Moreover, much as he hated to admit it, Rando drew a fair amount of satisfaction from his interactions with the black-shoe crew. Surface sailors were a different breed of people, that much was true. But they had their good points as well.

"Get your head back in the game," his copilot chided. "That submarine went sinker fifteen minutes ago. I don't know about you, but I want him bad, real bad. He's a damn sight too close to my stereo for my comfort."

"And just what the hell do you think I'm doing out here, playing with myself?" Rando snapped back. "If anybody would bother to give me a decent fly-to point, we might manage to get this mission started."

"Coming at you now." The copilot transmitted the location for the first sonobuoy to the pilot's console.

"You're right—too damned close," Rando said. His voice was markedly more serious than it had been a few minutes ago. "Think that lookout really saw something?"

"No doubt in my military mind," the copilot answered. "Besides, it wasn't only the lookout—the OOD saw it as well."

"And we'll see it last." Rando put the helicopter into a hard turn and headed for the first drop point.

0250 Local
TFCC
USS Jefferson

"So why don't we have him yet?" Batman asked. "People, I need answers—not excuses."

Gator spoke up, his voice cool and level in contrast to the admiral's. "Sir, the water gradient is for shit. There's a strong negative sound-velocity profile. That'll pull all sonar signals straight down to the bottom. And with as much garbage in the water as there is out here, the bottom's going to soak up most of the sound energy. Active sonar, sounds coming from the submarine itself." Gator shook his head. "This is a horrible ASW environment."

"Like I said—no excuses." Batman's voice was ragged from lack of sleep. "If you think the water conditions suck, try living with them in your stateroom."

Tombstone took one step forward and laid a hand on his friend's shoulder. There was nothing he could say, nothing he could do—not here, not in front of the watch team. Yet he knew too well the edge on which Batman was operating. Events were moving fast, too fast, and there were no decent explanations coming out of anyone. The crew, both on the ship and in the air wing, was getting jumpy.

But at least the aircrews could alternate Alert 15 watches. There was no relief for the admiral in command of a battle group, not really. Tombstone had experienced that all too often during the days when he commanded Battle Group 14. And now, even though he was on board, his presence provided no relief for Batman. It was *his* battle group, *his* ship, and *his* air wing. Not Tombstone's. To have offered to take off part of the load, to alternate in some sort of watch schedule with him, would not only have been tactically unsound, but would have amounted to an expression of no confidence in Batman's abilities.

I'm Sixth Fleet now. Sixth Fleet. This entire body of water and everything that surrounds it belongs to me— the carrier too, only because it's within my sphere of responsibility. The carrier from the outside. Everything inside and everything that leaves its deck is his.

Tombstone pulled his hand back, satisfied that he'd managed to restore Batman's perspective, at least for the moment. There were no long-term answers, and it was entirely possible that his own presence on board simply ratcheted up the pressure on Batman one notch higher.

But where else was he to go? His own flagship was an electronically gutted hulk, still underway to Gaeta for extensive repairs. A year, maybe two—his uncle had made it clear that he wouldn't be there that long.

Nevertheless, he hoped that his relief at Sixth Fleet got a better deal than this was shaping up to be.

"All right," Batman said finally. "Look, people—you know your jobs." He shook his head wearily. Then his expression softened. "A diesel submarine close to *Shiloh,* that's a tough target. I know you're doing everything you can, as are the aircrews we have out there now." He jerked his thumb in Tombstone's direction. "The admiral and I are going to go grab a cup of coffee." He glanced over at Tombstone, and saw the confirming nod. "If you see any indication of hostile intent or hostile acts, shoot the bastard. If you have a question, shoot first and call me later. If he's outside torpedo range when you regain contact, put everything you've got right on top of him. The second he ventures within torpedo range or makes any other threatening mood—hell, if its captain farts too loud, you kill him. Got that?"

Gator nodded. "Aye, aye, Admiral. We'll get him."

Batman led the way out of TFCC with Tombstone close behind. He paused outside in the empty conference room, sagging against one chair, holding onto the back of it for support. "I almost blew it, Stoney," he said softly. He shook his head ruefully. "As many times as I've been on the receiving end of it, you'd think I'd know better than to lose my temper like that. Hell, they're doing all they can—they've got tricks up their sleeve that weren't even dreamed of when you and I were in their spots. They're running ragged, and I let off steam at 'em, just because I'm short a little sleep."

"Get a hold of yourself, Admiral." Tombstone's voice was cold and sharp. "You did the right thing in there— but only after you fucked things up."

Batman recoiled as if Tombstone had taken a swing at him. "I suppose you never lost your cool when you were in command?" Batman demanded, his voice rising again. "Dammit, Stoney—"

"For the foreseeable future, I'm your reporting senior," Tombstone continued as though Batman hadn't spoken. "Here are your rudder orders. First, you will reexamine your priorities. You have left standing orders that you will be rousted out of your rack over matters that do not necessarily warrant your personal attention. Admiral, we don't know what the hell is going on out here. I understand your concern, and I applaud your diligence in trying to make every effort to ensure that another tragedy such as that which struck *La Salle* does not occur again." For the first time, Tombstone's voice softened slightly. "But there are limits to what you can do. One of the worst parts of this job is that you have to pace yourself—when the balloon goes up, you've got to be well rested, alert, or at least able to manage a reasonable facsimile thereof. You can't be there for every call. There's no way."

"That's what your predecessor thought too," Batman snapped back. "And as a result, he got his ship shot out from under him. That's not happening on my watch, Admiral. No way." He turned and started to walk away.

"And that's the trick," Tombstone said. "Deciding which ones are critical—and which ones can be handled without your intervention. Take this situation tonight, for example," he continued, nodding toward the TFCC hatch. "You just did exactly what you're paid to do— gave your people the information they needed about your intentions and wishes, clarified the tactical choices for them, and then left them to do their jobs. Batman—you don't need coffee, not right now." Tombstone pointed toward the admiral's stateroom. "You need sleep."

A long moment of silence stretched out between the

two, broken when Batman finally shook his head. "You don't miss a trick, do you?"

Tombstone almost smiled. "Some. But not the same one twice in a row. I learned something while I was out here. You will too."

Batman shot him a suspicious look. "Is that an order to hit the rack, Admiral?"

"Merely a suggestion."

Batman straightened. "Then may I assume that the admiral will be following his own advice? Because I'll be damned if I can recall a time when I was called to TFCC when you weren't right on my ass."

Tombstone shrugged. "Point well taken." He turned to leave the room. "If you need me, I'll be in my cabin. Other than that, you're on your own."

As the two admirals headed off at right angles to each other, each to his own stateroom, Tombstone paused at the hatch leading out of the conference room just as Batman reached his own entrance.

"Stoney?"

"Yeah?"

"We were never that young. And even if we were, we were a helluva lot hotter. Weren't we?"

Finally, Tombstone did smile. "We thought we were. And right now, that's all that matters."

"Night, Stoney."

"Night, Batman."

It was sixty-four steps back to his stateroom. Sixty-four steps and eight knee-knockers, each one threatening to gash open a giant bruise on his shinbone as he lifted his tired legs to clear the ten-inch obstacles. He turned left, then right along the starboard passageway, heading back toward the visiting flag spaces.

Two frames from his own compartment, Tombstone paused. He heard voices, one muttering angrily. At this hour of the morning, it caught his attention in a way that it wouldn't have during the day.

He paused outside the hatch, read the squadron insignia, and felt a wave of nostalgia wash over him. VF-95—his old squadron. How many times had he been up at this hour, going over some mistake he'd made in the air, swearing at himself for some trivial error. Feeling a little guilty, he tried to decipher the voices inside. There was only one, he realized—a man, talking to himself. A pilot, based on the phrases he caught. Mounted on the door frame was a small nameplate. It was Skeeter Harmon's room.

Tombstone stepped closer to the door, then paused. Should he?

No, he decided. He tried to remember what it was like to be a junior officer, tried to imagine the horror and chagrin he would have felt had an admiral knocked on his door at—it was almost three o'clock in the morning.

Every pilot has his or her own particular nightmares. For some it's a soft cat, for others it's the fear of ejecting. Each one finds his own ways to deal with it, and there is little that an admiral can do to speed the process along.

Tombstone dropped his hand down by his side and turned back toward his compartment.

0259 Local
Teletype Repair Shop

Inside the radio housing, delicate circuits clicked over microseconds, recording the passage of time far more accurately than was needed for the bomb's purposes.

Twenty seconds before the scheduled detonation time, two activating relays kicked over to their ready position. Poised just a millimeter over the metallic hard points that would complete the electrical circuit, they surged invisibly with the current poised over their tips.

As the timing circuit clicked over to 0300, both contacts closed the last millimeter of distance.

0300 Local
Starboard Passageway, 03 Deck

Tombstone took another step over another knee-knocker. The digital watch on his wrist chimed gently on the hour.

His world exploded.

Tombstone slammed hard into the bulkhead on his right. His shoulder hit first, followed a split second later by his head. His foot, still poised over the knee-knocker, caught the metal ledge on his heel, spinning him back into the angle formed by the knee-knocker hatch and the bulkhead. His chin slammed into the steel and he felt something crumple in his mouth. He slid down to the deck, barely conscious.

Fire erupted in the passageway, rolling down fore and aft on a wave of sound and smoke and flames. Tombstone felt the heat, searing and instant. Then it subsided slightly as damaged nerve endings shut down. Instinctively, he buried his head in his hands, shielding his face and eyes. It was a natural movement for a pilot—the eyes, his most critical personal asset aside from testosterone.

As his consciousness faded out, he noted how oddly quiet it was.

He slid to the deck, his cheek still scraping down the gray-painted metal bulkhead, and collapsed into an ungainly sprawl on the deck.

0301 Local

The explosion threw Shaughnessy down the passageway, slamming her into a fire hose coiled and mounted on the bulkhead. The impact stunned her for a few moments. She lay on the deck, heard the gonging sound of General Quarters begin, and feet pounding down the passageway, without entirely understanding what was happening.

"Shaughnessy!" A young man crouched next to her, shook her gently by the shoulder. "Are you all right?"

Full consciousness returned slowly. Shaughnessy stirred, and groaned as the numbness in her back seeped away. "I think so." Every second, her mind cleared more and more. "Help me get up."

The other sailor shot an anxious glance down the corridor, then held out his hand. "Come on. General Quarters—are you sure you're okay?" he asked, a frown on his face. "You don't look so hot."

Shaughnessy shook her head, took a deep breath, and shoved his helping hand away. "I'm all right. Let's get up to the flight deck."

The other sailor, Airman Mike Moyers, led the way. They darted down the passageway, keeping with the flow of sailors scrambling for General Quarters stations, then went up one ladder to the flight deck. Both were assigned to Repair 8 as their General Quarters station, the damage-control team that was responsible for the flight deck.

As they stepped over the knee-knocker and onto the

tarmac, Mike grabbed Shaughnessy by the shoulder again. He pointed aft to a cluster of people. "There it is—thank God, no fire."

Shaughnessy nodded. Of all the disasters they could face on board the carrier, a flight deck fire was one of the worst, second only to a fire in main Engineering. Uncontrolled, the flames could quickly engulf parked aircraft, weapons waiting to be unloaded onto wings, as well as the fuel outlets. In a matter of moments, a conflagration could destroy the entire fighting capability of an aircraft carrier. It had happened before.

"Let's get suited up." Shaughnessy took the lead as they darted toward their damage-control compartment. They joined a crowd of sailors thronging around it, struggling into asbestos-proofed firefighting ensembles, manning sound-powered phones, and generally gearing up for battle. It was the standard precaution. Even though there was no sign of fire now on the flight deck, there was no telling what damage the explosion had done below—and how it would spread.

Shaughnessy slipped the ensemble hood over her head, and the clear-tempered glass face mask immediately started fogging up. That was one of the worst parts about being suited up. While the gear provided excellent protection against most of the conditions a firefighting team would expect to encounter, the heat inside it quickly rose to a stifling temperature.

"Not yet," the damage-control-party leader said, motioning to Shaughnessy. "Stand by, though—so far it looks like all we've got is structural damage."

Shaughnessy gratefully took off the hood and took a deep breath of the fresh air.

"What happened?" Mike turned to her. "You were right down the passageway from it, weren't you?"

"Are you hurt?" the damage-control-party leader asked. He assessed her carefully. "Big raw gash on your forehead—what else?"

"I'm fine." Shaughnessy shook her head, aware of the ache that was already spreading down her back. "Knocked me around a little bit, but that's all."

"Well." The damage-control-party leader dropped the matter, relying on her assessment of her own condition.

"But what happened?" Mike demanded again.

"I don't know. I'd just passed an admiral in the passageway—Sixth Fleet, actually—and I was headed for the line shack. Then there was this big noise, and a flash. I must have hit the damage-control gear mounted on the bulkhead." She shook her head, remembering just how fast it had gone. There hadn't been time to react, not even time to be afraid. Suddenly, a thought occurred to her. "The admiral—what happened to him?"

"I don't know. I didn't see anyone else in the passageway, but it was dark too." Mike shrugged, and touched her gently on the back of the head. "Repair 2 will be on it. If he's there, they'll find him."

Shaughnessy nodded slowly. It wasn't her problem, not right now. Still, Admiral Magruder had been in command of her carrier battle group during her last cruise. He seemed like a good guy, as admirals went. Be a shame if something happened to him.

"What was the explosion?" she asked. "There's nothing in that part of the ship that could detonate like that."

Mike shrugged. "You're right about that."

An uneasy feeling wormed its way into Shaughnessy's gut. Disaster was possible in any part of the carrier—she knew that. The entire structure was honeycombed with electrical lines, fuel lines, and myriad other conduits.

There was nowhere that was entirely safe, not even the flag passageway.

But a fire in that area of the ship would more likely be electrical in nature, not explosive. Smoldering circuits, the stench of burning insulation—that was what she would have expected to find if she had been dispatched as primary investigator during a disaster. Not explosives. It was almost as though—

"You don't think somebody could have planted a bomb on the ship, do you?" she said, hearing just how very terrifying the words sounded even as she said them. "Not a bomb."

0308 Local
Starboard Passageway, 03 Deck

"Team Leader, Investigator." The point man on the fire team crouched down low in the passageway over the crumpled form. "One casualty—send a corpsman up ASAP."

"Investigator, Team Leader. Interrogative conditions in your area? The corpsman—can he make it up there?"

The investigator assessed the condition of the passageway. The bulkheads were charred and black smoke still boiled and eddied about him. Still, there were no signs of an actual fire. Not yet. That was his role on the damage-control team, to be the first in, to report back to the team leader, who could then decide how to dispatch his fire parties and desmoking teams.

"Put him in a suit, but I don't see any flames around. And get the desmoking teams on this—that looks to be the main problem right now."

"Roger."

The investigator knelt down by the body and ran his hands gently over it. There were no obvious signs of damage other than unconsciousness —it could be that the victim had simply been overcome by the smoke. But the position he was lying in indicated that he hadn't dropped gently to the deck.

The investigator glanced down the passageway, trying to locate the original source of the explosion. It couldn't be too far, and there was every chance that this casualty had been caught in the immediate vicinity of it. No, better not to move him—let the corpsman take a look at him first. If he had hit the wall, maybe slid down from there, he could have fractured his neck or his back. To move him now would be to risk permanent paralysis.

Leaning over him to look at the other side of the man's uniform, the investigator checked for a name. It was one of the things he would want to report immediately to the team leader, to answer questions about why the injured sailor hadn't shown up at his General Quarters station.

As his eyes lit on the collar, the investigator sucked in a hard breath. Stars. He brought his portable radio back up to his mouth. "Team Leader, I've identified the casualty. It's Admiral Magruder."

"The admiral? Are you certain?"

"Unless you know somebody else on board who's got three stars on his collar, that's who it is."

"Roger. The corpsman is on the way."

The investigator stayed with Admiral Magruder until two other team members showed up accompanying the corpsman. He left the admiral in their care, and proceeded on down the passageway to complete his preliminary examination.

Near the admiral's quarters, the nonstructural bulkheads were twisted and warped. The smoke was thicker, and the scent of it seeped in under his ensemble hood. He pulled it down tighter, breathing out a heavy breath to clear it out.

Around the corner now, easy, don't be getting in a rush. It looks like this is where—yes. The investigator picked up his radio for a third time. "Team Leader, in Compartment . . ." He glanced up at the overhead and reeled off a series of figures from the barely legible brass plaque. "I have a possible Class Alpha fire."

The investigator could hear the feet, the noises of a fire team moving as quickly as they could in their cumbersome gear. The hose slithered across the deck, clunking as the metal joints between sections scraped over the knee-knockers. A few moments later, he saw the lead hoseman materialize out of the smoke.

The investigator stepped back and let the rest of the damage-control team have complete access to the area.

Not a bad one—not as fires go. From the looks of it, most of the damage was done by the initial explosion. Just some residual fire—should be easy to extinguish.

The investigator left the scene and began circling through the adjoining compartments, checking for where the fire might have spread. Another investigator was also checking the decks immediately above and below, although Repair 8 would have primary responsibility for any damage on the flight deck. Still, it never hurt to double-check. Fire had a way of doing that aboard a ship, creeping along through empty spaces and between decks, getting out of hand before a fire party really knew what was happening.

Twenty minutes later, the investigator was satisfied that the damage was limited to the 03 level of the carrier in a small square centered around the admiral's stateroom.

0330 Local
Medical Department

"Admiral—do you know where you are?" The voice was kind, yet insistent. "I need for you to wake up now, Admiral. Come on, I know you can hear me."

Tombstone felt like he was underwater. The voice was barely audible, as though someone were talking a long way away. It sounded muffled, dampened by the sea. He tried to move, and felt the same sluggish restraint he always noticed when skin diving.

"Admiral—talk to me." The voice again, closer now, and louder.

Tombstone felt a groan shudder up from his gut. He twisted, and that small movement brought pain flooding into him from all over. The groan deepened, forcing its way out from between his lips against his wishes.

"Good—I knew you were awake. Open your eyes now, please."

Tombstone tried to obey, and felt the light slowly creeping up under his eyelids. It was lighter now, but the shapes around him were oddly fuzzy and indistinct. "Where am I?" he managed to croak. His throat felt as though it were on fire.

"You're in Medical, Admiral. There was an explosion and a fire in your quarters. You were injured—not seriously. You're going to be fine."

Tombstone squinted, trying to resolve the blurs into faces. Finally, one familiar to his eyes swam into view. "Batman."

Batman laid a restraining hand on his friend's shoulder. "Take it easy there, Stoney. I didn't believe it possible, but that bulkhead was harder than your head. You just lay back for a while, let the doc finish checking you out." Batman shot the doctor a concerned look. "He says you're going to be fine."

"Help me stand up." Tombstone's voice was weak but insistent.

The doctor shook his head. "Not a chance, Admiral. You check out all right, you stay with us for another thirty minutes, then we'll see about letting you move around. I'm not risking it at this point, not until I get the X-rays back and I'm sure you don't have a concussion. Tell me, how's your eyesight? Having any problem seeing me?" The doctor snapped a flashlight on, flicked it across Tombstone's pupils.

"No problems. I can see you fine," Tombstone lied. "Just let me—"

Batman increased the pressure on his friend's shoulder. "You lie your ass back down in that bed, Stoney, or I'm going to authorize the doc to put you in restraints. You got that?"

"Dammit, Batman, I—"

"It's my ship, Tombstone." Batman's voice carried with it a quiet dignity. "Quit being an asshole and let me go take care of it. The doc only called me down here because you kept trying to roll out of the bed."

"Okay." The efforts of the last few minutes had exhausted him, he was alarmed to find out. Tombstone lay back on the narrow mattress and stifled another groan. At least everything was moving, or seemed to be. He'd know for sure if they'd let him stand up. But there was no point in keeping Batman from his duties with a truculent childlike reaction from a senior officer. What he'd said was true—it was Batman's ship. At this point in time, there was absolutely nothing Tombstone could do except stay out of the way.

"That's better. Stoney, I'm going to leave, but I'll be back later to check on you."

"He'll be fine, Admiral Wayne," the doctor assured him. "Now that we've got him under control."

The explosion. Tombstone tried to summon up the exact details from his battered brain, but remembered nothing more than hitting the wall. He'd been headed back to his cabin, that much he remembered. There'd been a sharp flash, then—what? Nothing.

What on the ship could possibly explode that way? Nothing Tombstone knew about, not in that area of the ship.

A cold, clear dread settled in his stomach. It hadn't been the ship, he knew with compelling certainty. Not the ship at all. Someone else—something else—had caused the explosion.

Sabotage.

0400 Local
Admiral's Conference Room

"I demand to be briefed. Immediately." Bradley Tiltfelt's voice was cold, full of self-righteous rage. "It's imperative that I be kept fully aware of what's going on on this ship."

"How bad is it?" Batman asked the damage-control officer. The Captain of the carrier was standing immediately behind the grimy and sweating damage-control officer.

"Bad enough, Admiral." The engineer shook his head.

"The damage belowdecks is relatively minor. In relative terms, that is. A few staterooms, some personal belongings—nothing structural is damaged."

"And the flight deck?" Batman demanded.

"You've lost the waist catapult. There's no way around it, Admiral. The flight deck is slightly warped, and I can't be sure the shuttle run is even straight, much less that it retains sufficient structural integrity for launches. If we absolutely had to, like if we were in the middle of the war—well, you might chance it. But it would be just that—a chance. It might break loose the first launch and blast shrapnel into your flight deck crew and your aircraft, or it might actually work for a while. That's even assuming it's straight and it doesn't tear itself apart under the steam pressure. Or that it holds pressure at all." The engineer shrugged helplessly. "Without a lot more facilities than I've got on the ship, I just can't tell. For now, my recommendation is no flight operations whatsoever off the waist catapult."

"That's what I was afraid of." Batman's voice was cold and determined. "But at least we have the two forward catapults still working, right? No problem with them?"

The engineer nodded, the Captain of the aircraft carrier also nodding thoughtfully behind him. "As far as I can tell, there should be no problem with the forward catapults. There's enough separation that maybe there was a little stress on the deck there, but not enough to throw it out of true. There are no signs of damage, at any rate—I'd like to have the shipyard look it over next time we're in, but I think it's safe."

Think it's safe. Batman nodded. That would have to do for now.

"Admiral?" Tiltfelt's voice was sharp, demanding. "Did you hear me? What does all of this mean?"

Batman whirled to face the civilian. "It means that we've lost a part of our fighting capability. Sir." Batman let the last word drip venom. "Not so much that we're sitting ducks, but we can't launch as rapidly as we'd like to be able to. Is there any part of that you don't understand?"

"What do you mean by speaking to me in that tone of voice?" Tiltfelt's face was flushed.

"I mean that I have a job to do and you're getting in my way. Sir, I'll tell you everything you need to know—when I can. But I'm not going to let what amounts to a courtesy back-briefing to a civilian interfere with my ability to conduct operations off this carrier. Is that absolutely clear to you?"

"Why you—"

Batman cut him off. "Because if it's not, then it would make me happier than shit to strap your soft little civilian butt into a COD, throw it off the pointy end from one of my two remaining catapults, and send your ass back to the States. At least that way I won't have to put up with having a convention of saboteurs aboard my ship."

Bradley Tiltfelt stood and drew himself up to his full height. At six feet, three inches, he was an imposing figure. Even rousted from his stateroom in the middle of the night by the explosion and General Quarters alarm, he managed somehow to look as though he'd spent hours getting dressed. The clean, crisp white shirt, the old school tie so carefully knotted—in spite of himself, Batman was grudgingly impressed. Almost as much as he was dismayed by the State Department representative's inability to understand the situation in which Batman now found himself.

"If you are implying that any of our allies are responsible for this unfortunate occurrence, then I certainly hope you have the facts to back you up," Tiltfelt said coldly. "Otherwise, I'd suggest you keep your paranoid ravings to yourself."

"Just who on this ship do you think would want to set a bomb off, mister?" Batman exploded. "Some seaman pissed because he didn't get a letter from home? Or because the chief yelled at him? I don't think so. We're the ones who live here. We depend on this ship. And don't you think it's just terribly odd that the explosion occurred in Admiral Magruder's cabin?"

"The only logical cause of this explosion is one of two things," Tiltfelt continued as though Batman hadn't spoken. "First, one of your subordinates has failed to supervise some sort of system properly and it exploded." Tiltfelt waved one languid hand in the air as though filling in the details. "I'm sure if you look hard enough, you'll find that's certainly a possibility. The second, of course, is exactly as you've outlined—some disgruntled sailor under your command, no doubt alienated by your lack of concern for his physical well-being and morale, has become sufficiently disgruntled to make this sort of statement."

"That wasn't a statement, that was a fucking bomb. Just how many sailors do you think have access to that sort of material?"

"Probably all of them, judging from the degree of leadership and organization I see on board this vessel," Tiltfelt shot back. "And until you have hard evidence to back it up, you'd best refrain from idle and malicious speculation. Clearly, there is no reason for our guests to wish to disrupt the very peace process that they've initiated."

"The State Department—" Batman roared. He was cut

off by the appearance of a tall, shaken figure in the hatch leading to the passageway.

"Gets people killed." Tombstone stepped over the knee-knocker and entered the conference room. He looked at Batman, quelling his friend's rage with a supportive look, then turned his gaze to Tiltfelt. "That's how it always is, isn't it? State starts yelling about diplomatic solutions and the second it goes wrong, they blame the military. Well, mister, maybe Sixth Fleet draws a little more water than you think it does. You're excused, Mr. Tiltfelt. Please remain in your cabin until I call you."

"Just where do you people get off with this?" Tiltfelt sputtered. He turned and looked at his aides behind him as though for support. "First you provoke an attack, and then you try to blame the logical consequences for your actions on the same parties. Just who do you people think you are?"

Tombstone smiled. "I think I know exactly who I am. I'm the commander of Sixth Fleet. And you're here solely at my sufferance, Mr. Tiltfelt. Solely at my sufferance."

Tombstone turned to Batman and said formally, "Admiral, may I have the use of your communications officer for a few minutes?"

"Of course, sir," Batman replied in just as formal tones. "My ship is at your disposal."

Tombstone nodded. "Have someone call in for me, please. Tell them I need a secure circuit to the Chief of Naval Operations in Washington, D.C. He should be in his office at this hour, but if not, have someone hunt him down. It's imperative that I speak with my uncle immediately."

Tombstone turned back to Bradley Tiltfelt. "As you

reminded me right after you arrived on board, my uncle is Chief of Naval Operations."

Tiltfelt was almost apoplectic now. His color had deepened from red into a shade of purple that looked downright dangerous. "I don't care if the president is your mother. You're damned well not getting away with this."

"Oh, I think I am. You'll think that too after I talk to him." Tombstone's voice was almost mild, even more dangerous by the sound of it. "Please remain in your stateroom," he repeated. "I'll call you if I need you—if that ever happens."

Five minutes later, the communicator buzzed Tombstone on the intercom. "I have the CNO's office, Admiral," the communications officer announced. "His people are standing by for you."

Again, the delicate dance of elephants. The staff at the CNO's office was not about to leave their four-star boss waiting on the line for a three-star fleet commander. Staff and assistants took the ranks of their bosses almost as seriously as the officers themselves did. More so in some cases. Tombstone sighed and picked up the receiver. "This is Admiral Magruder," he announced.

"Admiral, good morning. Please stand by—the CNO will be on the line shortly." An annoying popular tune started playing softly on the line. His uncle's voice interrupted it seconds later.

"Tombstone. What the hell happened?"

"An explosion on board, sir." Tombstone quickly sketched the outline of what had happened and the damage to the carrier. He concluded with: "State seems to think they carry a pretty big stick around here,

Admiral. I need to ask you now—how much leeway do I have?"

He knows what I really mean, Tombstone thought. No matter how I phrase it, he's going to read between the lines. I don't have to tell him how much the whole idea of this conference pissed me off, that I know he sent me out of Washington before I could learn about it simply because of that. He knows what I would have said, how much I would have objected to it—and right now, sitting back there in D.C., he knows I would have been right. There were more advantages than his uncle had suspected to having a relative on the front lines, but this time the advantage was Tombstone's.

"Tell me what you need, Stoney." His uncle's voice was taut, white anger lurking underneath. It was a characteristic the Magruder males shared, the icy cold exterior that masked a hot, volatile temper few of their shipmates suspected. "Tell me what you need."

"A free hand," Tombstone replied promptly. "Sir, the political battles and diplomacy need to be run from D.C.—not from my carrier. I suspect we'll have evidence in the next several hours to prove that this incident was the work of someone outside of my crew or air wing. You know it was. Admiral, I've got twenty-eight foreign nationals on board my ship right now, half of them from a nation that already wiped out my flagship. In spite of what State says, this is not a diplomatic problem. It's a military one. And I'm the man on the front line. I need to know now, sir—do I have your support or not?"

"Stoney, calm down." His uncle's voice was quiet and reasonable now, although Tombstone could still hear the anger simmering just below the surface. "I sent you out there for a reason. And no, although you didn't say so, I didn't tell you everything. The final details weren't arranged when you left, but I suspected exactly this sort of ploy by the State Department, some sort of planning conference held on board your ship. I couldn't put someone else out there, Stoney—I just couldn't. The only one I can trust to give me a solid reaction, to do what I would have done if I were there, is you."

"So where does that leave us, Uncle?" Tombstone asked, his own anger deflated by the anguish he heard in his uncle's voice. "Where does that leave us?"

"With one slightly damaged but damned dangerous aircraft carrier," his uncle replied immediately. "And it leaves me with some ammunition. If you need any scientific or forensic assistance, just say so. Otherwise, I've got what I need—proof that State Department's ploy isn't going to work. In the end, we're going to save lives because of this, lives that would have been wasted on some NATO peacekeeping plan or cockeyed idea of a presence mission. We tried it their way—now it's our ball game."

Tombstone's load suddenly slipped off his shoulders. That he'd been in conflict with his uncle had made him acutely uncomfortable. During the years that he'd followed his uncle up the career ladder within the Navy, he'd felt a growing closeness to the man, a new appreciation of the hurdles his uncle had cleared so handily as a junior admiral himself. Now, as the Chief of Naval Operations, Admiral Thomas Magruder held ultimate responsibility for the performance of the Navy. Tombstone knew that, no matter how hard he tried, he could never appreciate fully the pressure his uncle operated under. Sure, now that he'd had his own tours as a flag officer, he might begin to understand it—but never really understand, not unless he ended up sitting in that seat himself someday.

"Admiral, this is what I'd like to do." Briefly, Tombstone outlined his plan.

"Make it happen," his uncle said instantly. "Here are your steaming orders—the formal Rules of Engagement amendments will follow, but for now I want you to know this. First, you will take all precautions necessary to prevent another attack on the carrier. I'm not there, and you're on scene. I'll let you make the call as to what that exactly entails. The tactical situation changes too rapidly for us to micromanage it from here. You make the call, Stoney—I'll back you up. Second, try to stabilize the situation there."

Tombstone started to protest, and his uncle cut him off.

"I know that's a broad order, but again—I'm not here to micromanage. You need to start with finding out exactly what happened in the attack on *La Salle* and go from there. You can't do that if you take any more damage. Those are your priorities, Admiral. Do you have any questions?"

"No, Admiral." Tombstone's voice was grim. "We won't take the first hit—not ever. You can be sure of that. And I'll do my best to get to the bottom of the rest of this tactical situation. As soon as I know anything, you'll hear about it."

"I expect no less." His uncle's voice took on a note of vicious glee. "And now I'm going to go cram your damaged catapult up somebody's ass."

0500 Local

Yuri walked back to the stateroom that he shared with the other senior Ukrainian representative. They followed a circuitous route, following behind a young seaman designated to guide them around the areas damaged by the bomb. Down two ladders, aft forty frames, then back up to the main 03 level. The acrid smell of smoke had already infiltrated the lower decks, although it was markedly less overpowering than it was on his own level.

It seemed to Yuri that his situation on board the carrier was increasingly precarious. His enemies were closing all around, both militarily and politically. The Turks as well as the Ukrainians were housed in this section of the carrier in a row of guest suites that ran partway down the corridor. He intercepted uneasy looks from them, pointedly accusing in some cases. He shook his head, trying to push away his fears. They couldn't know—they couldn't. There'd been no indications on his mission that he'd been detected at all, not even by his own radar.

And now the matter of the bomb. The missile, then the bomb—if the Americans uncovered any evidence, any at all, he dreaded to think what his future would hold. In his own country, there would have been a summary execution following a trial that might have lasted fifteen minutes. Although he'd heard protests to the contrary, and seen some evidence on his own while on board the carrier, he had no real deep conviction that in the end the Americans would deal any differently with him than his own country would have.

How had he gotten involved in this? His mind circled around that one question, trying to find a point at which to begin to think about it. All he was was a pilot, someone who wanted to strap a MiG on his ass and take huge bites out of airspace. He was a pilot. Yes, trained in tactics, trained to kill other aircraft. But in reality he suspected he had more in common with the American aviators than he did his superiors in Ukraine. He'd seen the looks on the Americans' faces as they walked the corridors on the way to the flight deck, watched them as they talked about the powerful Tomcat. At one point over dinner, the unreasoning impulse to join in the conversation had shook him like a strong gale. The urge to talk about airplanes, about flying, about all of the things that made life worthwhile for an aviator. From the carefully edited remarks and unclassified stories he'd heard in the mess, he knew that he had more in common with these aviators than anyone would have expected.

And the missile—God, the missile. The briefing had simply said that it was an advanced model, intended to detonate near the flagship. He'd thought it was conventional, had no reason to expect otherwise. There'd been none of the precautions he would have expected with a nuclear warhead, not the dosimeters, not the special protective gear, not the post-mission medical checks— nothing. Had that been meant to allay his fears, to deceive him? Or was it simply evidence of what he'd come to know as a complete lack of concern on the part of his government for the people who worked around fissionable material.

It was an old joke, one grounded in cold, hard reality: Sailing on a Russian or Ukrainian nuclear submarine was never a family tradition. Too true, since the lead shielding surrounding the reactor had been cut back to minimal levels to allow more space for weapons and higher speeds. The residual radiation leaking into the submarine living spaces was enough to induce a high rate of cancer and sterility in the men who sailed in her.

And what about him? How much had he been exposed to, flying with that thing on his wing all those hours? Probably not much, the technical part of his mind concluded. Not too much, at least.

And what would he have done if he had known it was a nuclear weapon? Refused the mission? He shook his head, seeing immediately the difficulties that would have opened up. Refuse one mission and spend the rest of his life tainted with the fatal label: politically unreliable.

"Perhaps there is something we can do to assist our American friends," Yuri said to the other Ukrainian. He glanced up at the overhead, wondering if there were listening devices planted in this area. Or perhaps the seaman escorting them even spoke Ukrainian—yes, that would have been easier to arrange than surveillance along a corridor they normally would not have used. "These last two hours—I overheard one aviator say there may be a problem with one of the catapults."

"How can we assist?" The broad, Slavic face of his compatriot looked puzzled. He gestured at the aircraft carrier. "This is American technology, not Ukrainian."

"But Ukrainians build the finest ships in the world," Yuri said forcefully. "Even the Americans would admit that was true. After all, we built the Russian carriers, did we not?"

"Yes, of course. The catapult on those is closely modeled on the American system," his compatriot said slowly. Comprehension began to dawn on his face.

"So if the Americans have some concern about their catapult, what better way to assist them than offer an inspection at our nearby Crimean Peninsula facilities? After all, Ukraine is well noted for her open and willing assistance to any nation in need. Even in the midst of this conflict, we provide assistance to Turkey to combat the aftereffects of their own aggression, do we not?"

Yuri waited, letting the point sink in. A smile played around his lips as he watched his companion begin to nod. "It would be a generous gesture," his compatriot concluded finally. "Moreover, it would offer the Americans an opportunity to demonstrate their trust, to cement their relationship with Ukraine. Their intelligence sources can tell them that we already have a working catapult system. Indeed, I would be very surprised if they do not have all of the details available immediately. And what we are offering is certainly nothing that would compromise their security. It is merely engineering services, the equipment and machinery and expertise that would allow them to assess the true operational status of one third of their launching facilities."

"With the Americans the only nation to stand between Ukraine and the Turks, their presence in the Black Sea would be most welcome." And that, Yuri thought, would be of particular interest to the admiral. Particularly if he is eavesdropping on this conversation and believes that we do not know it. And especially if he is concerned about that catapult.

"I will make the offer," the senior representative concluded finally. "After I check with my superiors, of course." He gazed approvingly at Yuri, the merest glint of acknowledgment in his eyes.

He understands, Yuri thought. Understands, and sees the advantages to it. Yuri felt chilled for a moment now that the danger had passed. He had been uncertain as to exactly how much of the entire plan the other man knew. Enough, it now appeared. Probably not all, but enough.

0600 Local
Admiral's Conference Room

By the time the first call for morning chow went down, the plan was finished. Tombstone lifted his head from the

chart of the Mediterranean and Black Seas spread out in
front of him. He scanned the faces of the other officers
seated around the conference room, noted the drained,
sober look in their eyes, felt the distinct stirrings of
pride as he thought about the last three hours. From
disaster—to a plan. Even as the smoke was being
cleared, the last traces of firefighting water siphoned
over the side of the ship, and reflash watches set, the staff
had done exactly what they were supposed to do—
analyze the situation and the alternatives and come up
with something that would work.

And his uncle—how could he ever have doubted him?
The same genes that had taken his father over to
Vietnam, never to return, had rocketed both uncle and
nephew up the ladder of responsibility within the Navy.
It would have been impossible to have misjudged him so
much, simply not believable. In the end, dealing with
issues and pressures that Tombstone could not fully
comprehend, his uncle had come through with the right
answer.

"Then it's settled." Tombstone reached out one finger
and circled a large area of the ocean. "Effective 0800,
we're declaring a no-fly zone one hundred and fifty
miles around the carrier."

"With a few exceptions, of course," Batman chimed
in. "I think we hammered that out pretty fairly. Commercial flights on a published schedule may proceed
within one hundred miles of the carrier if they contact us
ahead of time and arrange for a VID at the three-
hundred-mile point." Batman shrugged, evincing little
sympathy for the commercial air traffic. "It may slow
them down some, screw up some connecting flights, but
better them than us."

"I think they realize that," Tombstone said soberly.

"I'd be surprised if half the flights aren't canceled anyway." Tombstone leaned back in his chair and said, "There's one other matter. We've talked around it all morning and haven't really resolved it. Responsibility for this bomb attack." A quiet murmur started around the table as the officers discussed their theories with their neighbors. Tombstone cut it off with a wave of his hand. "Lots of arguments on both sides. But this one is my call." He turned to Batman. "Arrange a COD flight. I want all foreign nationals off this boat by noon. Every last one of them."

0630 Local

"Of course, you have my deepest apologies for the inconvenience," Bradley Tiltfelt said. The two Ukrainians stared at him impassively. "I assure you we have every intention of going forward with this investigation. As soon as I am able to contact the State Department again, this will be promptly straightened out. Promptly."

"We could continue the matter in Ukraine perhaps," the older of the two men suggested. "We would of course be willing to host those meetings ourselves."

Tiltfelt nodded agreeably. "I plan on urging my superiors to take advantage of that very generous offer. As for Turkey—well, she may be somewhat reluctant to join us. A shame—it is always preferable to have all concerned parties sitting around the table while these matters are resolved."

"There is one other matter as well," the elder Ukrainian said. "Your ship."

"As I said, sir, that will be straightened out as soon as

I can contact my superiors. Unfortunately, the one radio circuit that I'm allotted seems to be severely affected by local sunspot activity. The admiral assures me it should clear up by this evening." Tiltfelt let his voice express his utter disbelief in this statement.

"When you speak with him, there is one other matter we wish to offer," the Ukrainian continued. "We have heard about the damage to the catapult. It is a serious matter, as the Americans are the only force capable of standing between our country and Turkey. In return for continued protection by this aircraft carrier, we would offer the services of our excellent repair facilities in Ukraine." He held up one hand to forestall objections. "It is possible you do not wish the repair work to be done there. May I assure you, we will not be offended if that is the case. However, if the damage is less than you expect, we should be able to reassure you on that point. And you may consult your intelligence people as you wish. There is nothing about your catapult systems that we do not already know."

And have improved on, Yuri thought. Still, it would be nice to see one of yours myself.

"Why . . . why . . ." For a moment, Bradley Tiltfelt seemed to be at a loss for words. "A most generous offer. Really, this is so—I cannot tell you how gratified I am. I shall of course urge my superiors to accept immediately."

The two Ukrainians stood. "You will excuse us, but we have some preparations to make. I understand our flight is to be leaving shortly."

"Of course. And again, my sincerest apologies for this inconvenience. I hope to see you both in Ukraine in the near future."

The Ukrainians nodded. "Bring your aircraft carrier,

Mr. Secretary. We will show you how valuable a friend Ukraine can be."

As he watched the two men leave, Bradley Tiltfelt felt an overwhelming rush of exhilaration. This was what diplomacy was all about, and he'd been absolutely right to come here in person. Because of his personal intervention in this situation, a new bond of friendship was about to be forged between Ukraine and the United States. And it was all due to him, his foresight, his intuitive understanding of the ways of nations.

Bradley Tiltfelt was so happy he could almost cry. Vindication, particularly sweet following on the heels of the abusive treatment from the United States military. When this opportunity was presented to the United States, Tiltfelt's stock would soar to record levels. Never again would a man in uniform embarrass him as Admiral Wayne had earlier that day. And as for Admiral Magruder—both of them, now that he saw how their nepotistic relationship influenced national policy—both of them would pay.

0700 Local
Admiral's Conference Room

"Absolutely not." Tombstone felt his temper career up toward dangerous levels. He glanced across the table at Batman, and was not surprised to see a similar expression on his old wingman's face. "We are no more taking this carrier into port in the Crimean Peninsula than we are—" Words finally failed him, lost in the red haze of his outrage. "You understand that one of those men could have been responsible for the bomb planted on my ship?"

"And you would have us turn over custody of our ship to them?" Batman asked, his voice a dangerous, low growl. "I ought to have you shot."

Tiltfelt recoiled slightly. "You misunderstand, Admiral. There would be no 'turning over,' as you said, at all. We would simply make use of some superb shipyard facilities to determine whether or not your catapult is as damaged as you think it is. The Ukrainian workers will be accompanied by American sailors every step of the way. They will not be permitted belowdecks, except under escort to inspect and test certain portions of the catapult." Tiltfelt frowned for a moment, marshaling the facts he'd been briefed on only fifteen minutes earlier. "As I understand, you're concerned about two things. First, the structural integrity of the shuttle and its adjoining mechanisms. Second, whether or not the explosion warped the deck sufficiently to throw it off straight and true. This doesn't sound like it necessitates invasive testing. Not at all. Merely a correct truing and faring gear to ascertain the true extent of the damage."

"But in Ukraine!" Tombstone still sounded adamant. "For all we know, they were behind the bomb."

"I doubt it. It was most probably the Turks. After all, they're the ones who attacked *La Salle* in the first place."

Batman's face crumpled slightly. "I don't know, Admiral." He shook his head, reluctantly conceding a small point. "With *La Salle* out of commission, we could have a hell of a lot to handle in this part of the world. If that waist cat is okay, I'd sure like to know it. It wouldn't take long—maybe eight hours." He turned and studied his old lead carefully. "Maybe we should talk about this alone."

Tiltfelt stood. "I will be glad to excuse myself," he said stiffly. "But before you arrive at a decision, you should understand this—that I have little doubt that both of our superiors back in the United States will agree with this, at least in principle." He turned to Tombstone. "Your uncle because he needs every ounce of combat capability in this part of the world, or at least so he feels. And my superiors will see it for what it truly is—an era of unprecedented cooperation between Ukraine and the United States. If we turn this generous offer down because of old, outmoded hostilities, we lose the possibility of having extensive landing rights in Ukraine."

Tiltfelt's eyes narrowed as he assessed the possibilities. "Suppose your fears are true and there is someday a resurgence of Russian nationalism? What if you have to fight them again? Wouldn't Ukraine be a perfect staging area? Long airfields, the Black Sea as an entry point for an amphibious force, flat plains to accommodate tanks and other equipment in a dash north—doesn't that sound appealing?"

Tiltfelt tried to keep the disgust out of his voice as he delicately dangled the bait. "In short, would you throw away a superb strategic staging point just south of Russia based on something you can't even prove—that the Ukrainians were behind this bombing?"

He was quietly pleased when he saw Batman and Tombstone exchange a telling look, and felt the thrill of earlier exhilaration surge back through him. He was on a roll, riding the crest of his own superb abilities, and there was no way that the two admirals seated in front of him could withstand it. None at all.

"We'll talk about it," Tombstone said finally. He turned his back on the State Department representative as though dismissing him. He looked back over his shoulder at Tiltfelt. "And let you know. Now, if you'll excuse us . . ." Tombstone pointed at the door.

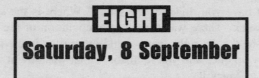

1300 Local
Istanbul, Turkey

*I've lost it—I know I have. For the first time in years,
I'm in the right place and there's nothing to report. This
is it—Istanbul—I can feel it! But there's nothing happening.*

Pamela Drake stared out at the horizon, so frustrated
she could spit. It was an article of faith that her instinct
was infallible, all-knowing, and at least twenty-four
hours ahead of any other reporter's. It had never failed
her, not in any part of the world. From the Aleutian
Islands to the South China Sea, from Norway to the tip of
India, Pamela Drake had been there. Been there first,
been there in the middle, and reported via ACN the best
stories of any news network in the world.

But after four days in Istanbul, rumors were starting to
fly that the famed Pamela Drake was merely a reporter
who got lucky sometimes.

Sometimes. As if that were even close to the truth.
She'd been right every time, been there before all of
them. But did they remember? More importantly, did her
editor? She shook her head, the unfairness of it raging

through her. All they remembered was the last story. What have you done for me lately? Where is the story this week? There was never any recognition of the fact that she'd been right every single other time in the past. Screw up once and you're history. That was how it was, and she knew it.

But it was here, of that she was certain. She leaned on the quay wall and stared out at the sea, silently demanding that something happen. Something, anything—hell, at this point she'd settle for two fishing boats colliding.

The story was here. She could feel it in the way the small hairs on the back of her neck prickled, in the uneasy tightness in her gut. Whether or not it was hers alone now was the problem. Every network kept track of her movements, she knew. They had their spies, their scouts in the major airlines as well as in her own bureau, no doubt. As soon as Pamela landed and established a presence in a particular theater, everyone played catch-up. Regardless of whether or not they knew what the story was, regardless of how absurd her destination seemed, everybody followed.

She grimaced. That was the problem with Istanbul right now—everybody else was also here. If a story did break, she'd just be one among the masses chasing after it. Someone might even scoop her. No, that would be entirely unacceptable. No, it wouldn't happen here, and it had never happened.

But where the hell was everybody? The line to an old song ran through her head—something about giving a war and nobody coming. "I wonder if I should call the Navy and tell them they're missing something," she said aloud.

The cameraman turned toward her with a weary, bored expression on his face. "What?"

She wheeled to face him down. "The story. There's one here, you know."

The cameraman nodded. "You've been telling me that. But where is it?"

She glared at him. "I don't know. But it'll be here soon. We just don't know where to look right this second."

The cameraman's face suddenly took on a degree of animation. He pointed out at the horizon behind her and said, "Maybe we should try out there."

"That's exactly what I mean. There's something happening out there, and I don't know what it is yet."

The cameraman began shaking his head violently from side to side, fumbling with the camera bag at his side without ever taking his eyes off the horizon. "No, I mean it's there—right there." He pointed again at the horizon, taking his eyes off it to dig out a new lens.

Pamela whirled and stared at the horizon. It *was* there—the pieces were starting to fall into place.

Right at the boundary between water and sky, a dark gray smudge broke the clean line of the ocean. She recognized it immediately, having seen it too many times from too many different angles not to. It was the USS *Jefferson*, steaming toward them with helicopters and aircraft arrayed overhead like an honor escort. "I told you."

"Dammit, set up for the feed." She moved in front of him, positioning for the sun and the favorable angle while still making sure that the camera could catch the shape of the aircraft carrier in the background.

1310 Local
Vulture's Row
USS Jefferson

"I don't like this, Tombstone. I don't like it one little bit."
Batman stared out at the calm, glassy water as the
massive carrier plowed through the smooth seas. "Con-
strained waters—that's no place for an aircraft carrier."

"I agree. You know I do." Tombstone stared off in the
sky, looking for the martial stack of aircraft orbiting.
"That's one of the reasons we've got so much in the air
right now."

"A hell of a lot it's going to do in these waters. And I
still don't see any justification for putting us at risk by
pulling into port in Ukraine. Hell, we can make do with
two cats—that's why we've got three."

Stoney sighed. The order from the Department of
Defense had been ambiguous at best, downright unclear
at worst. *Jefferson* had been directed to sail into the
Black Sea for possible repair in Ukraine "pending further
determination."

How many strings had Tiltfelt pulled? Enough, evidently. From what he'd heard on CNN and the other
networks, Congress was slavering over the possibility of
having a stronghold at Russia's back door.

"Let's look at the bright side," Tombstone said finally.
"At least we're not ordered to make port there. I think
Uncle Thomas is going to be playing this close to the
chest—get us in theater, within striking range of Turkey,
and wait to see what falls out from this little incident on
board. That's the only thing that makes sense to me."

His uncle, Tombstone knew, would be irrevocably opposed to pulling *Jefferson* into any foreign port right now. The prospect of making a transit through the Strait of Bosphorus and being confined to the Black Sea was not much better, but at least the Black Sea offered some elbow room. Once they were through the Strait, he'd feel better anyway.

"What I really don't understand," Batman said, pointing to mainland Turkey just starting to come into view off their starboard bow, "is why we're so convinced Turkey will let us through here. Isn't this whole area mined?"

"Of course it is. It's sort of a test, I suppose. Turkey is still claiming that they weren't behind the EMP attack, and the thinking is that if they let us sail through the Strait unmolested, then they probably weren't. Or at least possibly weren't. Or at least—oh, hell, I don't know. I don't like it any better than you do."

Both of the Naval aviators stared out at the calm waves, waiting for the first sign of trouble.

1320 Local
Istanbul, Turkey

"How fast can this tug go?" Pamela demanded. "Forty knots?"

The owner of the boat shrugged, and pointed at the sea. "Maybe twenty. As calm as the seas are today, we won't have the swells to contend with. But why the worry about speed?"

Pamela took two steps closer, bringing herself well within his personal range. She could feel his interest in her grow, see the sudden hungry look in his eyes. "I've got a plan. I need to borrow your boat—rent it, really. Could use you along, if you're interested." She let an alluring smile play across her face.

The man reached out one hand and laid it on her shoulder, stroking gently. "I might be."

"Work first." Pamela explained her plan to him. The man's face went through a cycle from lust to surprise to childish glee. He started nodding vigorously. "Come on. Let's see how fast I can get her going."

1345 Local
Hunter 701

"Man, I'm hungry," AW1 Harness moaned. "Come on, guys—didn't anybody bring something to eat?"

Rabies and his copilot exchanged a snide, knowing look. Harness could be the best antisubmarine technician in the Navy—neither of them had any doubt that he was—but he could be a real pain in the ass on a mission.

"Didn't you eat before you left home?" Rabies inquired innocently. "I know I told you to."

"After last time, sir, I thought it might be better to go light on lunch," Harness replied stiffly. "You know, just in case you wanted to start down and take another real close look at those waves again."

Rabies burst out laughing. "Harness, you're such a pussy."

"I resemble that remark," the TACCO said from the backseat. "Last time I checked, he wasn't allowed in our heads." Lieutenant Sara Andrews was one of the first female TACCOs to fly in an S-3 Viking. "Besides, even if he were—he'd still get hungry."

"Thanks—I think," Harness muttered. "Come on, what happened to the team concept here?"

"Oh, all right." Rabies fumbled around in a flight suit pocket and drew out a candy bar. "Here."

"Thanks, sir."

Rabies could hear Harness peeling off the paper, the muffling little noises barely audible over the ICS.

Wait for it, wait for it—now. "Oh, by the way, Harness," Rabies said casually. "It doesn't bother you that I keep that in the same package I have your full piddle pack, does it? I don't know why the hell I forgot to take it out after the last mission—it's been, what— three days?"

The copilot and TACCO howled. Rabies burst into song. He could hear just what he'd expected to hear from the backseat—Harness gagging.

The S-3 Viking was flying lazy, low-level circles around the aircraft carrier as she approached the Strait. Once *Jefferson* commenced her transit, the Viking would dart ahead to the Black Sea and orbit there, waiting for the ship to arrive. The technicalities of maneuvering by aircraft over international waterways were complicated, and Rabies wasn't sure exactly why the rules were the way they were. All he knew was how the mission had been briefed by Intel, with a JAG officer sitting right next to him.

"Look! To starboard."

Rabies glanced over as the copilot craned his head back to see. "I don't believe it." Rabies threw the S-3 into a hard, starboard turn, descending rapidly to two thousand feet. From that altitude, the sight that had so intrigued the copilot was readily visible. The clear, calm waters of the Mediterranean were a massive barrier of odd acoustics and soggy bottom. Detection by sonar, including sonobuoys, was problematic at best. On the worst day, S-3 could virtually hit a submarine with a sonobuoy and not hear it acoustically.

There was, however, one advantage to the shallow waters on a calm day—visibility was excellent. As more than one Mediterranean sailor could testify, being submerged wasn't a blanket of invisibility in the Mediterranean, not on a day like this.

Living proof of that theory was making a slow transit through the water below them.

Sara whistled softly. "He must be fifty feet down," she said, quiet wonder in her voice. "I'd heard the stories—but it sure is something to see it yourself. Wait, I can almost—what about it, Rabies, can you see what type it is?"

"Let's get a little closer and see if we can figure it out." Rabies tipped the S-3's blunt nose down and executed a steep descent toward the waves. The dark shadow under the water abruptly started to turn to port. "He hears us—I'm sure of it," Rabies said over the ICS.

"But what kind of submarine?"

Rabies and the copilot studied the sleek underwater form, trying to make out the class identifiers. Both had done several tours in the Mediterranean, and the variety of diesel submarines located in its shallow waters were familiar to them. Both were expecting to see a Turkish Kilo, or perhaps one of the myriad German varieties that populated these waters. Either one of them would have been cause for worry, the Turkish Kilo particularly. With the current state of affairs between the United States and Turkey, neither Rabies nor the copilot would be inclined to believe the Turkish submarine had friendly intentions, lurking as it was in the trail of the American aircraft carrier.

When Rabies finally made out the silhouette of the submarine, he sucked in a hard breath. He'd been prepared to worry over a Turkish Kilo, but what he saw bothered him even more. Not because of the capabilities of the submarine, though that was cause for concern as well. No, what this classification meant this close on the trail of the aircraft carrier was about to throw a wrench into every bit of tactical planning that had gone on to date. He turned to the copilot. "You'd best get Homeplate on the circuit. That there is a Juliet—an old Russian ship-killer. She's capable of over-the-horizon linking with surveillance aircraft, and she's too damned close to our carrier."

"A Juliet?" The copilot leaned forward as though getting closer to the glass would improve his vision. "You're right—Juliet, no doubt about it."

During the Cold War, the old Type II Juliet-class diesel submarine was a mainstay of the Soviet Union. It alternated anticarrier operations in the Mediterranean with other SSG diesel boats as well as the then-new Echo II nuclear submarine.

In the last decades, the Juliets had been increasingly reluctant to stray far from home port. Age and poor maintenance had rendered them virtually unseaworthy. For this one to be here in the Mediterranean, lurking outside the entrance to the Black Sea, must have required a major maintenance and resupply evolution.

"Turkey doesn't have any Juliets," Rabies said over the ICS. "Do they? Anybody know different, you speak up."

"No." Harness's voice was crisp and clear. "They were sold to several nations around the world, but the only countries who still have operational ones are Ukraine and Russia."

"Then what in the hell is this boat doing out here?" Rabies demanded. "From her position on the stern, it looks like she's herding us, like a sheepdog."

"I don't know, but I don't like it," Sara said. "Hold on, Homeplate's talking."

They all listened as the directions came from the aircraft carrier. Hunter 701 was to maintain close contact on the Juliet, pinning it down inside a barrier of sonobuoys including active sonobuoys that would hold it even if it went sinker. In addition, two SH-60-B helos were being vectored off the aircraft carrier for coordinated antisubmarine operations with the S-3. The S-3 was to maintain tactical control of the situation. Weapons free was authorized if the Juliet approached within three thousand yards of the carrier.

"Weapons free," Rabies said quietly. "Oh, deep holy shit. Weapons free."

1400 Local
Bosphorus Strait

"There it is. Get closer." Pamela's voice was harsh and demanding. Her cameraman glanced at her uneasily and then stepped away from her as though to distance himself from what he suspected she was about to do.

An uneasy murmuring arose from the crew. The cameraman held up one hand as though to quell protests, listened, and then turned back to her. "They don't want to get very close to the carrier. It is not good seamanship, they say. The carrier, it is so heavily laden, it cannot maneuver to avoid them should they run into problems."

"We're not going that close. Circle around to the other

side." Pamela had spotted the rescue helicopter making lazy orbits on the starboard side of the carrier.

"We'll pass astern," the captain said.

"Fine, fine—just hurry up and do it." Pamela kicked at the gunwales of the battered fishing boat. The engine roared to life, a good deal more steady and satisfying than she would have thought possible, given the outward condition of the boat. The boat picked up speed, traced a parallel course to the carrier, then pitched and bobbed as it steamed over the massive vessel's wake.

Finally, as the waves died down on the leeward side of the ship, Pamela saw the helicopter again. She waved her arms at it, trying to attract the pilot's attention. There was no indication that it saw her, although she was certain the helo's crew members were checking out every one on deck on the vessels near the carrier.

Frustrated, she reached down at her sides, grabbed the edges of her white pullover, and yanked it over her head. Stunned silence, followed by a low chorus of appreciative wolf whistles, greeted her as her head popped out of the sweater. She put her hands on her hips, glared at the fishing boat's crew members, then turned back to the helo.

Raising her right hand holding the sweater, she began vigorously waving the new signal flag at the helicopter. She saw it stop in midair, change course, and vector toward them.

She grinned, thinking how horrified Tombstone would be if he knew his stories about the predilections of sailors on watch on both ships and helicopters had inspired her.

She waited until the helicopter was almost directly overhead, certain that its crew was watching her. She turned to the cameraman. "Have them come to a dead stop. Then you get the hell out of here. Explain it to the crew if the captain doesn't. If he doesn't clear the area at his best possible speed, there's a good chance his boat will be impounded when he returns to shore. He needs to get lost—and you make him understand it. Now give me your camera."

"What?" The cameraman started to say something else, but his words were lost.

"The camera," she repeated. She reached out and snatched it from his hands, silently thanking the powers that looked down on reporters that he'd had the foresight to bring the waterproof camera. Field offices had been bitching about the extra cost for combat undersea-hardened equipment for years, but it always paid off in the end.

She slung the camera strap around her neck, then looped her belt over it to hold it close to her body. Then she stepped up onto the gunwales, balanced carefully for a moment, and executed a perfect racing dive into the calm waters.

The chill in the water took her breath away immediately, but she stroked determinedly underwater, trying to put as much distance as possible between herself and the churning screws of the fishing boat. Finally, when she could stand the oxygen deprivation no longer, she clawed her way gasping and coughing to the surface. She treaded water, still feeling the chill seep into her bones, and scanned the ocean around her.

The fishing vessel had evidently taken her advice. It was rapidly leaving the area, its wake from powerful twin three-bladed propellers churning up the water in a rooster tail behind it. Pamela treaded water, watching the helo now closing in on her, hoping and praying the United States Navy was as chivalrous as it claimed to be.

1405 Local
Seahawk 601

"Look at that crazy bitch!" The helicopter pilot followed that comment with a string of obscenities. The woman in the water had gone from being a pleasant, welcome source of free entertainment to being part of his job. "Get Mother on the circuit—we've got a problem here."

The carrier's reaction was immediate and predictable. The helicopter was equipped for sea-air rescue, which was why it was assigned as the angel helo during flight operations. The pilot was ordered to execute a standard SAR mission on the woman in the water.

"Now this is something different," the rescue diver murmured as he shrugged into his harness. He looked at the other flight crew member standing by the winch. "Course, it's all business with me. You know that."

The other man eyed him sternly. "You start copping feels on the way up, you're gonna hear about it later. Who knows who the hell that crazy bitch is?"

The diver affected an offended look. "Who, me? You think I'd do that just because some broad takes off her shirt and dives into the water just to meet me? Hell, all the trouble she's gone to—I don't want to disappoint her." But his serious face belied the smart-ass comments. Both men were completely focused on their mission. Too much could go wrong during any sea-air rescue, as well they knew. Sometimes the downdraft from the helicopter overwhelmed a struggling swimmer, or an unexpected cramp took the victim beneath the waves before the rescue crew could get to him. That meant hours of heartbreaking searches underwater, trying desperately to recover a body—hopefully, within the first few minutes, when there was a chance of reviving the victim.

Four minutes later, the Seahawk now stable and hovering directly overhead, the flight crew lowered the rescue diver to the water.

1410 Local

The downdraft from the helicopter was strong, flattening out the water around her and trying to drive her head underwater. She fought back, treading water furiously. She was a strong swimmer, but nothing had really prepared her for the force of the downdraft. With it coming as it did immediately after the shock of cold water, she could already feel her strength leaching away.

Pamela kicked off her shoes, and felt a small increase in buoyancy at the loss of the weight. As the helicopter lowered itself, extruding the winch that tethered the rescue diver to it, she breathed a sigh of relief. A few more minutes—certainly she could hold out that long.

Two minutes later, the rescue diver released himself from the winch and dropped ten feet into the ocean below. She saw him pause for a minute, get his bearings, then proceed over to her with strong, certain strokes. Moments later, he was by her side.

"You speak English?" he asked.

"Yes."

He fiddled with the harness, pulling it toward her and linking it around her body. Finally, with that done, he said, "What the hell did you do that for? Don't you know how much trouble you just caused us? I wouldn't be surprised if the admiral chewed you out himself."

Despite the cold, despite the biting sensation of the harness cutting into her ribs, Pamela smiled. "That's exactly what I was hoping for."

"It's who?" Tombstone roared. The denial was almost automatic, but he realized as soon as he asked that he'd known all along it might be her.

Pamela Drake. What would she not do to get a story? Who else would she put in danger besides herself?

"Get her dried off—find her something to wear," Batman said. "Then I want to see her." His voice was cold. He glanced over at Tombstone. "My helo, Admiral—unless you have other wishes?"

Tombstone shook his head wearily. "No, I don't think so. Not after this week. About the last thing in the world I want to do is see Miss Pamela Drake of ACN."

Yuri loitered to within fifty miles of the aircraft carrier. Although the carrier was out of sight, he was receiving data relay from surveillance aircraft and had a clear picture of it on his radarscope when tuned out to maximum range. He and his wingman were careful to stay at least minimally in compliance with the keep-away zone—not precisely, of course. They were exercising their own freedom of navigation by declining to remain outside the three-hundred-mile zone. Still and all, it was a good compromise distance—close enough to assert their right to independent operations, yet not so close as to provoke the American carrier.

Listening to the encrypted radio transmissions, he followed the progress of the submarine toward the battle group. Two helicopters had it pinned down now, and at his last report, the submarine commander had tersely stated that he was breaking off further communications to concentrate on evasion. Not such a difficult problem when you considered the wildly erratic sound characteristics of the Mediterranean. The fellow had been stupid to have been sighted at all, and Yuri thought that he at least partially deserved the harassment he was now getting from the helicopters.

He was less sanguine about his own role in the conflict now rapidly developing. He wondered for perhaps the millionth time what his reaction would have been had he known he was actually launching a nuclear weapon. Pride, perhaps, for having been selected for such an essential mission? Or would he have—could he have— found the courage to refuse to fly?

Not likely. It would have completely ended his career, as well as most probably his life. Besides, even if he'd been willing to sacrifice his own life for his principles, he still had a substantial number of relatives on the ground in Ukraine. It was one thing to risk your own life— another to risk that of your *babushka*.

And since the attack on *La Salle* and the bomb on board the carrier, Yuri now had no choice. He was committed. At any point in time, if Ukraine wanted to resolve the conflict with the Americans, they had only to turn him over as the ultimate scapegoat. Certainly, there would be questions about how the nuclear weapon had found itself on his wing to start with, but he had a feeling that an ever-widening conspiracy would be discovered that would undoubtedly encompass the ground crew responsible for the on-load. People would die—junior people, the ones who had no say in their own destiny.

1530 Local
Admiral's Conference Room
USS Jefferson

The bond between Bradley Tiltfelt and Pamela Drake was immediate and obvious. As she walked into the conference room, hair still damp, clad in a utilitarian set of coveralls, Bradley Tiltfelt stood and offered a small, courtly bow. "We're delighted to see you survived your ordeal in such admirable fashion," he offered genially. His eyes stayed locked on hers, although it was obvious to Tombstone that his mind was wandering over the taut curves under the rough coverall fabric.

Pamela slipped into a chair without asking. She waved a lazy hand at the men still standing and said, "Now that I'm here, don't you think we ought to talk?"

Batman exploded. "Jesus, woman, just who in the fuck do you think you are? You diverted my SAR helo with your little stunt. If we'd had an actual in-flight emergency, you could have cost lives—useful lives—men and women that are out here protecting their country. And for what?"

Bradley Tiltfelt held up a placating hand. "Now, now, Admiral—that kind of attitude gets us nowhere." He pointed at Pamela Drake. "Had you been cooperative with the press to begin with, and acknowledged the American public's right to know, this young woman would not have been pushed to such dangerous lengths to exercise her First Amendment rights."

"Rights." Tombstone filled the word with disgust. "Her rights end where my right to keep my pilots safe begins."

Bradley edged a little closer to Pamela. "I understand completely," he told her. "You see what I deal with every day."

Pamela appeared to barely hear him. She was staring at Tombstone, the familiar glare and fire surfacing behind her brilliant green eyes. Her mouth twisted into something that might have been a frown—but uglier.

"You think you can sail an American aircraft carrier into the Black Sea and not have the press asking questions? Or the American people?" She leaned forward in her chair, pointing an accusing finger at him. "Just remember who you work for, Admiral."

Tombstone drew up straight and stiff. "I work for the president of the United States, serving American national security interests. You work for a paycheck. Don't ever confuse our two roles, Miss Drake—not ever."

"I think there's a way we can work out a compromise," Tiltfelt continued smoothly, as though Tombstone had not spoken. "Since Miss Drake is already here, and will undoubtedly be followed by hordes of requests for information, it's in our interest to cooperate." He shot a hasty look at Tombstone, wincing a little at the anger he saw there. "Not, of course, in any way that might compromise safety or security. But a background briefing, perhaps the chance to observe certain operations— surely that wouldn't hurt, Admiral?"

Pamela turned to Tiltfelt and focused the full force of

her smile on the State Department representative, the storm clouds clearing instantly from her face. "I think it would be helpful to have the broader perspective as well, sir. By the way, I didn't catch your name." She offered her hand. "I'm Pamela Drake, ACN."

Tiltfelt preened. "Bradley Tiltfelt, at your service madame." He followed that with a brief recitation of his history in the State Department and his current assignment, concluding with; "I'm a great fan, Miss Drake. The reports you made from the Aluetians—absolutely stunning." A look of consternation crossed his face. "On this same ship, I believe."

Pamela smiled warmly at him, then turned a frigid look on Tombstone. "There were difficulties on that assignment as well, Director Tiltfelt." She moved her chair closer to his until their knees were almost touching. "Now how exactly do you spell your last name?"

Tiltfelt preened again.

"This is going to shit, Tombstone," Batman said gloomily. "I can't believe she's here—dammit, why is it that everywhere we go, she turns up?"

Tombstone sighed heavily. "You know the answer to that. Two answers, actually. First, she doesn't mind embarrassing me whenever possible. I should have known this would happen when I broke off our engagement."

Batman scowled. "A woman scorned—that's it?"

Tombstone paused and looked reflective. "Not completely. There's one other reason. Pamela Drake is very, very good at what she does. In her own field, she is as exceptionally capable as you are." He held up a hand to forestall objections. "Now, no false protestations of modesty—you know what I mean. As much as we may hate it, the fact is Pamela's here and she's a force to be dealt with. And regardless of what we think of her, we must never forget that—that she's very, very good. You copy?"

"Roger." Batman slumped down in his chair as if drained of energy. "But I don't have to like it."

"Nobody said you did." Tombstone's face was a sober, graven mask. "We just have to live with it."

1545 Local
Hornet 301

"Got a visual on that MiG," Thor said laconically over the radio. "Dirty wings—but he's staying almost outside the exclusion area. Any orders?"

"Just fly the mission as briefed," the TAO on the carrier responded. "VID and escort—if he makes a move into us, you know what happens at two hundred miles."

"Roger, copy." Thor put the agile Hornet into a tight turn, falling into killing position behind the MiG.

In a contest between the two aircraft, the outcome might be in doubt, he admitted to himself finally. The MiG was a sleek, sharp-looking bird, with performance characteristics that almost matched the Hornet. Flown by a sharp pilot, it would be a bitch to take on.

A harsh, shrieking noise inside the cockpit captured his attention. He frowned, looking over at the ESM warning gear. "What the hell—?" He flipped a switch to silence the alarm and called the carrier. "You get that? I'm getting downlink indications from that MiG. Is he talking to that submarine?"

There was a moment of silence on the radio. Then the

TAO came back. "Maybe. Right now we've got his playmate pinned down, so I doubt if he's getting any response. But this is bad shit, Thor. If he's passing targeting information to the submarine, you need to be ready to take him out."

Thor moved the Hornet back slightly from the MiG and climbed, settling into his favorite killing position on the MiG's tail. The MiG gave no sign of noticing.

"What the hell is he thinking?" Thor wondered.

1550 Local
MiG 31

Yuri shifted uncomfortably in the cockpit, nervous about the American Hornet on his ass. It was something he was expecting, something he was equipped to deal with, but that didn't make him any more comfortable.

If anything went wrong with the timing of his countermeasures, he could kiss his MiG—and his ass—good-bye. The Hornet was a formidable opponent, much more dangerous than the heavier and slower-turning Tomcat.

He glanced down at his radarscope and saw the distance-line indicator spooling down the numbers. Just before he reached the two-hundred-mile mark from the carrier, he turned back. It would be close, just as the mission was briefed. He only hoped the American's range indicator was just as good.

Mike Packmeyer leaned back in his chair and rubbed his face with both hands. His skin felt oily, as though he'd been too long without a shower, and the small muscles in the back of his neck were starting to complain from the tension.

Nothing unusual—it was always like this when a story was starting to roll off the wires. Hell, this wasn't even a story yet—just a rumor. He stared at the phone, wondering if it could divulge any answers. After ten years in Istanbul, he had enough contacts to be able to track down almost any story. But this one was a little bit different.

The telephone call he'd just received outlined detailed preparations that Turkey was making for military mobilization. It puzzled him, since he hadn't seen this sort of reaction before the attack on the USS *La Salle*.

Puzzled him, and worried him. Usually the people on the ground had at least some warning before an international situation went to shit, but there had been no such warning during the previous attack.

Why was Turkey spinning up now, after the attack? Were they planning another strike? Or was there something else brewing in the tumultuous region that he hadn't yet tumbled to.

He sighed, felt a sharp stab in his gut, and wondered if his ulcer was kicking up again. It was almost a badge of honor, a medical complaint suffered by most frontline journalists. He kept a stash of medication in his upper right-hand drawer just to cope with this hazard of the profession.

Who could he call? He ran over in his mind a list of contacts. Then he shook his head. No, if there were really something in the offing, he would need more than mere rumors. He needed some actual facts.

And where the hell was Drake? That was another factor that worked against the story, incredible as that might be. If something significant were happening, Drake would be around—she always was. But he'd had no word from either her or her assigned cameraman in the last eight hours. Another piece of the puzzle that bothered him.

Maybe it was just possible that Miss Drake's luck was finally changing. Mike smiled gleefully, picturing the look on her face when she realized she'd missed the beginning of a major assault from Turkey on United States forces. Sure, there'd be an element of personal danger—there was for all of them, even people like Packmeyer, who'd been in the region for over a decade. But that wouldn't have stopped her—it never had before.

No, if this were really a breaking story, Pamela would have been here. Been here and been in the middle of it.

Then again . . . Newsmen believe in the concept of luck almost religiously. It was an article of faith that each reporter carried his own particular type of luck with him, something that followed him or her around until the day the reporter committed some egregious sin and pissed off the powers that be. For a moment, he wondered if Pamela's had finally started to evaporate. It would be a shock to her, one that most of her colleagues would watch with undisguised glee. They'd been scooped too many times, made to look like shirkers in too many parts of the world, not view her downfall with some small degree of relish and personal pleasure.

Well, this might just be the story that Miss Drake missed. Funny, he didn't feel bad about it at all. Not at all.

The telephone rang, piercing his pleasant reverie. He frowned and stared at it—his private number—then snatched it off the cradle. "Packmeyer," he snapped.

"Mike?" Pamela's dulcet tones were unmistakable.

"Where the hell are you?" Inwardly, he sighed. It looked like Pamela's luck hadn't left her after all. She was undoubtedly calling to report some of the rumors he'd just received from other sources.

"You're not going to believe this—I'm on board the USS *Jefferson*. The carrier is headed through the Bosphorus Strait, as you've undoubtedly heard by now, probably en route to the Black Sea for offensive operations." Tersely, Pamela outlined her dramatic dive into the sea and subsequent rescue by the American helicopter. She concluded with: "I'm getting background information, some access—Mike, you can take this for gospel. I don't know what's going on yet—not yet—but the *Jefferson* is a part of it."

After five minutes, Packmeyer hung up the phone, his mood darkening. Whatever thoughts he'd had about Pamela Drake's luck disappearing had just been dispelled.

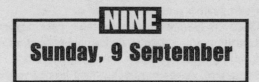

NINE
Sunday, 9 September

0700 Local
ACN Headquarters
Istanbul, Turkey

With his feet parked on the corner of his desk, Pack-meyer leaned back in his chair and lifted his butt off the seat cushion. He stretched, feeling the tight muscles around his lower spine resist. It was a routine of his, a daily exercise to try to combat the inevitable backaches and joint problems he acquired as a result of his sedentary job. With the phone plastered to his ear, he started tracking down the story.

As he waited for a mid-grade career employee at the embassy to take him off hold, his second line rang. His private line, the one number that he gave to important sources. It was indicative of his relationship with the embassy that no one inside the United States government had that particular telephone number. He replaced the receiver on his public line, cutting off the bland music that had been serenading him for the last ten minutes while the attaché got around to answering his call. He picked up the private line: "Packmeyer."

"Mike, it's me. You recognize the voice?" The man

spoke fluent English, the edges of his vowels tinged with a clipped British accent.

"Of course I do. What's happening?" Packmeyer came right to the point, knowing that if this particular source were calling him, then time was at a premium.

"No names. And deep background—not even a hint where you got this information. Agreed?"

"Of course."

A heavy sigh. Then, more slowly now that the preliminary conditions of their conversation were established, the man continued. "Everything's going to shit. By this afternoon, a radical Shiite sect will be making a statement condemning United States interference in this area of the world and promising retaliation and vengeance for the damage done to Turkey's international reputation. Mike, they're absolutely serious about this—not a one of them believes that a Turkish platform actually fired that missile."

Packmeyer snorted. "And you believe them?" Both men had a long history with the Turkish government, and his contact should have known better than to believe any public pronouncements.

His contact. A strange way to identify the cultural attaché of the Russian embassy. But then again, Chernenko was an odd sort of cultural attaché. A real one wouldn't have been armed at all times.

"Yes, yes—I know. But this time, I do believe them. Every source I've got—and I've got sources you wouldn't even dream of—has called me in a cold sweat over this entire incident. It's not just disinformation this time—this is for real. Mike, someone's trying to implicate Turkey in this, and they don't like it one bit. There's no way the moderates will be able to hold the Shiites in check this time."

Packmeyer let out a low whistle. "What have they got planned besides the statement?"

"That's the reason I'm calling. They're going to be seeking out U.S. targets in Turkey for retaliation. It's all dressed up in fancy diplomatic language, but that's the gist of it."

"ACN?" Mike felt a sudden cold tingle of fear. The ACN bureau had generally positive relationships with most of the Turkish political entities, but there was always that chance. . . .

"An epitome of American capitalism," the voice over the phone continued dryly. "At least that's the line. You take some special precautions, at least for the next couple of weeks until this shakes out. I wouldn't put it past them to—"

The window glass in Mike's office shattered, showering him with a spray of sharp shards. He yelped, dropped the phone, and dove out of his chair and onto the far side of his desk. The receiver dangled in front of him. He snatched it up and plastered it to his ear. "Are you still there?" he asked, his voice shaky as adrenaline flooded his system.

"What's going on?"

"Some asshole just shot out my window. Dammit, are they—?"

He cut his question off in mid-sentence. The telephone line was dead.

Still crouching down, Mike darted across to his office door and crept out into the main newsroom. Most of the reporters were already sheltered behind desks, and a few still clutched telephones in their hands. He felt a momentary frisson of pride—under fire, they were still doing their jobs. Pamela Drake wasn't the only one who had guts around here.

"Gather around!" He was pleased to find that his voice was steady. "Everybody, over here."

The resulting editorial conference looked as much like a children's game as a business meeting, but there was nothing entertaining about it at all. All the reporters, even the administrative staff, all refused to cut and run, refused to be driven off the story by a terrorist attack. Finally, Mike convinced them to take at least some elementary precautions.

In the distance he could hear sirens wailing, tires screeching as local law enforcement officials pulled up in front of the building. He scuttled over to the door and let himself out into a hallway before standing again.

The exchange was brief and foreboding. The officers appeared oddly unconcerned about the attack on ACN. While they promised more frequent patrols in the area and a full investigation, Packmeyer was convinced that they either knew about the attack, or were already certain that they knew who had conducted it.

After they left, he rejoined his staff. Many of them had already moved computer monitors and keyboards down to the floor and were busy typing, cross-legged in front of their monitors, their keyboards resting across their knees. Phones littered the narrow passages between desks as investigative reporters started tracking down their sources.

Mike went back to his office to put in a few calls of his own.

A half hour later, he had as many questions as answers. All across the country, particularly along the coast, Turkish military troops were mobilizing, going to their scheduled strike-launching points. But there was no pattern to it—units were deployed to the north as often as they were deployed to the coast. In particular, the mine-control facility at Izmir was in a heightened state of alert. Yet despite his best efforts, he could not get the slightest lead on any possible targeting information. Indeed, his sources sounded puzzled, confused—in some cases actually angry that they knew so little.

Finally, as he hung up the phone after talking to his last source, Mike Packmeyer sat back to think.

Random violence against U.S. businesses and institutions—no, that wouldn't be enough. He shook his head, certain that the Turkish national mentality would hardly deem that as fitting vengeance for their grievances. There would be something larger, more spectacular.

The aircraft carrier. Of course. A perfect target. And now, en route to the Black Sea and transiting the Strait of Bosphorus, it was a perfect target. Most nations knew that the Strait was heavily mined, the weapons inert and harmless until they received an underwater radio-activation signal from the facility at Izmir.

Publicly, the purpose of the mines was to prevent a Russian sortie from the Black Sea with the Black Sea fleet, but most agreed that, like any trapdoor, this one worked two ways. The mines in the Bosphorus Strait could be used to keep the Russians in—or the United States out.

That was the easy answer, the most likely U.S. target. But Mike still had to unravel the actual causes behind the initial attack on the United States and Turkey's reactions. Why, for instance, were amphibious forces loading onto transports within the Black Sea? And why were ground troops concentrating not only on the coast but to the north as well? Of course Turkey was not going to invade

the United States—that was beyond even the most
grandiose of Turkish plans. But ground troops—why?
His thoughts took a new direction as he contemplated the
map of Turkey. To her east, Iraq, always an uneasy
neighbor. To her north, the smaller former Soviet states
of Georgia, Azerbaijan, and Armenia. North of that,
Ukraine.

Ukraine—she was the key, he suddenly knew. Ukraine
was the only other powerhouse nation, or what passed for
it, in the vicinity of the Black Sea. Since the breakup of
the Soviet Union, Ukraine had suffered through horren-
dous economic and social turmoil. Her relations with
Russia had been cool, verging on uneasy at best.

Russia—another wild card. He pondered that one for
a moment, trying to trace out the circuitous and subtle
motives and objectives of the nations involved.

His contact was Russian—definitely Russian. Normally reliable, but not above using his sources—and
Mike knew that the attaché viewed him as just that—to
achieve his own objectives.

What, then, was the hidden agenda behind the attaché's call? The sudden conviction seized him that if he
could unravel that part of the puzzle, the rest of the
pieces would fall into place.

Reaching a decision, he walked back in a crouch into
the newsroom, waddling ducklike over to his number-
two man. "I'm going out." Packmeyer made it a statement, not a question.

His assistant editor nodded. "Be careful. It's not going
to be any better out there than it is in here."

Mike nodded. "I know." He managed a small chuckle.
"It's been years since I've been a field reporter, but I
think I remember the drill. There's a story out there, and
somebody needs to get it."

"Our viewers?" The assistant editor wore a wry, sardonic look. "Anything for the scoop, heh?"

"Something like that." Mike followed this cryptic pronouncement with a detailed list of instructions, finally patting the fellow on the back and saying, "Just run things like they ought to be run, George. You know how to do it." He stuffed a cell phone and pager into his satchel as he spoke.

Packmeyer hoisted the bag onto his shoulder and crawled over to the door, standing upright once he went out into the passageway. There was a back stairway. He turned and crept down it, feeling unexpectedly excited and adventurous.

Yes, the ACN viewers depended on the bureau to get the story. But there was more at stake than that—more than Pamela Drake certainly would have ever admitted. With his sources and contacts inside Istanbul, Packmeyer knew without a doubt that sooner or later he'd tumble onto the link between Russia, Ukraine, and Turkey. It was just a matter of time. And as urgently as the ACN viewers might want to absorb his in-depth analysis from the safety of their Stateside homes, there was one other entity that would value the data even more—the United States Navy.

0831 Local
Hunter 701

"Little bastard's gotta come up sometime," Rabies muttered. He turned partway in his seat, throwing a dark glance at the TACCO and enlisted technician in the backseat. "Harness, you got your head up your ass? Haven't heard you say a word back there."

Harness shrugged, the gesture almost imperceptible in his ejection harness. "I can't find what isn't there."

"He's there, all right," Rabies said firmly. "I can feel it—dammit, do I have to do your job too?"

"No, sir," Harness answered, putting slightly more emphasis than was necessary on the last word. "I think I'm probably capable of handling this."

"Then find me a submarine." Rabies put the S-3B Viking into a tight turn, maintaining station above the line of sonobuoys strung across the Strait. "He was in the Med last time we saw him. He'll be after the carrier—that's his only mission in life. Unless you want those helos to claim all the glory, shut us out of the prosecution like they did last time, we need to come up with something. And fast." He shot a glance in the direction of the carrier, now only a vague blur on the horizon. "Trapped in that strait, she's got nowhere to run."

"And we've got lousy water, sir," Harness said sharply. "Sir, I recommend we try something radical. Acoustics aren't gonna cut it in this environment—not a bit. Let's reverse-engineer this—figure out what distance she wants to be from the carrier to shoot, and start running MAD runs across the area. We'll come up to altitude intermittently, take a look at the buoys, see if there's anything interesting. But in this circumstance, since we're not going to get a visual during daylight hours, I think MAD is our best bet."

"Now you're thinking," Rabies said approvingly. "Any objections?" The magnetic anomaly detector, or MAD, was the sensor of choice in this situation.

"Go for it," the TACCO said.

Rabies put the S-3 into a steep dive, heading for the deck. Finally, five hundred feet above the water, he pulled her up, leveling off a mere fifty feet above the water. "East and west okay with you?"

"Just fine. Here's your first fly-to point." A small symbol blipped up on Rabies' screen, transmitted by the TACCO.

"We're going hunting bear, boys," Rabies said softly. "Sometimes you get the bear, and sometimes the bear gets you."

Halfway through the second pass, Harness yelled, "Bingo! Boss, we got him bigger than shit."

"Madman, Madman," the TACCO sung out. "Rabies, I need a cross-fix—turn zero, zero, zero, then come back south on him."

The nimble ASW aircraft reversed the plane of its search, cutting north-south lines in a ladder pattern above the point at which Harness had first gotten the positive detection of the submarine. On the third pass, Harness sang out another Madman call. "We got him cold."

"Hold on, boys." Rabies' voice was jubilant. "It's time to call home and get our marching orders. I think I know what they'll be—let's get that torpedo spun up."

0832 Local
Admiral's Briefing Room
USS Jefferson

"In conclusion, Admiral, we've—" Lab Rat broke off abruptly as the insistent, high-pitched ringing of a cellular telephone cut through his briefing.

Pamela shrugged impatiently, reached into her pocket, and withdrew a tiny cell phone. Without even glancing at the admiral or Lab Rat, she flipped it open and answered tersely with her last name.

"Pamela—thank God I got you." Mike Packmeyer's voice was low and urgent. "You're still on the carrier, right?"

Pamela drummed her fingers impatiently on the tabletop, and finally looked over at Tombstone. Her fingers stopped when she saw the rage growing in his face. "I am. And I'm kinda busy right now, Mike," she said quickly.

"Listen, I just need to tell you a couple of things."

Pamela cut him off. "I said I'm busy." She punched the power button, breaking off the connection. "My apologies for the interruption, Admiral. I've turned the power off—it won't happen again."

The unexpected apology spun Tombstone's temper down three degrees. He nodded, softening his frosty glare slightly. "No telephones in the briefing room, Miss Drake—that's my policy."

Pamela nodded courteously. "It won't happen again," she repeated. She turned back toward the front of the room.

"Just out of curiosity," Tombstone added as an afterthought, "who was it?"

Pamela shrugged. "Just another reporter. Jealous, I think."

0833 Local
Hunter 701

"Hunter 701, take with torpedoes upon visual ID," the aircraft TAO's voice said calmly. "Or positive acoustic identification."

Rabies swore quietly. "We're not gonna get VID—

that would mean she'd have to come up to the surface, and she's not going to do that during daylight hours. And if we could get acoustic, we would. But we won't, not in these waters." His voice was hard, belying his earlier harassment of Harness. Rabies knew as well as the AW that acoustic contact in the strait was damned near impossible.

"Those are the Rules of Engagement at this point, Rabies," the TAO said. "Too many possible friendlies in the area to risk an incident."

"If they're friendly, what are they doing so near our aircraft carrier?" Rabies demanded. "Anyone who's on good terms with us is staying well clear of this, as per our stay-away zone."

The TAO sighed, his frustration evident even over the encrypted circuit. "Like I said—until we know who it is, you stay weapons tight."

"Get me some data," Rabies snapped at Harness. "Dammit, Harness, if anybody can, you can. You heard the man—now make it happen."

"Roger." Harness's voice was calm. "Let's saturate this area with sonobuoys. Sooner or later, somebody's gotta flush the toilet—then I'll get her."

The TACCO snorted. "And just how are you going to tell a Turkish toilet from a Russian? Or, for that matter, any one of the other nations that owns these sewer pipes?"

"We'll solve that problem when we get to it," Harness said.

0834 Local
Admiral's Briefing Room
USS Jefferson

The messenger slipped into the compartment and handed Batman a scribbled sheet of paper. He waited, taking a step back as the admiral stood up.

Batman turned to Tombstone. "Submarine activity. I'll be in TFCC if you need me, Admiral."

Tombstone shifted his weight as if starting to stand, then settled back in his chair. "Call me if you need me," he said. "I'll be right here."

Batman strode into TFCC and assessed the situation with a glance. The symbol designating a hostile submarine was six thousand yards aft of the carrier, its speed leader pointing toward the carrier and *Shiloh,* now stationed seven thousand yards ahead of the carrier. The submarine was closing on them as they spoke. He turned to the TAO. "Kick her in the ass."

The TAO nodded. "The bridge is already coming up to twenty knots, Admiral, but this part of the water is lousy with fishing boats. Even at twenty knots, we're unsafe. Not unless we want to take the risk of running over a civilian craft."

"Damned sight cheaper to buy them a new one than to replace a shaft on this aircraft carrier," Batman said tersely. "Twenty-five—if the Captain thinks he can."

0834 Local
Hunter 701

"Got it," Harness crowed. He jabbed his forefinger at the waterfall display. "I classify this as Russian—or at least, built by the Russians. You understand, I can't tell you who owns it now."

"That's the problem with those damned Russkies," Rabies snapped. "Dammit, selling their submarines to every pissant little nation that wants one. Is there anything to tell you that it's not Turkey?"

"It's not Turkey," Harness said thoughtfully. "They made some modifications to the electrical system—this isn't one of theirs."

"At least that solves our problem," the copilot said. "If it's not Turkey, then we shouldn't have to worry about them."

Rabies shot him a scornful look. "We always have to worry about submarines, shipmate. That's our job."

"How 'bout we go down and take a look?" Harness suggested. "This water's for shit, but maybe we'll see him just under the surface. Maybe."

Rabies shrugged. "Worth a shot." He tipped the S-3 back down and headed for the surface of the water. "Are you holding contact enough to track him?"

"I just got a couple of hits—enough to say that he's probably headed north, right in behind the carrier."

"Whoever she is, we're staying right on top of her," Rabies answered. The S-3 skimmed along, too close to the surface of the ocean for comfort. Rabies put her in a gentle circle, orbiting around the spot at which they had gained acoustic contact. All four crew members peered out of the windows, desperate for a glimpse of the submarine.

Suddenly, just ahead of them, the ocean exploded. Water geysered up sixty feet, almost grazing the bottom of the aircraft. With a sharp yelp, Rabies yanked the S-3 into a steep climb and slammed the throttles forward to avoid a stall. In the backseat, Harness howled and snatched the earphones off of his head.

"What the fuck was that?" Rabies demanded. "Jesus, did we—?"

"No, we didn't," the copilot said firmly. "All of our weapons are still hanging off the wings."

"Then what was that? Harness, stop that damned caterwauling!" Rabies snapped.

"It was a fucking explosion," Harness finally said. His voice was high and tremulous. "Damn, just about blew my eardrums out."

The TACCO next to him leaned over and looked at the waterfall display. "No doubt about it," he confirmed. "A huge blast of noise all across the spectrum, on all buoys. Something damned big went boom down there."

"Look." Rabies tipped the jet over to the left to get a better view of the water below. The Bosphorus Strait was a major waterway in this part of the world. As such, the surface was usually glazed with debris and dirt, an oily film mixing with the surface layer of the water to form a thin emulsion. Even given the dirty water, though, the evidence was clear. The massive oil slick was spreading out below them, cluttered with bits of debris and odd unidentifiable parts.

"Jesus, that submarine—what the hell happened to her?" Rabies finally said. "We sure as hell didn't do it. Did we?"

"Absolutely not." The copilot's voice was firm. "You want to go outside and check yourself?"

Rabies shook his head. "Then what happened?"

"A mine," Harness said. His voice was steady now, all traces of his earlier pain gone. "A mine—you know how this strait is—that's what it had to be. The submarine trailer hit a mine."

"Then why didn't it go off earlier when the carrier passed over it?" the copilot asked.

"You know why," Rabies retorted. "At least you would if you went to all the intelligence briefings like you're supposed to. Those mines are command-activated—some of them are on counters. They don't hit the first contact that passes through, but they nail the second one. That's in case there are mine sweepers going out in front of the major target—don't want to waste a mine on a small boat when you can nail the big one right behind him."

During this exchange, the copilot was talking to *Jefferson,* filling her in on the explosion and giving her a running commentary on their conclusions. The others could hear the carrier TAO agreeing, could hear the urgency stark in his voice. From their Link data, they could see that the carrier was slowly accelerating through twenty knots, still headed straight north in the Strait, *Shiloh* steaming ahead of her. If the minefield were now active, whether on a counter or not, both ships stood every chance of taking a hit.

As they watched, the water churned violently behind the carrier as she threw her engines into reverse and sought to slow her frantic dash through the Strait. *Shiloh* executed a sharp turn to port, slowing quickly and clearing the channel for the larger ship. Each aviator said a silent prayer that it would be enough.

0840 Local
TFCC
USS Jefferson

"Dammit, I gave explicit orders," Batman stormed. "What the hell—" His sentence broke off as he listened to the report from the S-3 coming over the speaker. His anger seeped away as his face turned pale. Everyone in TFCC felt the deck shudder as the aircraft carrier tried to slow eighty-four thousand tons of metal through the water at twenty knots. The General Quarters alarm was barely audible over the shuddering through every structural member of the ship.

0841 Local
Admiral's Conference Room

Pamela slipped a hand into her pocket and surreptitiously thumbed the power switch on her cell phone on. Her fingers sought out the speed-dial codes, and she punched the code in for ACN Istanbul. She could hear the busy signal sound faintly as the officers in the conference room dashed for TFCC.

She hit the disconnect switch but left the power on, intending to try again in a few minutes. She'd overheard the conversation from TFCC, and ACN was going to be the first to break the news of another attack on the aircraft carrier.

Her telephone rang. Annoyed, she thumbed the answer switch. "Drake."

"Pamela, don't hang up," Packmeyer said. His voice was frantic. "Listen, you've gotta listen for just a minute. I've got evidence that Turkey is mobilizing for a full-scale attack on American forces and assets around here. Jesus, Pamela—they machine-gunned my office. Nobody was hurt, but—"

"What did you say?" Pamela said, cutting him off. "About the mobilization. Give me the details." Her voice was hard and uncompromising.

"My sources say that every military force in Turkey is mobilizing. They're pissed, Pamela—real pissed. I've never seen anything like it. If I didn't know better, I'd say that they were not behind the first attack on the USS *La Salle*—but they will be behind the next one. You can count on it."

"I think they just were." Pamela briefly described the gist of the conversation she'd heard over the radio circuit. "Where are you now? We need to get this out immediately."

Packmeyer laughed. "Not in my office, that's for sure. The story's out here, Pamela—and I'm on scene."

Pamela thought for a moment. "Why are you calling me?" she asked finally.

"Because you're on the carrier. And if anybody needs this, the battle group does. Pamela, please—you're an American citizen," he said, almost pleading. "Our viewers—yes, we work for them. But we've got other responsibilities as well, whether you admit it or not."

"Of course I know," she snapped. "Just what the hell—"

"Pamela, for once in your life, think about something besides the story. Think about the sailors who may get killed, the soldiers who are going to be dead on some battlefield if we don't stop this. I don't know what started this—it has something to do with Russia or Ukraine, I know—please, Pamela."

"Hold on." Pamela looked at the phone thoughtfully, trying to assess the emotions warring inside her. The story was breaking, probably one of the biggest she'd ever covered, and she was in a perfect position to report it. Yet, as Packmeyer had said, she had other responsibilities as well. If it ever got out that she'd known about this—known, and deliberately endangered U.S. troops by keeping her information to herself—ACN would never have access again to any military reporting pool.

Tombstone had often taunted her about her driven need to get into the middle of the action, saying she put the story above everything.

"Maybe above my love life—but not above my country." She stood up and walked into TFCC and handed Tombstone the telephone. "I think you may want to talk to this fellow—his name's Mike Packmeyer."

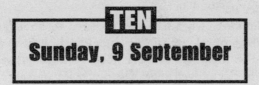
0900 Local
The Crimean Peninsula
Sevastopol Naval Base

"It's working—there's no doubt about it." The Naval Aviation captain first rank looked pleased.

"But the Americans? We believe they're headed toward our facilities for an examination of their catapult." Yuri spread his hands to indicate his lack of comprehension. "How does that show that we have been successful?"

The captain's smile broadened. "You have not heard the news, obviously. The foolish Turks have done exactly as we anticipated. They have activated the minefield in the Strait." The captain's voice turned grim. "Unfortunately, the first casualty was our submarine."

"Then the Americans—" Yuri started.

"Are trapped in the Strait. An excellent tactical position—unless you are an American." The captain chuckled lightly. "It certainly makes our targeting and antiair-defense problems much simpler, does it not?"

Yuri nodded, letting a smile settle on his face. It would not do to appear anything other than completely enthusiastic at this point. It was clear that there were circles within circles, aspects of this plan that he had never been briefed on.

But since when had they bothered to brief him on anything of relevance? Even the details of this weapon hung on his wings were classified. A ridiculous state of affairs, not to even know what weapon you were firing.

"Moreover, I believe a window of opportunity is now opening," the captain continued, evidently satisfied with Yuri's expression of understanding. "We have many sources of information—two nations cannot be this close together without developing certain sources."

"Sources?" Yuri immediately wished he could call the question back. An officer was told what he needed to know—he did not question. It was all too easy to see how his one-word query could be taken as a sign of political unreliability, particularly in these unstable times.

Evidently, however, the captain was in a garrulous mood. "The entire Turkish command structure," he confided, "is riddled with spies. Our spies. We know exactly what they're going to do moments after they decide themselves." A self-satisfied look spread across his face. "Many of these sources I helped develop myself."

"Impressive." Yuri breathed a sigh of relief. A brief expression of admiration always went well with the captain.

"And we now know that they are planning to avenge their honor—that is how they put it." The captain laughed. "As if they had any. And they certainly won't after today."

"They never did," Yuri commented idly.

"They will be launching an air attack on the aircraft carrier. An air attack—imagine it. It will be devastating to both sides. The aircraft carrier already has many of its fighters airborne, and it can rely on the weapons aboard the Aegis cruiser *Shiloh*. If the Turks have any sense, they'll hold until the aircraft are running low on fuel, then launch."

Yuri could see the picture now, unfolding in all of its complexity. By shooting a tactical nuclear weapon at the Americans while pretending to be a Turkish aircraft, he had provoked the aggressive stand of the Americans. At the same time, Turkey was outraged that the Americans believed she had provoked the attack. To avenge Turkey's honor—he nodded his head, now understanding. Yes, that would have been a cultural certainty. And based on his experience with the Turkish air force, he would bet that they would have considered the question of fuel.

"So you will prepare to launch in one hour," the captain continued. "While they are preoccupied with Turkey, we will launch a massive preemptive strike, along the same mission plan as before. We can circle with ease over Turkey—after all, all of their interceptors will be otherwise occupied at that time, will they not?"

"Truly brilliant," Yuri said numbly. The weapons load— what would he be launching with? Another nuclear weapon?

It bothered him, even though the tactical first use of tactical nuclear weapons was well established in their military thought. It had always been viewed as a normal part of any battle for the Soviet Union—and now Ukraine—to take an aggressive posture against any force by introducing overwhelming force at the earliest possibility. Tactical nuclear weapons had always been part of that plan.

But why wouldn't they tell him? If it were truly in accordance with military doctrine, and truly a part of the

Ukraine's national military strategy, then why weren't officers allowed to know that? Why were they launched blindly, carrying weapons about which they'd been inadequately briefed?

And what were the possibilities of collateral damage? In particular, to his own aircraft. Had he not immediately dived low and put airspace between himself and the first launch, there was a good chance that the EMP would have wiped out the avionics on his aircraft as well. He shuddered at the thought of being downed by his own weapon.

Yuri stood, carefully concealing the confusion whirling in his brain. "It will be an honor, of course," he said, saluting sharply. "I will go prepare for briefing immediately."

0915 Local
Tomcat 201

"Where the hell is the carrier?" Bird Dog fumed. "Dammit, she's—"

"She's a little busy right now," Gator pointed out mildly. "You think there's a possibility of mines ahead, you wanna be real careful where you take your only airport. Makes sense to me."

"Me too, I suppose," Bird Dog admitted. "But dammit, we're going to be getting low on fuel before long."

The Tomcat, along with twenty other fighters off the carrier, was loitering just inside the Black Sea. *Shiloh* and *Jefferson* were supposed to be through the Strait by now, their reliefs launching from the ready deck. At least that was the plan before the whole situation went to shit.

"Besides, we've got a tanker airborne," Gator continued.

"The Hornets are already sucking down," Bird Dog said grimly. "Thirsty little bastards, they are."

"I heard that," the sharp voice over the tactical circuit snapped. "We ain't thirsty, we just got a high metabolism. Accounts for all that muscle, you know."

Gator laughed. "Muscle, huh? The only muscle you've got is from doing push-ups on the flight deck."

"That's Thor," Bird Dog said, disgusted. "Goddamn Marines ought not to be flying—they ought to be down in the mud, like they're supposed to be. Do you know what the Army calls the Marines? Pop-up targets."

"Funny guy. There'll be enough mud up here, if it comes to that," Thor pointed out. "Besides, against one of those little MiG bastards, you want a Hornet. Not a Tomcat."

Bird Dog yanked the Tomcat back into a steep climb, effectively reducing his speed over ground to zero. The jet rocketed up, its high power-to-weight ratio sending it screaming past the lighter Hornet. "Muscle, huh—can you do this?"

"Bird Dog, cut it out." Gator's voice was sharp. "Gas ain't something we wanna be wasting up here. Get back down to most economical loiter speed."

Reluctantly, Bird Dog leveled off into stable flight. The Hornet, which had given chase, was still five thousand feet below him. "If he wants a muscle car, he ought to be in a Tomcat. Not that lightweight piece of shit."

"You got a thing about wingmen?" another voice snapped over the circuit. "Because if you do, you'd better tell me now."

"Oh, shit," Bird Dog groaned. "I forgot about the kid."

"Didn't forget—just decided not to think about it, right?" Gator said out loud, his voice barely audible in the cockpit.

"Whatever." Bird Dog flipped one lazy hand toward the backseat. "Don't know why I have to be baby-sitting him. Damned nugget's just on the boat a week."

"Because this is a training mission. At least that's what it was briefed as. That's the only reason you're flying, you know. And me too." Gator's voice was infinitely patient. Over the last several cruises, he'd been a prime baby-sitter himself, keeping his feisty young lieutenant pilot in check from the backseat.

Baby-sitting—if anybody knew anything about that, it was Gator.

"Still, I don't see why we have to do it," Bird Dog continued, blithely oblivious to Gator's sarcasm. "After all, you and I are the most experienced combat pilots around."

"For now." Skeeter's slow Southern drawl was grim. "That crap about baby-sitting—from what I hear, you need one yourself. Sir."

"He's got you, Bird Dog," Gator said, laughing. "Any pilot who'd go off and leave his wingman needs one."

"Yeah, yeah, yeah, yeah," Bird Dog muttered. He glanced down at the fuel gauge again. His stupid little stunt had cost him more than he wanted to admit. "Let's go see if we can hit the tanker, how about it?"

"On your wing," Skeeter chimed in. "We could use some too."

"Skeeter, the only thing I want to hear from you from here on out are two things: the word 'two,' acknowledging my directions, or the phrase 'Lead, you're on fire.' You got that?"

"Two." The other Tomcat moved in closer, glued itself

into the appropriate position on Bird Dog's wing, and cycled through the gentle turn toward the carrier with him.

Gator flipped over to the ICS. When he was certain that no one else could hear him, he said, "Bird Dog, sometimes you are such an asshole."

1000 Local
The Crimean Peninsula
Sevastopol Naval Base

Yuri walked out of the hangar and paused for a moment to survey the aircraft arrayed up and down the flight line. A slight breeze blew in off the Black Sea, warm and humid in the temperate early fall. The dull roar of aircraft engines turning over, winding up into a high-pitched feral scream, filled the air, accompanied by the sharp staccato of aircraft maintenance workers and technicians. Aviation fuel mixed with salt air, forming the peculiar tang he always associated with this base.

His MiG was parked at the end of the line, away from the rest of the aircraft. A junior technician stood a lackadaisical guard watch over it. Yuri headed for his aircraft, walking slowly to survey the other craft parked along the line in order to later compare them with his own bird.

The MiG-31 was not a radical departure from previous airframes—lighter, packed with advanced avionics, with a peculiar jutting radar dome near the front. Her skin was smooth and bright, washed daily to prevent the salt air from corroding her. She was still new, so new that no maintenance dings and dents marred her finish. The patina laid down by the factory still glistened in the sun.

He exchanged a few words with the guard, then dismissed him. No one had attempted to approach the aircraft. Despite the alleged secrecy of the project, almost everyone on the flight line knew that there was something special about this bird. Even if the rumor mill had not been operating at full force, the presence of an armed guard alongside the bird would have sparked their curiosity.

He pulled out his laminated checklist and began the preflight. Tires, struts—he jiggled each fuselage panel to make sure it was securely latched. He paused at the weapons hung on the wing, checking the safety streamers plugged into the firing circuit. His plane captain accompanied him.

Plane captain. Spy, most likely. Ukrainian politics intruded on almost every aspect of a pilot's life. No doubt the secret police got regular reports on his conduct around his aircraft. If his political reliability were ever called into question—no, he wouldn't let that happen.

Still, even aware of the scrutiny of the man, Yuri paused to examine the weapon more closely. It looked like any normal antiair missile, sleek, deadly, and far larger than a civilian would have thought. There were no special markings on it, no indications of its warhead.

But there was something odd about it—there had to be, based on the mission briefing he'd been given. He spent a few more seconds looking at it, always aware of the plane captain's scrutiny. Finally, he finished his circuit around the aircraft, and approached the pull-down stairs inset into its left side.

"A good flight, Comrade," the plane captain said. He followed Yuri up the ladder, leaned over into the cockpit, and helped him secure his ejection harness to the safety points. Finally, satisfied that everything was in order in the cockpit, the plane captain climbed back down. He walked under the aircraft, pulled the safety streamers out of the weapons lockout, and held them up for Yuri to see.

Yuri made a motion with his hand. The technician spread the streamers out so that he could count them.

Finally, satisfied that his weapons were ready for use, Yuri gave the technician another hand signal. The plane captain nodded, moved over in front of the aircraft, and began signaling him to turn on the engines.

The light-up sequence went smoothly, the plane captain in full control of the aircraft's conduct while it was still on the ground. After all preflight checks, and a final sweep of the stick by Yuri to ensure full and complete movement of each control service, the plane captain snapped up to attention and rendered a sharp salute.

Yuri returned it, then slowly eased off the brakes and turned the nimble jet toward the landing strip.

With his release by the plane captain, control of his aircraft shifted to the tower. Shortly after he was airborne, the ground-control-intercept officer would take control, giving him detailed instructions and vectors. Yet even chafing under the continuous and all-pervasive surveillance, Yuri felt the familiar sensation of freedom slip over him. At least here, inside the aircraft, there was no one watching every expression on his face. No one to comment that he took too long over lunch, was late for a political-reliability meeting, or otherwise exhibited some small sign that could wreck his career. There was no one—just him and his aircraft, with the GCI officer a tolerable annoyance as merely a voice over the radio circuit.

After waiting for a flight of MiG-29's to vacate the airstrip, Yuri commenced his rollout. The MiG-31 took barely one third of the runway to come up to rotation speed. He felt the general shift in the aircraft's center of gravity as it eased up off the concrete and grabbed air, gently buffeted by ground effect. Seconds later, he rotated and was free.

1020 Local
Outside Izmir Naval Base, Turkey

Mike Packmeyer loitered at the small cafe near the Naval base. It was almost deserted, as most of its customary clientele were still at work at the base. In the next thirty minutes, the first of the early lunch crowd would start filtering in. Until then, only two other tables were occupied, and those with pensioners.

The cell phone rested on the table in front of him, fresh from the recharger. It should be good for another twelve hours, if the advertisements were correct. Still, he counted on no more than six. After that, he'd swap battery packs.

With events proceeding at this pace, twelve hours looked like a long time away.

So just what was going on? Once again, he entered the circular logic of motives and opportunities that defined international relationships in this part of the world. He was still no closer to an answer, but his gut conviction that everyone had the wrong read on this situation was growing.

That was the reason he was here. The lunch crowd was often noisy, and he'd eaten here often enough that his presence would go unremarked by the regular patrons. A few comments, someone slipping up and letting out a small piece of the puzzle, and he'd have it. Have it, and *the* story would be all his. Pamela Drake might be out on the aircraft carrier, but he was right here, right here where the story was breaking. He felt a gleeful satisfaction at being the first one to beat Pamela to the punch.

The cell phone rang, startling him out of his delightful reverie of edging out Pamela Drake. He reached for it, jabbed the answer button, and snapped, "Packmeyer."

"Uh—Mr. Mike Packmeyer?" a voice on the other end said cautiously. "The reporter?"

"Yes. You've got him. Who's this?"

American—most definitely, from the accent. That's not one they acquired in four years of college or through self-study. No, that's the genuine thing.

Still, he proceeded cautiously. "You've got this number—you must know it's me."

"Yes. Of course. Mr Packmeyer, my name is Commander Hillman Busby."

"United States Navy?"

"Yes. I'm not prepared to go any further than that in identifying myself. Not on an unsecure line. There's no chance you can get to a STU-3 phone?" the voice inquired hopefully.

Mike grimaced. "Not hardly. You folks haven't been too eager to give reporters access to top-secret secure telephone lines."

"The American Embassy—"

"Listen," Packmeyer broke in, "if we go through all the security bullshit, we're going to be sitting out in the cold. Things are moving too fast—too fast to bother with that."

A long silence. "I think you're right," the voice said finally. "You're on scene—I'm not. You made a call this morning—is there anything I should know about? My source at this end vouches for your reliability."

The aircraft carrier. Mike knew it to a certainty, although the solid endorsement from Pamela Drake puzzled him momentarily. His motives at this point were a little bit different from hers. "Things are gearing up. I'm at Izmir—you know it?"

"All too well. Izmir has—certain capabilities. How much of that are you familiar with?"

"Very familiar with the capabilities someone in your position would be concerned about," Mike replied with grim satisfaction. "That's why I'm here. I'm hoping to pick up something from the luncheon trade that may shed some light on our situations—both yours and mine."

"No specifics yet?" The officer's voice was suddenly hard and demanding. "I need anything you can tell me—we'll sort it out here, but give it all to me. No filtering—even your worst rumors. And your opinions, if you will clearly indicate that's what they are."

"Got it." Mike proceeded to fill in the anonymous voice on the other end. "Increased troop movements, and ships seem to be gearing up to go to sea. I see black smoke, people moving, and lots of traffic headed into the base—but none coming out."

"These other facilities—you understand we're quite interested in them."

"No information," Packmeyer reported with regret. "Is there a number I can reach you at?"

"Yes." The officer reeled off a series of numbers preceded by the international code for accessing one particular satellite. "It'll cost you about nine bucks a minute, but we'll cover the cost. I think you know where to find us."

"I do indeed. And from the looks of it, you're not going anywhere else anytime soon."

"Thank you, Mr. Packmeyer," the officer said politely.

"We appreciate your assistance in this matter. Rest assured it will not go unnoticed. Or unrewarded."

"Thanks, buddy, but there's one thing you people seem to forget sometimes. The rest of us are Americans too."

Another silence. "Some people have different priorities."

"Not me," Mike shot back promptly. "Sure, I want the story—but for now, it takes second place behind this. As soon as I hear something, you'll hear it from me first. Not on ACN."

"Good enough." The line went dead, hissing static and odd echoes that were so common on cell-phone circuits in this part of the world.

Packmeyer toggled the phone off and set it back down on the table. Interesting, that—a telephone call from, if he were not sadly mistaken, the USS *Thomas Jefferson*. And just who the hell was Commander Busby?

1030 Local
TFCC
USS **Jefferson**

"And that's the gist of it," Lab Rat said, finishing up a summary of his conversation with Mike Packmeyer. "A good source, and it sounds like he knows what he's doing."

Tombstone turned to Pamela. "Does he?" he said bluntly.

Reluctantly, Pamela nodded. "He's been in this area of the world for a long time. He knows the people, knows the normal movements—and what's not normal. He's been on a desk for a long time, but Packmeyer has good instincts." A guarded expression crept across her face. "Are you going to tell me what he tells you? I mean the next time?"

Tombstone considered the matter. "Maybe. It depends."

"On what?" Pamela said, pressing the matter.

"On whether or not I decide to at the time," Tombstone shot back. "No promises, Pamela. I'm not certain about this Packmeyer fellow, but I know what your priorities are. If he's telling us the truth, then his are a bit different. At the same time, I'm not going to screw him over by feeding his stories to you if it's going to hurt him."

Pamela shook her head angrily. "You just don't get it, do you?"

Tombstone shook his head. "No, I get it. You're the one that won't."

1035 Local
Admiral's Conference Room

"We're only five miles from open water," Batman said. "Five miles—dammit, you can see it from the bridge."

The staff assembled around the table was silent. They all knew what their status was. Surrounded by a potentially activated minefield, the safest course was to simply sit where they were and wait for minesweeping help before proceeding.

But they didn't have that luxury—not this time. Activating the minefield by itself was an act of war, and that didn't even take into account the earlier attack on *La Salle*. Trapped here, not even moving forward at bare steerage, the carrier had lost its most potent weapon—

the ability to launch and recover aircraft. Additionally, there were twenty fighters orbiting forty miles ahead over the Black Sea. Sooner or later, the tankers would exhaust their reserves and the fighters would be running on fumes.

Within the next hour, Batman would have to make the decision whether or not to bingo the fuel-starved aircraft to the naval base in Greece—that is, assuming that Greece would grant them landing rights.

Or Ukraine. He frowned, not wanting to consider that possibility. Ukraine's offer of assistance with the catapult had seemed wrong to him from the very first, as it had to Tombstone. Had it not been for the insistence of the State Department, the carrier would have remained in the relative safety of the Med, able to turn into the wind and generate enough airspeed across the deck to launch and recover aircraft. With the bare twenty fighters bingoing back and forth from an airfield somewhere, the carrier was almost completely exposed. Exposed, and trapped.

"Admiral, at least the *Shiloh* is with us," his Chief of Staff said. "She's a pretty potent ship."

Captain Daniel Heather, CO of the *Shiloh,* who had ferried over by helo for the conference, nodded. "If we let the Spy One run the engagement, we can target and engage more incoming missiles and aircraft than any ship in the Navy." He frowned. "Of course, you all know the problem with sea-skimmers. The probability of kill is high—but not that high."

"And this close to land, the odds go down dramatically," the Air Operations officer chimed in. "Admiral, we need air cover—there's no way around it."

"I know that," Batman said heavily. "We need our deck back." He turned to Captain Heather. "And as much as I hate to say it, there's only one way I know to do that—break out of the Strait and get into the Black Sea."

Captain Heather was a tall, muscular man. Pale blond hair cropped short topped blue eyes and a genial open face. He stared at Batman for a moment, a puzzled expression on his face. Then he paled markedly. "You're serious?" he said, reading the admiral's mind. Heather's soft Georgia accent made the question sound mild. "We can do it, Admiral, but the cost is going to be hellacious."

Batman nodded. "I know. But we've got no options right now. None at all. We can't go back the way we came—that's too far. Clear water lies five miles ahead, and there are no minesweepers around. As much as I hate to say it, the priority at this point is on the carrier. That means *Shiloh* takes point. You've got minesweeping duty, Captain."

Captain Heather tried for an optimistic look. "It could be worse. Most of these are older mines, tethered near the surface. Some good lookouts, the motor whaleboat going out ahead, sonar will probably pick up most of them. The fifty-caliber-gun crews can detonate some of them, and we'll vector around them if they can't."

Batman recognized and silently applauded the man's courage. He was overstating the odds by a good deal, but you had to give him credit for recognizing the situation and realizing that Batman had only one possible choice. "You'll want to get back to your ship soon, Captain," Batman said gravely. "You have some preparations to make. For starters, I'd recommend having everyone up above the waterline."

The captain nodded. "We'll be buttoned up completely, you can count on it. If I may take my leave, Admiral?"

Batman nodded. "Godspeed. We'll see you in the Black Sea. Be ready to get underway in twenty minutes."

1100 Local
USS Shiloh

Precisely twenty minutes after his conversation with Admiral Wayne, Captain Heather began inching *Shiloh* forward. Two motor whaleboats as well as his own gig were in the water, arrayed in a loose half-diamond formation in front of the Aegis cruiser. They were each manned with a boat crew, and were proceeding slowly ahead, carefully scanning the water in front of them. Gun crews were just inside the skin of the ship, waiting to try their skills on any mines.

Shiloh herself was buttoned up for battle, setting full General Quarters stations. The ping of the sonar reverberated throughout the hull as she searched the water ahead with her underwater sensors, trying desperately to generate an active return off any mines ahead.

Captain Heather was on the bridge, pacing back and forth, adding his own eyes to the barrage of faces turned toward the water ahead.

The *Shiloh* was tough, built for survivability, especially against EMP—but not that tough. Even an ancient mine, cheap and easily obtainable by any nation in the world, could do her serious damage. At the very least, if it hit the forward part of the ship, it would blind her, ripping off the massive sonar dome that protruded down into the water from her bow twenty-eight feet.

"Another possible," the OOD announced. It was th

third alert in the last five minutes. "They're vectoring to check it out."

"Anything from sonar?" The captain tried to keep his voice calm, but despite his best efforts, tension edged up on the bridge.

"No, Captain. Not a thing."

"Warn the gun crews. We'll detonate it if we can."

He took a moment to watch the others on the bridge, noting the stark concentration and fixed gaze on every man and woman's face. This was one of the most deadly effects of a mine, much like the effects of a submarine— the sheer terror, the gut-wrenching uncertainty that it evoked in any surface ship. There was danger beneath the waves, unseen and undetectable. The small metal casings of the mines were generally below the ship's detection threshold. A minesweeper, equipped with an SQR-14 sonar set, a high-frequency, specialized piece of gear designed specifically for this purpose, could ferret them out of their hidey-holes. If he had one. That, and a Special Forces team to disarm the ones too deep to reach with the fifty-cals.

But they didn't. All they had was the *Shiloh*, and the aircraft carrier two thousand yards behind her that desperately needed open ocean.

"Sir?" The OOD turned toward him, his eyes fixed on the water ahead. "There may be counters," he concluded quietly, "and we might not see them in time."

"I know. Let's just make sure we find them before we have to worry about that." He tried to smile.

"We'll get 'em, Captain." The OOD's voice was firm and clear. He took a deep breath, turned back toward the watch crew, and issued a stream of orders and encouragements that steadied them.

A good man—how the hell do we build them like that?

Not a one of them over thirty, most of them are under twenty-five, and they're doing a job that no one else in the world can do.

In that moment, the Captain of the *Shiloh*, a man with twenty-five years in the Navy and five at-sea commands, was so proud of his crew he could have cried.

He turned away from the OOD to hide the expression on his face. Just as he did, the ship rocked violently to starboard. Seconds later, water geysered up on the port side, spewing against the bridge window glass and splashing against the closed bulkheads.

The captain lost his balance as *Shiloh* pitched further and further to starboard, and loose gear and sailors slid across the deck toward the starboard side. He felt himself skid, and hit the deck hard with his right hip.

His eyes sought out the inclinometer. Twenty degrees, twenty-five—the red needle tipped toward thirty, then passed it. Thirty-five degrees, forty. He knew a moment of despair, and yelled, "Come on, *Shiloh*! You can do it, you can do it," urging the ship to recover from the roll.

The screams from the crew on the deck and throughout the ship almost drowned him out. Even braced as they were for the possibility of a mine, sailors would be thrown free, rammed into gear, and pinned by sliding equipment. *Shiloh* was built to take punishment, but serving as a minesweeper had never been in her design specs.

The moment lasted forever. Slowly, imperceptibly at first, he felt the ship hesitate in her downward swing. She hung there, suspended between water and sky, the ocean clearly visible through her starboard hatch porthole, far closer than it had any right to be.

The heel back to port started slowly, the barest shift in her deck evidence of her center of gravity taking control of the problem. The rate of change accelerated markedly, and *Shiloh* rocked violently to port, almost as far as she had to starboard. Injured sailors slid back across to the other side of the bridge, frantically grasping for a handhold, arms flung around the radar repeater, the corner of the plotting table—anything to stop their mad plummet from side to side as the ship rocked.

It seemed an eternity, but three minutes later the *Shiloh* settled into a five-degree list to starboard. Damage-control reports began pouring in from the outlying teams.

The captain swore violently and turned to the OOD, who was just regaining his feet. The OOD had his weight all on one leg, the other one trailing oddly behind him. He clutched his arm close to him, white and pasty-faced.

"Are you okay?" the captain asked.

The OOD started to crumple. The captain darted forward, grabbed him, and laid him out flat on the deck. He turned to the boatswain's mate of the watch. "The corpsman—get him up here as soon as you can."

"Aye, aye, Captain—but Damage Control just reported he's down in the mess decks with two critically injured sailors."

The captain turned to the junior officer of the deck. "You have the deck, mister. Get me a damage-control status." He glanced at the JOOW—the junior officer of the watch. "You still have the conn." Noting that both men looked stricken and shaken, he added, "Just do it the way we've trained. That's all I ask. If you have any questions, speak up. But for now, you have my complete trust and confidence. Get hot."

He turned his attention away from the ship and back to the frantic messages from the damage-control teams being relayed over the sound-powered telephones. They'd taken a hit to port and the mine had opened up a

two-foot, almost circular jagged hole on the forward
bow. Sonar had dogged the compartment down. They
reported there was little chance of repairing the damage,
but that they would simply maintain watertight integrity.

"Did everyone get out?" the captain asked tersely. He
could see it in his mind, one of the moments he dreaded
and saw in his nightmares—men trapped behind a
dogged-down hatch, struggling against rising water,
drowning while still within the confines of the ship. He
shuddered, trying to think.

"They all got out, Captain." The Damage Control
phone talker looked as relieved as he felt. Instead of
cheering, however, the captain nodded. "Very well." He
dismissed the matter and turned his attention to the next
crisis.

1120 Local
Tomcat 201

"What are they doing, Bird Dog?" Gator demanded.
"Dammit, I can't see from back here."

"Hold on, I'll give you a look." Bird Dog's voice was
grim. He put the Tomcat into a tight circle, edging closer
to the mouth of the Bosphorus. "We could overfly."

"No way." Gator's voice was firm. "That Aegis is
going to be one pissed-off cruiser, and we're not getting
anywhere near the edge of her engagement envelope.
You're not anyway—not as long as I'm in the backseat."

The two aviators gazed down at the ship ten miles
from them. Aside from the cloud of dirty, debris-laden
water churning around her starboard side, there wasn't
anything apparently wrong with her. Sure, there were no

sailors on the weather decks, and she was not making any way. That and the motor whaleboats arrayed out in front of her would alone have been enough to cause them concern.

They listened to reports *Shiloh* made to the carrier on the mine strike, each one silently thanking their higher powers that they were aviators instead of surface sailors. If they were going to die in battle, let it be in freedom, in airspace, and by their own mistakes—not trapped in a ship, maybe even below the waterline.

"Dammit, I wish there was something we could do to help," Bird Dog muttered.

"Not a thing except keep the bad guys off them," Gator said. He shook his head. "That ship—hell of a captain on her."

"Lead, Two." The quiet voice over the tactical coordination circuit was from Skeeter. "Is there anything we can do?" he asked, unconsciously echoing Bird Dog's comment just moments earlier.

"Not a thing, Two. You heard the report. How's your fuel state?"

"Seven thousand pounds—enough for now."

"Roger. Don't waste it, Skeeter. The tanker's still out here, but those Hornets suck down gas like it's going out of style. Loiter speed, most conservative airspeed—you know the drill, straight out of the books."

"Just like you did a little while ago?" Skeeter asked innocently.

Bird Dog sucked in a hard breath at the young pilot's audacity. Evidently, his wingman was not going to quickly forget about his dash on afterburner. He started to answer, then gave it up as a lost cause as Gator howled in the backseat with laughter. "Whose side are you on anyway?"

Gator ripped off his oxygen mask, choking and sputtering. "Dammit, it's about time I saw that—that young'un's gonna give you a taste of your own medicine, Bird Dog. Oh, shit, I can't believe he said that—" Gator's voice broke off as a new peal of laughter ripped through him.

"Yeah, well—it's about teamwork, isn't it?" Bird Dog muttered.

The squeal of the RHAWS ESM warning gear cut through Gator's jocularity. The RIO swore and reached for the silent switch. "F-14's inbound, Bird Dog—and they ain't ours. Based on their direction, I make them from Turkey."

"Concur," Bird Dog said crisply. He flipped over to the tactical circuit. "You getting it, Skeeter?"

"Got it."

"High-low—I'll take high." Bird Dog goosed the jet up, settling in the classic high-low combat spread that was the favorite fighting position of the United States Navy. Separated by altitude, with the higher aircraft slightly aft of the lower one, this combination gave the two-fighter team superb visibility. Additionally, it allowed the high station to back up the low as the low engaged the incoming target.

They fought the way they trained, in twos. Bird Dog just hoped Skeeter remembered that.

"Got him—bogey inbound. Fifty miles, bearing zero-nine-zero."

"Tomcat 201. Weapons free, weapons free." The carrier TAO's voice was calm and assured. "Good hunting, gentlemen."

"How many of them are there, Gator?" Bird Dog said, maintaining station on Skeeter. "A number."

"I make it to be thirty-two—give or take a couple,"

Gator said. "Jesus, they're launching a full-scale strike at us."

"We need to get at least two of them real fast then. With twenty of us, and no ready source of fuel, we don't have time to knife-fight it. Not for long anyway."

"Skeeter, Phoenix—let's get 'em broken up a little bit. Who knows, we might even get lucky and hit something."

"Fox Three, Fox Three," Skeeter said immediately.

Bird Dog smiled. Evidently the younger pilot already had had his finger poised over the weapons-selector switch and had already acquired a tone lock on the lead target.

Over the tactical, he heard the other Tomcats and Hornets identifying their targets, selecting their Phoenix, and unleashing a barrage of the long-range missiles on the incoming targets. At the very least, it would force Turkey on the defensive, give the American fighters a little maneuvering room as the raid streaked in toward the trapped carrier below.

"Twenty miles and closing," Gator reported. "They're coming after us first, Bird Dog—not the carrier."

"Good thing too," Bird Dog said, "those assholes are—missile inbound." Bird Dog rocked the Tomcat into a hard driving turn. The missile had just appeared on his heads-up display and was only four miles away. He swore quietly. "What the hell was that, Gator? How the hell did it get so close so fast?"

"I don't know—keep an eye out for another visual," the RIO reported, his voice muffled.

Bird Dog twisted and weaved in the sky, shaking the missile easily. It streaked on past him, tried to home in on a Tomcat behind him, and was just as easily evaded.

Finally, its fuel spent, it ceased forward motion and plunged into the ocean below.

"Got one," a voice over tactical crowed. "Ain't never saying another bad thing about a Phoenix."

For a few moments, the circuit was cluttered with jubilant cries as five Phoenix missiles found their targets.

1130 Local
USS Shiloh

"Get this ship underway." The captain's voice was cool and confident. "We've got the damage under control, and whether or not we're underway won't make any difference to the corpsman."

The situation around him was becoming increasingly desperate. The twenty fighters that had been loitering just north of them were fully engaged with the incoming Turkish fighters. They were holding their own for now, but under the constant pressure of attack, there would be no opportunity for them to refuel, and sooner or later they'd run out of missiles. The battle was already edging forward into the edge of *Shiloh*'s air-engagement envelope, but there was no way she could take a shot, not without risking taking out a friendly fighter instead. Not with the furball that they were in.

"Indicate zero-two-one revolutions for three knots," the OOD said. The captain watched as the helmsman carefully rang up the ordered rounds on the engine-order telegraph.

The cruiser inched forward slowly, preceded by her escort of motor whaleboats. She was still listing to starboard, and the five-degrees tilt on the deck felt much more significant than it actually was.

For the next ten minutes, she proceeded by fits and starts, creeping forward at three knots, going into a full-astern bell at the slightest indication of trouble from her waterborne lookouts. They edged closer and closer to the edge of the Black Sea.

The second mine caught *Shiloh* just under the bow. The ship slammed up, her bow tossed out of the water by the violence of the explosion. The crew, braced unconsciously for another hit on the beam, was thrown back against the aft bulkhead. Again the screams, the wails of the dead and dying, as the explosion catapulted already injured sailors into cold steel surfaces.

The bow crashed back down on the water, the forward weather deck completely submerged. The sea coursed up over it, lapping hungrily at the forward bridge windows before subsiding. The fore-and-aft pendulum motion dampened out more quickly than the side-to-side roll had. Within a couple of moments, the ship was bow-down and still listing to starboard.

"Damage report." The captain's voice was a harsh croak, but still understandable. The reports started pouring in.

He made his assessment quickly, still somewhat dazed by the hard blow he'd taken against the chart table. The forward part of the ship below the waterline was a complete casualty. The explosion had ripped off the sonar dome, buckled steel plates, and twisted stanchions. The sea was pouring in, had completely inundated the forward boatswains' locker, as well as the first twenty frames of the ship. The damage control team had already established watertight boundaries, but there was no hope of pumping out the flooding.

Most worrisome was the indication that some of the watertight doors forward had been buckled by the stress to which the steel frame of the ship was exposed. Damage Control teams reported leaking around some of the hatches, controllable for now, but likely to get worse. The captain ordered secondary boundaries set and casualties evacuated, and ordered the ship forward.

1140 Local
MiG-31

Yuri led his flight of MiGs due east, then cut southeast across the Caucasus mountain range. Skimming above the towering peaks, they rendezvoused with the tanker, took on fuel, and topped off tanks. Finally, when the last hungry MiG was at max capacity, they turned south-southwest.

The ancient Ottoman Empire below them was invisible through the light haze and cloud cover, but Yuri remembered the smells and sounds of his last trip to Istanbul. These people—close cousins but still so different. For a moment, he wondered why there couldn't be room enough in the world for both of them.

No, it was a historical impossibility. Since the earliest days of their history, the Turks had sought to dominate the region. That they were now backed by Pan-Islamic nationalists from the Middle East did nothing to stabilize the area. Unless the Americans could be forced to intervene and stem the burgeoning tide of Muslim radicals, a second Ottoman Empire under the control of Shiite reactionaries would soon dominate the entire region. The Caucasus Mountains would not hold them off for long—soon enough they'd cast greedy eyes on the fertile plains of Ukraine.

"Feet wet," Yuri announced to his GCI, indicating they were now over the water. They outchopped into the Aegean Sea, then vectored northwest toward the entrance to the Bosphorus Strait. The weapon under his wings—just what was it? Remembering the damage that the last one had caused, Yuri had plenty of reason to be concerned. With a flight of forty-eight MiGs hot on his heels, another EMP pulse was not acceptable. Though it might prove a decisive victory over the Americans, it would also wipe out the delicate electronics that kept them all aloft.

Were his superiors willing to make that sacrifice? He knew the answer to that—of course they were. Balanced against the future of Ukraine under Muslim domination, the sacrifice of forty-nine fighter aircraft was insignificant, especially when the current Naval inventory held more than 250, and production facilities were in full gear to produce more.

He fingered the weapons-selection switch, still set in its off position. There was one setting—no, it didn't bear thinking about. If he did that, his entire future was gone. Gone as surely as if it had disappeared in a nuclear blast.

Yet his thoughts kept returning to the possibility. Could he do it? Jettison his weapon, go empty-winged into the conflict ahead? He shook his head and dismissed the option. His career, not to mention all the family he still had remaining in Russia and Ukraine, was at stake. He had no choice but to follow the mission as briefed.

Heroes come in odd shapes and sizes, a silent voice insisted.

1155 Local
USS Shiloh

They were passing Istanbul now, and the sight of the city shook the captain almost as much as the mine attacks had. The waterfront was still and silent. The piers were crowded with fishing vessels tied up and vacant. Not a soul moved, not even the shipfitters and fishermen that normally crowded the waterfront and piers.

Ahead, the Black Sea beckoned. To the captain, it was probably the most beautiful sight in the world—free, open water, probably devoid of minefields. Probably. The thought made him pause. Who was to say the Turks hadn't seeded the entire Black Sea with mines. Mines were cheap, readily available, and one of the easiest defensive emplacements to deploy.

But intelligence reports had been fairly uniform. There was no indication that there were mines past the point about five hundred yards ahead. Like it or not, he would have to rely on those reports.

Five minutes later, *Shiloh* slipped past the breakout point. She was battered, waterlogged, and clumsy in the water—but she was free.

1200 Local
USS Jefferson

"Flank speed," Batman snapped. "Send a signal to *Shiloh*—well done and clear the area. How bad is her damage?"

"She's still afloat, Admiral," the TAO reported. "Barely."

Batman nodded. "I'll see that her captain gets so many decorations he walks with a port list. In the meantime, get us back into this fight. I've got aircraft overhead that need some company right about now."

1201 Local
USS Shiloh

"Right full rudder." The captain felt the ship respond slowly, too slowly. She sluggishly veered off to the right, steadying up on a new course to clear the area. He walked onto the bridge wing to stare aft.

Behind him, the aircraft carrier plowed through the ocean like a behemoth. Huge bow waves sputtered up around her hull, an indication she was balls to the walls. The captain stuck his head back into the bridge and ordered another five knots of speed. Best to be clear of the carrier. In any conflict over who had the right of way, tonnage always counted.

1202 Local
USS Jefferson

"What's our relative wind?" Batman asked.

"Spot on," the bridge answered. "Ready to commence flight operations."

"Make it so." Batman had barely finished the sentence when the overhead reverberated with the deep-throated roar of a Tomcat at full military power. During the transit through the Strait, the Air Boss and handlers had prestaged the entire complement of the air wing, prepositioning Tomcats on the two forward catapults.

The waist cat—was it usable? Batman wondered. An extra catapult could make all the difference in the world in getting gas and air support in the air right now. He glanced up at the plat camera, and noted that the Air Boss had staged aircraft within easy reach of all three catapults.

Was it time to take the chance? It was one thing to launch pilots into the air with weapons loads and ask them to risk their lives against incoming adversary air. Another matter entirely to have them trust their lives to questionable catapults. Besides, if they lost birds off it, that was just as effective in depleting their forces as a missile strike by an incoming raider. An aircraft loss was an aircraft loss—the cause didn't matter.

"Just the two catapults for now," Batman decided. "And tell the Air Boss I want to see him setting a new record in launches."

The TAO turned to face him for a moment, his face grim. "I think you're going to get that wish, Admiral."

1204 Local
Tomcat 201

"Now who the hell are these guys?" Gator shouted. His fingers flew over the distinctively shaped control knobs for his radar, his face pressed hard against the soft plastic hood. "Bird Dog, we've got a ton of new bandits inbound, coming directly from the east. Looks like forty, fifty of them. Jesus!"

"One at a time, Gator," Bird Dog said grimly. "That's

how we kill them—one at a time." He toggled over to tactical. "Skeeter, you holding the new bad guys?"

"Affirmative. Lead, we need to start taking this first wave out. We don't have time or gas for ACM."

"Agreed. Go with the Sparrow. Pick your target— here's mine." Bird Dog centered his targeting blip over one radar paint and pressed Enter. "Got it."

Bird Dog felt the aircraft shake itself like a dog coming out of a creek as the Sparrow left his wings. He shut his eyes as it left to cut down on the afterimage it would paint on his retina. When he was sure it had a solid lock and was underway, he toggled off another one. Just for good measure, he picked out another blip and dumped a Phoenix at it. It might not hit—then again, it might, considering the success they'd had so far—but at least his fuel consumption would drop with the heavy missile off the wings. Besides, it might keep the Turks on the defensive.

"Tomcat Flight, help's on the way," the carrier announced over the open circuit. "Launching now—stand by, fellas, the cavalry's on the way."

Bird Dog glanced down at his fuel indicator. "They'd better be the damned Pony Express if they're going to get here before I'm in trouble."

1207 Local
MiG-31

Yuri craned his head back, could see the other fighters peeling off from the pack as they vectored in to engage the small cluster of American forces already beating back the Turkish marauders. He snapped his head back for-

ward and took a quick visual scan on the sky around him.
It appeared clear. No one was watching him. He reached
out and toggled on the sensitive skin that covered his
airframe, completely engaging the stealth capabilities.

Had they been watching, the other aircraft would have
seen him waver in and then blip off their radar screens.
He doubted that they were—there were too many
missiles, too many bogeys in the air for a pilot or an RIO
to concentrate on anything but survival.

He tipped the fighter forward and dove for the deck.
As briefed, he pressed in straight toward the carrier,
ignoring the smaller escort floundering in the water
before it.

Forty miles away, he got a warning on his ESM gear.
He scanned the sky around him, annoyed—why the hell
was somebody paying any attention to him with all the
ACM in the air all around? He saw the aircraft before he
could even pick it out on his radarscope. An American
Hornet—the worst possible choice.

The Hornet, unlike the Tomcat, was a close match for
the MiG in weight-to-thrust ratio and maneuverability.
With a Hornet, Yuri would find himself more equally
matched, less able to exploit the slower turning radius of
a heavier aircraft.

He glanced back down at his range indicator. Still too
far away from the ship to fire—although who knew
exactly how critical the briefed distance from target was?
Not very, probably—not if the weapon under his wings
was what he thought it was.

In a small way, the appearance of the American Hornet
was a relief. It bought him time, a few more minutes to
try to answer the questions that kept nagging him about
the use of tactical nuclear weapons. If they could have
listened in on his thoughts, his superiors would have

been appalled that he dared to even question the nature of his mission. But that was the nature of a fighter pilot—to take responsibility for his own life, to make his own destiny in the skies. They might think he was simply a glorified carrier pigeon, but Yuri knew better.

Yuri tipped the nose of his MiG up to grab altitude, climbing to meet the Hornet.

1208 Local
Hornet 301

Thor bore down on the MiG that was separated from the rest of the pack. It puzzled him momentarily why this one bird seemed to be avoiding the growing furball behind him. Was the other pilot frightened, running away from the battle? If so, why wasn't he headed back the way he'd come, to the east? Or would that take him within range of his own radars, quickly exposing him for the coward he was? Maybe the MiG was looking for a nice, safe corner of the sky to hide out from the battle, hoping to join the survivors after the action and finesse his way back to home base. Attracting Thor's attention had just eliminated that possibility.

"Kill them all and let God sort them out," Thor said aloud. He waited until the MiG began its maneuver to gain altitude, then fell in behind it, easily pacing it.

As soon as he was in position, he selected a Sparrow, waiting for the tone lock telling him he had a good radar fix for the semiactive guidance head to follow. No tone—what the hell? He tweaked and peeked, trying to regain radar contact on it, but there was simply nothing on his scope.

Too far for a Sidewinder—have to close him. Maybe even get in guns range if he could. Thor kicked his Hornet in the ass and headed off after the aircraft. The only contact he had on it was visual, and he was damned if he was going to lose that.

The MiG streaked upward, then rolled into an oblique turn that was the beginning of a maneuver to circle back on him. With two fighters of relatively equal performance capabilities, battle often came down to this—a matter of maintaining the proper angle of separation to enable a lock on the bogey.

But how was he going to get a lock? Whatever it was about this MiG, it sure as hell looked like a ghost on radar. That left only guns and a Sidewinder, the heat-seeking missile that didn't give a damn about the radar-reflective characteristics of an aircraft. All it saw was the hot, burning hell of jet engines and afterburners.

Thor let the MiG begin its oblique roll and descent to the left, holding his own hard turn until he judged he was directly over the bandit. He snapped the Hornet over at the top of his turn, dove back down, and was annoyed to find himself slightly leading the bogey.

A rolling scissors—that's what we're getting into. Not a bad tactic against a similar fighter, but a dangerous way to live, at least half the time. The aircraft in the top of the serpentine maneuver generally had the better firing position, and as they looped through the sky, alternating altitudes and relative advantage, Thor's Hornet would be exposed to a rear-quarter-aspect missile during the period when he was at low altitude.

Well, it was better to cut this short. Thor rolled out of the scissors, then threw the Hornet into a tight starboard turn, all the while watching over his shoulder to see what the other pilot was doing. With any luck . . .

Luck was with him. The other pilot continued evasive maneuvers, but continued pressing in on the carrier. Now just what was so damned urgent about the carrier? Thor checked his radar again to see if there were any heavy bombers coming in behind the fighters, but his radar screen showed nothing. Not that that meant anything, not with the lack of contact that this bogey was generating. Still, it was possible that there was a flight of stealth-equipped bombers carrying antisurface weapons just behind the fighters.

Thor tucked the jet into a tight roll and dropped back into a high rear-quarter position on the MiG. He was just barely within range of his Sidewinders, and had only two on the wings. He debated waiting, trying to gain a more favorable position on the MiG, but decided against it. The MiG seemed bound and determined to head for the carrier. Ergo, Thor was bound and determined not to let him do it.

But what was the bogey carrying? Thor replayed his last glimpse of the aircraft's undercarriage in his mind, simultaneously readying the Sidewinder. He heard the low growl indicate a lock, and toggled it off.

The missile on the undercarriage had looked like a standard antiair missile—now why the hell would he want to be close to the carrier with that? A number of possibilities flitted through his mind, and suddenly the only reasonable one seemed obvious.

Another tactical nuclear weapon—that had to be it. Thor felt his blood run cold. Even if the missile didn't strike anything, the resulting EMP would effectively wipe out every aircraft now in the air, as well as destroying the combat capabilities of all ships within range. He reached forward and jammed throttles into the slots as hard as they would go, desperately seeking a few more knots. The Hornet responded, almost exceeding the design specifications on the books. Thor urged her on silently, rocking forward in his seat as though he could help her gain a few more knots.

He toggled the weapons-selector switch to Sidewinder again, waited for the growl, then let it rip. The first one was still en route the jet.

The first missile locked onto the MiG's starboard tailpipe. It bore in at Mach 2, entranced by the blazing infrared radiation coming out of the tailpipe and the jet's hot exhaust.

Another target—the missile wavered for a moment, confused by the sudden profusion of bright heat spots around its primary target. It settled on the strongest one, changed course slightly, and headed for it. Four seconds later, it exploded harmlessly in the middle of a flare in a cloud of chaff.

Thor swore vehemently. The MiG had ejected flares and chaff and executed a hard port turn. The first Sidewinder was decoyed. He fixed all of his hopes on the second.

The second missile had a steady lock on the port exhaust. The MiG's turn only served to present it a more favorable aspect. The MiG spat out a last-minute flurry of chaff and flares, but even if the missile had been decoyed, its momentum would have carried it straight on. It rocketed up to the exhaust, poking its nose into the broad flow of hot air before exploding.

MiG-31

I'm going to dump it. Even with a Hornet on his ass and odds that he was just moments away from having to

eject, Yuri felt an odd sense of relief. He closed his hand
around the bar labeled Weapons Jettison. Just as he
started to yank it, he saw the second missile, felt the cold
clear knowledge that this one wasn't going to miss. Rage
engulfed him, an overriding regret for the rest of his
life—or what could have been the rest of his life were it
not for his superiors, for the Hornet welded to his ass. *It
isn't fair—all I wanted was a little freedom.*

Without even pausing to reach for his ejection switch,
he slapped his hand against the stick and fired the missile
under his wing.

Hornet 301

Thor shut his eyes against the glare as the MiG exploded
in midair. A violent black and yellow fireball, shot
through with red and white flames, erupted. He heard the
small ping of shrapnel hitting his fuselage, and broke
hard right to avoid it. That would be a hell of a thing—to
shoot down a MiG and then get dumped in the water
himself with shrapnel in his engine intake.

Over tactical, Thor could hear the cries and victory
yelps from his compadres. The first aircraft launched
from the carrier were just starting to arrive on station,
and the desperate fighters that had held the line alone
were breaking off one by one to seek out the tanker.
He glanced down at his own fuel status—fine for a
while. He went buster and rejoined the fray.

As he selected his next victim, Thor's mind scampered
back briefly over the odd, stealthy MiG. Had it been
carrying nuclear weapons? Someone on the carrier would
know. No doubt the explosion would have spewed

radioactive material through the air, and the damage would be detectable by the ship's radiac meters. Still, at least he'd gotten it before it detonated. It took a helluva lot more than a fireball to set off a nuclear tactical weapon.

"Vampire inbound!" the E-2C TACCO howled. "Thor— he got it off just before you nailed him!"

Tomcat 201

"Just in time." Bird Dog saw the tanker off in the distance, and cut the Tomcat sharply to the right to swing around and come up behind it. Another Tomcat was currently glued to the basket trailing behind the KA-6, greedily sucking down fuel. At this point, the original fighters had been ordered to take on just enough fuel to take a pass at the boat, land, and be rearmed. They'd be completely refueled on the boat.

"Two thousand pounds," Gator confirmed. "Man, we're cutting it close."

"How is our wingman doing?" Bird Dog asked.

Gator pointed off to his right. Skeeter was welded into position, hovering virtually motionless off their starboard wing. "Doing fine. Gonna make a fine pilot, he is."

"Maybe," Bird Dog grumbled. "Got a little attitude problem."

Gator stifled a chortle. If he'd had to design a scenario to brighten his day, it was this—to see Bird Dog get a taste of his own medicine from another young hothead.

The tanker was positioned halfway between the carrier and the furball, providing easy access to gas both for fighters refueling to rejoin the battle and those headed for the deck. As Bird Dog started his final approach on it, the Tomcat in front of him drew back slightly, withdrew his probe from the basket, and peeled off back to the furball.

Bird Dog lined up on the flexible basket trailing behind the KA-6. His refueling probe, located on the forward portion of the cockpit fuselage, was extended. He slid the Tomcat forward, keeping his eyes fixed on the basket, not watching the relative motion of the aircraft. Of all the maneuvers a fighter pilot was required to perform, this one was second only to a night carrier-deck landing for stress. The two aircraft flew less than ten feet apart, linked basket-to-refueling-probe. There was no room for any mistake in judgment.

Bird Dog slid up slowly, felt a slight plunk as the probe seated, then glanced down at his instruments to check the fuel flow. As expected, he was taking on fuel at the optimum rate.

"Headed back for the boat, aren't you?" the KA-6 pilot said. "Looks like your wing's empty."

"That's affirmative." And it made a difference, it did, during the approach on a tanker. It was much easier to bulldog a lightly laden Tomcat into position behind the smaller jet than one carrying a full combat load. "Be back soon, though, I expect."

"If there's anything left for you to do. Looks like the Turks are dropping like flies."

"We do what we can. Okay, I think I'm good to go."

"Roger. Securing fuel flow."

As the instruments indicated that the flow of aviation fuel had ceased, Bird Dog eased back slowly on the throttle. The two aircraft separated, the distance between them growing at an almost imperceptible rate. Finally, when he was well clear of the tanker, Bird Dog peeled off to starboard and headed for the martial stack to wait his turn.

Five miles off the carrier, Gator started yelping. "Bird Dog, contact—Mach 2—Jesus, it's a missile!"

"Where, where?" Bird Dog hollered, frantically scanning the sky around him. "I don't have it."

"On our six," Gator snapped, his voice now cold and steady. "Come right, steady on four-zero-four. I've got it on radar—recommend we find a use for those Sparrows on your wings."

Bird Dog followed the orders instantly, sluing the jet around in a violent turn that pushed her up to max Gs. As he came out of the turn, he saw it, a wavering glittery speck just dead ahead. He continued to turn to starboard, increasing their lead-angle geometry. As the radar lock growled, he turned off first one Sparrow, then another.

"They know—the carrier's already screaming bloody murder," Gator reported. "Bird Dog, we're out of this—no more weapons. But Skeeter has two Sparrows left. Put him in chase—now!" Gator's voice was demanding, urgent.

Bird Dog glanced over at his wingman, still rock-steady in place. "You heard the man—here's your chance. Get out ahead of that bastard, take it nose-on-nose. The carrier's got a close-in weapons system, but it's for shit. If we wanna knock this baby down, it's gotta be now."

Two clicks on the tactical circuit acknowledged Bird Dog's order. His wingman rolled hard to starboard, dived to gain speed, and headed out for front position on the missile.

"Bird Dog—what was his fuel status?" Gator said urgently. "He was just starting to take it on when I called the Vampire."

"I don't know," Bird Dog said grimly. "Little shithead

probably thinks he's got enough. He knows how fast he's going to burn it up—at least according to the books—but he doesn't really know, not like you and I do."

"Let Mother know to get SAR ready," Gator said grimly. "I have a feeling your wingman is headed for the drink."

Tomcat 202

Skeeter let out a loud howl as he gave chase. The missile was still ten miles away, and if he played it right, he had just enough time to get in front of it and take it out with a nose-on-nose shot. He fingered the weapons-selector switch, making sure it was in position for the Sparrows. There was nothing else that had even a chance of catching the missile at this point, not from a nose-on-nose aspect.

Behind him, his backseater, a new guy he'd never even had a chance to talk to, muttered vector information and guidance. Skeeter followed the orders mechanically, watching the missile, relying on his eyeballs to warn him if the geometry got radically out of synch. So far, the backseater seemed to know what he was doing.

"Recommend you fire now—now, now, now," the RIO said finally.

Skeeter toggled the missiles off—one, two—then made the Fox call over tactical. He could see the bright flares of the engines of his own missiles, tracked them readily as they dove down toward the incoming missile.

"Skeeter—get the hell out of there," he heard another voice say over tactical. He glanced back over at Bird Dog, as if he could see who was talking.

"Skeeter, that's Thor—Marine jarhead. He just took out the bastard that launched that missile." Bird Dog's voice was almost frantic. "Head for the deck, Skeeter— that missile's probably a tactical nuke—you stay within range of it and you're going to catch the EMP blast head-on. It'll wipe out everything you've got, even if the buffet doesn't knock you out of the air. You hear me? Get out of the way."

"I can't—the Sparrows haven't shifted to independent tracking. I've got to keep the radar lock on—got to." Skeeter's voice was determined. "If you think it'll do some damage to me, just think what it'll do to every aircraft in the air, not to mention the surface ships. I'll get out of here as soon as I see it dead, not before."

"Skeeter!" Real anguish permeated Bird Dog's voice. "The Sparrows will make it, they're close enough now— get the hell out."

Skeeter bore on, following his missiles into their target. Finally, as the two tracks were intercepting, he rolled violently to starboard and dove for the deck. Seconds later, a hard wash of air buffeted the massive Tomcat like a boat bobbing in the water. He fought the aircraft, lost control, and the Tomcat spiraled down to the deck in a flat spin.

Skeeter let the aircraft go, fighting with the controls to establish a stable flight attitude. The violent spinning slowed slightly, then stopped completely as Skeeter pushed the nose down and traded altitude for airspeed. The increased airflow over the wings, coupled with the manual extension of the wings, gave him back control of the aircraft.

But they were close to the sea, so close. At one thousand feet, the Tomcat had broken out of its spin, but was still headed at a steep angle for the deck. Skeeter howled, yanked back on the yoke, not even bothering to warn his backseater about the maneuver. It either worked, or it didn't. He suspected the man's hand was poised over the ejection-seat handle—that is, if he could get to it under the driving G forces of their flat spin.

At the last second, the Tomcat pulled out of the dive, returning to vertical flight a bare forty feet above the ocean.

Skeeter howled again, this time in victory. He heard the backseater breathing raggedly over the ICS, and said, "What's the matter, man?" His bravado masked the real fear he'd felt just a few seconds earlier.

"Nothing—everything's fine back here," the backseater snapped. "There's just one little problem—when we get back to the carrier, I'm gettin' the fuck out of your cockpit and never gettin' back in again."

"Now, now, now—didn't I just pull us out of one of the nastiest spins you've ever seen in your life?" Skeeter inquired, recklessly confident with the adrenaline screaming through his veins. "What more could you ask from a pilot?"

"The common sense God gave a gnat would do for starters." With that, the backseater fell silent.

1230 Local
TFCC
USS Jefferson

"The air battle is still a standoff," Batman reported to Tombstone. He sighed, feeling the weight of responsibility of sending young pilots out to die. They were the finest pilots in the world, flying the most capable aircraft, but air combat was still unpredictable. Most would come back—but some wouldn't.

"They don't have a sustainable force," Tombstone said shortly. "I notice there're no tankers reported—that means they have to land to refuel. Lost time—we'll take them eventually."

The Turks were proving to be surprisingly tenacious, remaining engaged against the American fighters even after a second wave of Hornets and Tomcats arrived from *Jefferson,* even after it was clear that the Americans were outperforming their adversaries in all categories of skill. One by one the Turkish F-14's dropped into the water, either accompanied by billowing parachutes as their aircrews escaped or raining down on the water in a fireball. "Sooner or later, they've gotta quit."

Batman frowned. "There's something else odd about it—that last wave of MiGs," he said slowly. "They're not Turkish—they're Ukrainian. Oh, they've got Turkey's colors painted on their tail, but it's absolutely clear at this point that they're not what they seem to be."

Batman turned to Lab Rat. "Isn't that so, Commander Busby?"

The senior Intelligence Officer nodded. "We caught one of them transmitting in the clear—otherwise, they stayed on secure lines. Definitely Ukrainian."

Tombstone tossed his pencil on the table, and leaned back in the chair. "Ukrainian—that explains it, I suppose." He looked at the two men steadily. "So what do we do now?"

Batman turned to Lab Rat. "Go ahead and brief him."

Lab Rat took a deep breath. "I've taken the liberty of preparing two strike packages. One is aimed against Turkey, the other Ukraine." He passed over a large-scale chart with hastily scribbled pencil markings on it. "Here you can see the two command centers, one in Sevastopol and the other in Izmir. *Shiloh* can have her Tomahawks retargeted against either one of them in a matter of minutes. Once we take out command-and-control facilities, the fighters may become confused, pull back some while they wait for an alternate command center to take over with new orders. You know how dependent they are on their ground-control-intercept officers."

Tombstone studied the charts. He tapped the penciled target symbol on the Crimean Peninsula. "These bastards started it all—that first attack on *La Salle*. It looked like Turkey, but at this point I'm willing to bet it was Ukraine. That's the first target. Let's teach them a lesson."

"You'll get flak from State over this," Batman cautioned. "After all, we're supposedly en route to their shipyards for technical assistance."

"I don't give a fuck about State," Tombstone blazed. "Their calls already got us into this—dammit, neither you or I would ever have been caught dead in this strait, not under these circumstances."

"I agree," Batman put in. "Just wanted to bring it up. But to hell with them all." He turned back to the Intelligence Officer. "You've got your orders—let's retarget against Ukraine."

Busby nodded. "Just as well—I was afraid you were going to say both. That would complicate matters a bit."

"I can take out the command centers, but where does that leave us in the end?" Tombstone said, staring down at the chart. "This whole tactical scenario—dammit, one aircraft carrier is not enough. *Shiloh*'s doing her best, but we need an additional show of force, a battle group stationed with some airpower just off Turkey's Mediterranean coast, while we quell the Black Sea. The U.S. Air

Force base in Turkey at Incirclik is no help—they scrambled their aircraft out to safety when *La Salle* got hit. Greece bitched about allowing overflights, so they're staging out of the United Kingdom for now. Too long a lead time to use them for immediate support, but just where the hell am I gonna get another carrier and some fighters?"

Just then, a voice called from TFCC. "Admiral Wayne? I think you might want to see this."

The two admirals exchanged glances, then stood as one and walked into the TFCC. A new symbol had just popped into being on the large-screen display, something that had been happening all too often in the last three hours. With one big difference—this one bore the symbology of a friendly unit.

"Who the hell—" Batman started to say. He fell silent as the name of the ship flashed up beside the symbology: *La Salle*.

"*Jefferson,* this is *La Salle,*" a voice said over tactical.

Batman reached for the handset, paused, and then handed it to Tombstone. "Your ship, Admiral—I'll let you sort this out." Batman's voice was grim. "I've got an air battle to win." He turned his back on Tombstone, and his attention back to the large-screen display.

"Captain?" Tombstone said, his voice sliding up the scale in incredulity. "What are you doing out here? I thought—"

"Pardon me for interrupting, Admiral, but you did give me a free hand," said a familiar voice. It was the captain of *La Salle,* the man to whom Tombstone had given complete discretion in getting the ship back into the ball game. "You wanted your ship back—well, here she is."

Tombstone glanced at the telephone, making sure that

the light indicating secure transmissions was lit. "What are your capabilities?" he asked, still not believing that the flagship was cruising toward him. "God, man, you're an answer to a prayer." The *La Salle* had just entered the tactical link, transmitting its positioning data to the aircraft carrier and all other units. It was still in the Mediterranean, headed for the Aegean and the eastern coast of Turkey.

"We've been following the battle from your transmissions, Admiral," the captain continued. "I can offer you the surface-search radar and six Harriers."

"How in the world are you even steaming?" Tombstone demanded. "From the condition of that ship that I saw, there's no way you should even be underway."

"New challenges demand special solutions," the captain replied, satisfaction in his voice. "We had enough spare parts on board to cobble together some electronics— we're not fully mission-capable, but I've got my close-in weapons systems operable, a surface-search radar, and all of my Link capabilities. And as for power—Admiral, did you have a chance to tour the ship? The entire ship, I mean."

Tombstone thought for a minute. "Not all of it," he said finally. "Mainly the flag spaces—that and the flight deck."

"With all due respect, you missed a very important part of the ship. Underneath the flight deck that you aviators think so much about, there's something called a well deck—it's open to the ocean, and it's where we keep all of our amphibious vehicles. Plenty of room in there for a couple of tugs."

Tombstone was speechless for a moment. "Tugs?" he said finally, not believing what he was hearing. "You can't be serious."

"Well, it's not that radical a solution. We use tugs for propulsive power all the time, don't we? It's just that they're usually made up to the outside of the ship, getting us off a pier or into port. Fortunately, as we've just proved, a couple of oceangoing tugs can handily fit inside the well deck. They push as well as they pull. Besides, Harriers aren't all that picky about wind across the deck for flight operations."

Tombstone began laughing. "I don't believe it. You mean to tell me you've got two tugs inside your well deck? And they're shoving you around so that you can get underway?" He laughed again, shaking his head in disbelief. "Captain, of all the—"

"Creative solutions you've ever seen, Admiral?" the captain finished. "Thank you very much, sir. After all, you did tell me to get the ship squared away."

"Okay, you're here," Tombstone said. "Get those Harriers ready to launch—I'm going to need them for backup in case Turkey needs some additional convincing." He spent the next five minutes reeling off a set of orders, directing the *La Salle* to take station on the west coast of Turkey. Finally, after a last congratulatory comment, Tombstone replaced the receiver. He stared at it for a moment, then started laughing again.

1250 Local
USS Shiloh

"It's done, Captain." The fire-control technician looked up at him with bleary, battle-worn eyes. "I've downloaded a complete retargeting package."

"Let's hope it works," Captain Heather answered. He

walked out of Combat up and forward to the bridge. Normally his station during a missile launch would be in Combat, but this one he wanted to see himself.

Could the vertical launch tubes take it? He shook his head—there was still no real answer on that. The flooding had been contained, and the tubes appeared to be structurally sound, but there was no way to really tell how much damage the mine explosions had done. The delicate circuitry of the missiles might have been fatally jarred, the tubes cracked somewhere they couldn't see and unable to maintain the air pressure that they needed to lift the missiles out of their tubes. He stared down at the hatches on the deck, wondering just how much of his combat capability he had left.

Finally, he turned to the Officer of the Deck. "Weapons free. Fire when ready."

"Weapons free, fire when ready, aye, sir," the OOD echoed. He picked up the bitch-box speaker and relayed the order to Combat.

The captain held his breath and waited. A slow rumble shook the ship, deepening and spreading throughout every structural member. The square cover on the first tube popped open, and the captain gazed down into the blackness inside it. The sound built, higher and higher, until it encompassed his entire world. Finally, with a final shriek, a Tomahawk missile burst out of the vertical-launch cell, then seemed to hover over the deck for the barest instant before its motor ignited. It splashed fire down on the deck, charring the nonskid, then tipped over and streaked away from the ship at speeds almost impossible to imagine.

Moments later, the scenario repeated itself. In all, four Tomahawk missiles lifted out of their cells and headed for Ukraine.

The captain released his breath, giddy from pain and lack of oxygen. "Good job, people." He let his voice convey more than words ever could. "Someone find me the corpsman. I think—" The engineer caught him as he crumpled to the floor.

1300 Local
USS Jefferson

"Here they come," Batman said as he glanced at the Plat camera. "First thirsty Tomcat on board." With the carrier now in open water, the fighters that had taken the initial brunt of the raid were coming back on board for refueling and rearming. *La Salle*'s Harriers took over the air battle, decimating the already thin ranks of Turkish fighters while the American air base steamed threateningly toward their coast.

Batman kept his eyes moving quickly between the large-screen tactical display and the Plat camera. As fast as the technicians were working, it looked like it might not even be necessary. One by one, starting immediately after the missile attack on Ukraine, the Turkish fighters were breaking off and heading for home, escorted by *La Salle*'s Harriers and the remaining Tomcats.

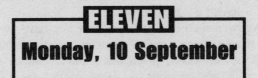

ELEVEN
Monday, 10 September

0800 Local
Izmir, Turkey

Packmeyer was so tired he could barely keep his eyes open. They sagged, threatening to snap shut at any second. He took another swig of coffee, trying to concentrate on what the men were saying. It was starting to make sense, such as it was.

What startled him more than anything was not the facts of the situation. He could understand Ukraine's motivation, and while not sympathizing, could view things from their perspective. The five Turks gathered around the table in front of him would no doubt disagree, but Packmeyer had to admit a grudging admiration for both their technology and their tactics. It might have worked—almost had.

"So where are we now?" he asked again, all too aware of how thick his tongue felt in his mouth, of the slight slurring at the edge of his words. God, he was tired. After running on adrenaline and coffee for forty-eight hours, he had absolutely no resources left. There was nothing, short of an incoming missile raid on his position, that could get him excited now. Or so he thought. Seconds later, it turned out he was wrong.

"We have sources—and we know you have contact with the American carrier." The senior military officer shrugged. "However, given our political climate right now, it is not possible for us to contact the carrier directly. You understand." He spread his hands in a gesture of requesting understanding.

"The carrier's not likely to want to talk to you anyway," Packmeyer said, aware that the words were blunt and unpolitical, but beyond caring. "Your mines damned near took out one of their ships, and the carrier has sustained damage as well. They've lost men, aircraft— hell, they're not likely to talk to you at all."

"We know that. That is why we wish to enlist your assistance," a second man said.

Mike assessed him carefully. A moderate, he knew from the man's reputation, one who'd been gaining political power for the last five years. Some had even mentioned him for the presidency of Turkey, but that had vanished about six months ago as Muslim radicals gained ascendancy. Now, all bets were off.

"You want me to call the carrier for you?" Mike asked.

"Exactly," the second man said. "From the Naval base."

"Huh?"

"We are taking you to the mine-control facility," the second man continued. "There, we will allow you to observe all operations as we stand down the field from tactical activation. You will thus be able to assure the carrier that we have corrected the mistakes made by our predecessors and have assumed a neutral posture. They will not believe it from us—perhaps they may from you."

"Don't tell me that Izmir is the only facility you have," Mike said accusingly, now feeling a slight trickle of anger. How could they think he was so ignorant after all these years in Turkey? He was a reporter, by God. He knew what went on in this country.

"The other facilities are standing down as well," the man continued. "There is not time to take you to each one of them immediately, but we will if you require it. Indeed, we would invite a team from the American carrier to inspect each one individually. We will even offer our own vessels as escorts for the Americans as they leave the Black Sea. You see, mistakes have been made—not only by Ukraine, but by our former government as well. We wish to rectify those immediately and return to a civil, supportive relationship with the United States."

Mike shook his head wearily. In the last forty-eight hours he had gone from being a bureau chief and producer for one of ACN's main overseas stations to resuming a long-forgotten position as a field reporter. And now this—damn, he was practically an ambassador.

Oddly enough, he felt some of the weariness start to seep out of his bones. It was a responsibility—one that he had to try his best to fulfill. He stood up from the table, feeling his knees and hips creak as he stretched. "Let's go," he said simply. "The sooner the better for both countries."

0930 Local
USS **Jefferson**

"If we can believe it, then it represents a major change in our tactical situation," Lab Rat said. "And I'm inclined to believe that the Turks are sincere about this."

"Especially if they provide escort," Batman added. "Frankly, I agree with Commander Busby. If Ukraine was behind this from the start, and Turkey was undergoing a coup d'etat at the same time, it's easy to see how the political scenario could get totally cluster-fucked. It sounds like they're on the right track for straightening things out. I wouldn't mind giving them a hand if we can."

Tombstone grimaced. "Twenty-four hours ago, I was ready to bomb Izmir to Hell and back. Now you're telling me to trust the Turks?" He shook his head. "It's like Reagan used to say—trust, but verify." He turned to Batman. "Get together a team of intelligence officers and specialists—take some engineers if you want. I want a team ready to board a CH-46 within the next thirty minutes to fly to Izmir. We'll verify for ourselves that the minefields are deactivated, and then accept Turkey's gracious offer of an escort back through them. How does that sound?"

"Just fine." Batman turned to his Chief of Staff and began rapping out a series of orders.

Lab Rat said, "Admiral, how much of this information do you want to release to the press? If I could, I'd suggest we be circumspect about this until we've actually verified the status of those minefields. Besides, Mike Packmeyer appears to be an excellent source in place. If we put the media on this right now, we'll have blown him—and we may need him later."

Tombstone looked thoughtful. "I'm inclined to agree with you. For now, no details. If anybody asks, the CH-46 is en route to Izmir to render humanitarian assistance. Will that do?"

Lab Rat nodded. "Packmeyer may think he's become a diplomat—and I guess he has. But there's nothing to say that he can't do just as much for his country by remaining exactly what he is—a damned fine reporter."

An image of Pamela Drake appeared in Tombstone's mind. Pamela, the one first to every story, the one who had to be there, on scene. She was cooling her heels in the outer waiting room, still in the dark about the latest scenario. She would be furious, he knew, if she knew how much influence Mike Packmeyer was having on the course of events—furious, and first on the air with it, trying to take as much credit as she could for being his initial point of contact on board the carrier. Tombstone shook his head, a grim expression crossing his face.

Well, not this time. Pamela might have been on station on the carrier, but this story wasn't hers—it was Packmeyer's. And Tombstone was determined to see that Packmeyer got every bit of credit he was entitled to.

He turned back to Lab Rat. "Slight change in plans— tell Packmeyer that I'll give him an exclusive. Tell the team to bring him back on board *Jefferson* on the CH-46 when they return from their inspection tour. I'll make all the facilities he needs available to him—satellite communications, cell phones—whatever. Tell him he's got my word on it."

Lab Rat turned to go. Tombstone stopped him with a gesture.

"One other thing. Tell him he rendered his nation an important service. And it won't be forgotten. On my word." Tombstone turned back to Batman. "We've got one other little matter to resolve—the State Department."

Batman looked grim. "What the hell do we do with Tiltfelt?"

"My problem, not yours, my friend." Tombstone clapped him on the shoulder with one hand. "Why don't you just have your Chief of Staff escort Mr. Bradley Tiltfelt up here? And have him bring Pamela Drake along with him. I think they'll both be interested in seeing how this plays out."

Twenty minutes later, Bradley Tiltfelt and Pamela Drake were seated alone in the admiral's conference room. Pamela reached out, shook the coffeepot, and grimaced. The least they could do was keep it full.

"Outrageous," Tiltfelt said. He glanced over at her, assessing her mood. "To bomb Ukraine—conduct what they call a surgical strike against a military base— absolutely outrageous in view of the Ukrainians' gesture of friendship."

Pamela toyed with the empty coffee cup. "I wouldn't be so certain about that," she said noncommittally. "Tombstone usually has a reason for what he does. I may not always agree with him, but I've never known him to act foolishly. Not often anyway," she finished, her eyes narrowing as she thought of Commander Joyce "Tomboy" Flynn. "At least not in tactics."

"I can see no justification for his conduct," Tiltfelt said solemnly. "When I return to Washington, my top priority will be to have him relieved of command. A loose cannon in today's Navy—the world situation is far too delicate for this sort of unilateral activity. The conduct of nations, international relations—they belong in the appropriate hands, not negotiated at gunpoint."

The hatch opened and Tombstone Magruder stepped into the room. He stopped and surveyed both of them coldly, then stepped forward and took the high-backed chair at the end of the table. "This will constitute my only briefing on this matter—for both of you. There is a helicopter leaving in fifteen minutes. I expect you both to be on it. You will be ferried back to Greece for further transportation to your respective destinations. This is non-negotiable." He quelled the question starting on Pamela's lips with a harsh glare. "You've both caused enough damage as it is."

With that, he turned toward Tiltfelt. "In the very near future, it will become apparent that your decision to lobby in favor of sending this carrier into the Black Sea will have been the most foolish of all possible mistakes. You have two choices at this point. First, you can take your chances as your case is tried in the media, and most probably wind up the scapegoat as the Department of State recognizes the enormity of its mistake. Second, you may decide to take an offensive posture and admit that you were in error. Believe me, the subsequent facts are going to make that quite clear. If you take the second option, you have a chance of retaining your position within the State Department. And as an inducement to do so, I offer you this. I will say that I relied upon your advice in deciding to conduct the strike against Ukraine."

Bradley Tiltfelt's mouth fell open. He sputtered for a moment, then said, "That's absolutely insane. I had no hand in that attack—none at all. What you're asking is—"

"Your only possible hope," Tombstone finished coldly.

"I'll know what your choice is by the time you leave this ship. Understood?"

Tiltfelt shook his head angrily.

Tombstone turned to Drake. "Before you disembark, you will file one last story. It will be along the lines of the two choices I have outlined for Mr. Tiltfelt. I will personally review your copy—print only, at this point— prior to your departure. If you choose not to draft a story for my approval at this time, I will have you held on board, incommunicado, until federal agents arrive to charge you with treason."

"Treason? Just what the hell—?"

"Listen, don't talk," Tombstone ordered. "By throwing yourself off that fishing boat, you interfered with Naval operations during a time of conflict. You personally managed to endanger the lives of several men, starting with the pilots who had to pull you out of the drink. In the end, I may be proved to be wrong—but you'll still spend at least four days incommunicado on board this ship. If there is a story to report, you'll miss it completely. Got that?"

Oh, she got it. Indeed she did. Pamela's color rose, her face twisted into a mask of fury. She leaped to her feet, pointing an accusing finger at him. "You can't do this!"

"I can, and I will. Come, Miss Drake, do you really doubt me?"

The color drained from Pamela's face as quickly as it had risen. The air seemed to go out of her and, deflated, she sagged back down into her chair. She nodded without looking up at him.

Tombstone turned back to Tiltfelt. "Your decision?"

"Number two." Tiltfelt's voice was low, beaten. The all-pervasive self-confidence that had infused the man since he'd come on board was gone. He looked like what he was—a political hack, caught in the middle of a scenario he neither understood nor could solve.

Tombstone nodded. "Very well. You have fifteen minutes to pack your belongings. The Chief of Staff will escort you to the flight deck."

"I'll file the story," Pamela said sullenly. She lifted her head finally and glared at him. "But you'll pay for this Tombstone, I swear you will."

TWELVE
Wednesday, 12 September

1300 Local
Newport, Rhode Island

Bird Dog pulled up in front of his apartment in his rental car. He parked at the sidewalk, leaped out, and ran to the door. Fumbling with his keys, he finally got the knob to turn. He slammed open the door.

"Callie," he yelled. "Callie, where are you?"

"Bird Dog?" Her voice rose, high and excited. "You're back!" Callie Lazure came hurtling out of the back room, barely pausing before she threw herself at him. He pulled her close to him, felt the warm familiar curves of her body.

"Oh, Callie, I've missed you so much."

She buried her face in his neck, murmuring nonsensical phrases and almost crying. Bird Dog wisely remained silent and held her.

"Don't ever do this to me again, Bird Dog," Callie said finally, pulling away from him.

"Do what?"

"Go off and leave me like that. Promise me." Her eyes were pleading. At that moment, no one would have guessed that Callie was a career Navy officer herself.

"There'll be cruises, dear," Bird Dog said gently. "For you, and for me. You know that."

"I can't do this again." She returned to the safe embrace of his arms, holding him hard against her.

"Callie Lazure—will you marry me?" Bird Dog startled himself, the words out of his throat before he could even think them through. Get married? What in the world was he thinking? He was headed back to sea after this, and there were so many things he had yet to do. Yet at that point in time, all that mattered to him was that Callie agree to spend the rest of her life with him.

She pulled back slightly and looked up at him, her face streaked with tears. "Marry?" Her voice was tentative and uncertain.

"Marry," Bird Dog said firmly. "That is, if you want to." An awful feeling that he'd just stepped on his dick invaded him.

"Okay." Callie snuggled back up to him.

Bird Dog clasped her to him, an odd mixture of terror and delight sweeping over him.

1400 Local
Chief of Naval Operations
Washington, D.C.

"You did well, nephew," Thomas Magruder said. He gazed levelly at his nephew, his eyes unreadable.

"Thank you, Admiral," Tombstone said. He swayed slightly on his feet. The last sixteen hours had been a frantic rush of airlifts, commercial airliners, and one final last harrowing taxicab ride to the Pentagon. He'd caught a few catnaps, but not nearly enough sleep to keep him going. At the moment, Tombstone felt light-headed.

"That captain on *La Salle*," his uncle said, shaking his head in disbelief. "Your idea?" He shot Tombstone a look under bushy eyebrows.

Tombstone shook his head. "Not mine. That was sheer surface-warrior ingenuity all by itself. Surprised me as much as it did you."

His uncle grunted. "Well, she's hardly operational— your relief is going to have to stay on *Jefferson* for the time being. Six months at least in the shipyards, maybe longer. But she was there when it counted, wasn't she?"

Tombstone nodded. "She was indeed."

"Well." His uncle seemed to be grappling for a way to broach his next subject. "Are you ready for another job?"

Tombstone laughed. "I'm ready for some leave," he said bluntly. "Sir, I have some personal things to take care of before I take command of SouthCom. The last couple of weeks have been interesting, but—"

His uncle waved aside his objections. "Take two weeks. SouthCom can wait, although I have to tell you that the situation down there is getting critical." He arched an eyebrow and smiled at Tombstone. "But from what you've been through, you're just the man to handle it."

Tombstone stood, turned toward the door, then paused. He turned back to his uncle, an odd expression of uncertainty in his eyes. "Do you have a few minutes for some family business, sir?"

Caught off guard by the change in his nephew's voice, the CNO simply motioned him back down into the chair. "What's on your mind, Matt?"

Tombstone took a deep breath. "It's probably nothing. Just something one of the Ukrainians said on board *Jeff*—it was about my father."

The senior Magruder sucked in a hard breath. "What about him?"

"He said Dad survived. That he was taken to Russia after he was shot down. I think he meant—Uncle, he wanted me to think that Dad might still be alive." Tombstone stared off in the distance. "I know it was probably just a psychological ploy but—is there any chance?"

His uncle shook his head slowly. "You know there've been rumors for decades about that. The faked photos, the false reports. Matt, you can't even begin to think about it being a possibility. It'll eat you up if you do. And there's no chance—none." His voice was filled with sympathy but decisive. He motioned at the office around him. "If there were any chance there were survivors, don't you think I'd know?"

Tombstone nodded slowly. "Yes, you should." He sat silent, appeared to reach some inner decision, then stood. "Thanks." He started for the door.

"Matt—you do believe that, don't you? That we did everything we could?" There was an almost pleading note in his uncle's voice.

Tombstone paused, his back still to his uncle. "I don't know. But I'll find out." He left quickly, not waiting for his uncle to answer.

Matthew Magruder, son of Sam Magruder—it felt odd thinking of himself in those terms instead of just as a Naval officer. The Ukrainian's claims—well, there were ways of investigating them, he supposed.

He retrieved his GTO from the parking lot, and inspected it for damage. Somehow it had managed to survive without a nick. He slid behind the wheel, and started it. It roared into life, sounding as close to a

Tomcat's howl as anything he'd ever run across ashore.

Tomboy—he could see her now, feel the shape of her body, breathe the smell of her hair. With a little more force than necessary, he slammed the gearshift into reverse and screamed out of the parking lot.

1600 Local
ACN Studio
Washington, D.C.

"So, Miss Drake, you actually had a hand in deciphering the events over there?" the anchor queried. Pamela gazed at him for a moment, tempted beyond all endurance. She started to speak, then remembered the last time she'd seen Tombstone.

Finally, she shook her head from side to side. "No, I'm afraid not."

The anchor looked startled. The back-briefing he'd received had indicated that Pamela had been on the carrier the entire time of the incident, and he'd been expecting her usual detailed firsthand account of her intervention in the conflict.

"Then what happened?" he said, unable to come up with a more piercing, provocative question.

Pamela took a deep breath and began. "Most of the credit goes to Mr. Bradley Tiltfelt of the State Department. Once he realized the error of taking the carrier into the Black Sea and discovered the depths of Ukraine's treachery, he was fully involved in all decisions from that point on." She turned to face the camera, pasting her most sincere, believable expression on her face. "Had it not been for him, matters would not have worked out as quickly as they did. This nation owes him a debt of gratitude."

The anchor concluded the interview quickly, still at a loss as to why Pamela Drake had not proved to be the center of controversy once again. As soon as it was possible, Pamela slipped out of the studio and headed back to her luxurious apartment.

As she fought the traffic, maneuvering her black Porsche recklessly between the competing lines of traffic, her thoughts returned to Tombstone.

He'd humiliated her, embarrassed her—and worst of all, forced her to slant her news report to suit his own agenda. As she veered to avoid a heavily loaded schoolbus, she made herself one promise.

Tombstone would pay for this. He would pay—and pay big.